" 'Love' " and Other Stories of Yokomitsu Riichi

" 'Love' " and Other Stories of Yokomitsu Riichi

translated and with an introduction
by DENNIS KEENE

UNIVERSITY OF TOKYO PRESS

Previously published in Japanese:
"Onmi" ("Love")
"Warawareta ko" (The Child Who Was Laughed At)
"Maketa otto" (The Defeated Husband)
"Aoi ishi o hirotte kara" (After Picking Up a Blue Stone)
"Aoi taii" (The Pale Captain)
"Machi no soko" (The Depths of the Town)
"Haru wa basha ni notte" (Spring Riding in a Carriage)
"Hanasono no shiso" (Ideas of a Flower Garden)
"Kikai" (The Machine)
"Basha" (The Carriage)
"Bisho" (Smile)

Published in English in Japan by arrangement with Orion Press

3-7-1, Kasumigaseki
Chiyoda-ku, Tokyo
Japan

Published by
UNIVERSITY OF TOKYO PRESS
UTP 3093-87139-5149
Printed in Japan

ISBN 0-86008-116-8
Library of Congress Catalogue Card No. 74-81987

The Japan Foundation Translation Series

Contents

Preface	vii
Introduction	ix
"Love"	1
The Child Who Was Laughed At	21
The Defeated Husband	29
After Picking Up a Blue Stone	69
The Pale Captain	97
The Depths of the Town	109
Spring Riding in a Carriage	115
Ideas of a Flower Garden	131
The Machine	151
The Carriage	181
Smile	227
Bibliographical Note	265

Preface

The making of this translated selection of Yokomitsu's short stories arose out of a doctoral thesis written for Oxford University with this author as its subject. Some of the translation was done as material preparatory for, or actually used in, the thesis, but the bulk of it would most likely not have been done without the suggestion from The Japan Foundation that it was worth undertaking. I should thus like to express my thanks to this body, to the head of its Editorial Section, Mr. Tomotada Iwakura, and in particular to Miss Aya Morishima of the same section, who read through the translations with great care and pointed out a number of mistakes I have since rectified. I should also like to thank Professor Donald Keene, who, as a member of the selection board of The Japan Foundation, encouraged me, on the evidence of one page then translated, to make a complete translation of "The Machine," something which on my own initiative I should perhaps not have undertaken.

In referring to Japanese works that have been translated into English (in this selection by myself or elsewhere by others), I give the title in English, followed in the first instance by the romanized original. In the case of works that have not been translated, I give the romanized title, followed by an English version of that title. Names are written in the Japanese order, with surname first and given name second.

The translation of "Ideas of a Flower Garden" first appeared in the *Japan Quarterly*, vol. XX, no. 2, for April-June 1973. My thanks are due to the editor of that journal for permission to reprint a slightly altered version of the one that appeared there.

Introduction

Yokomitsu Riichi was born in 1898, and thus belongs to what one might call the third generation of modern Japanese writers, the first generation being those born around 1870 (the "naturalists," such as Shimazaki Toson), the second those born around 1885 (the "Shirakaba" writers, such as Shiga Naoya). The division of writers into fifteen-year generations is a game that perhaps creates more questions than it answers, and the distinctions it makes obviously lose their validity, or at least their edge, with the passage of time; and yet it is necessary to see any writer within the situation in which he began to write, and since the literary situation in Japan was altering so rapidly during those early years of the twentieth century when Yokomitsu was growing up, some emphasis upon the facts of literary history is required.

Put very simply, what happened during the first decade of the twentieth century was that the colloquial language established itself as the medium for literary prose at the same time as "naturalism" became the main literary movement, and the two are clearly linked. "Naturalism" meant a concern with the "real," with what life was "really" like, and since the life that the writer really knows about is his own, there was a tendency for Japanese "realism" to be concerned with personal confession, a development no doubt encouraged by the fact that there is a long tradition in Japan of the diary as a literary form. This concern with the real as that which is personally experienced was also shared by the next generation of writers, of whom Shiga Naoya is the supreme representative, although the dramatic, confessional aspects of the naturalists are hardly present in his work, since his realism is that much closer to real life in which dramatic events rarely occur. The tone of any work by Shiga Naoya is constantly under control, played down, a control reflected in a style where the colloquial language finally becomes a medium in which a writer can work with ease. This emphasis upon the experience of the "I" is shown in the name of the basic literary genre of the Taisho period (1912–26), which is referred to as the "I-novel." It was against this image of literature, according to his own account, that Yokomitsu wanted to write; he wished to create "fictions" and not record the falsifications, "the enormous lies" that go under the name of a diary. This does not mean that he then avoided the autobiographical, since he did not, and perhaps no novelist ever totally does; instead he wished to transform that life into a fictional work of art, unlike Shiga Naoya, who seemed to feel that life as it had been lived was a work of art already.

European modernism of the 1920s also began as a reaction to the idea of the "real" in literature (the opening of Breton's first surrealist manifesto is an attack upon the way Dostoevsky describes the objects in a room), and although the connections between what happened in literary Paris at that period and what happened in literary Tokyo are tenuous (Japanese dadaism, for example, is a marginal affair, and has virtually nothing to do with the parent manifestations in Europe), the starting points of both modernist movements have something in common. Also, if one believes that the avant-garde in the West was, if not created, at least given great impetus by World War I, then a counterpart also occurred in Tokyo with the great earthquake of 1923. Yokomitsu himself certainly believed that the effects of both events upon their respective cultures were similar. Again, if one sees European modernism as a continuation of the symbolist movement in literature, then it is of some interest that Yokomitsu saw his own modernist writings as symbolist also, and not so much as the "literature of sensations" that the manifesto statements of his literary group, the "Shinkankakuha," claimed it to be.

The importance of Yokomitsu's early literature, of which the bulk of this selection consists, is that it is perhaps the one serious attempt in Japanese to write a modernist literary prose, a prose which has something in common with what was going on in Europe in the 1920s. It is certainly true that one can find things written in Japanese in the 'twenties which seem much closer to European counterparts, such as futurist poems and manifestos, cubist and surrealist poems, prose works more aggressively modernist than Yokomitsu's, but these look now like merely the sad detritus of dead fashions, and even in terms of literary history it is difficult to give them any kind of serious attention. Dada, for example, made a real impact in Paris, whereas in Tokyo it was the plaything of a small and ignored number of individuals; and Jean-Paul Sartre, despite his loathing of surrealism, at least felt himself obliged to admit that it was the one important poetic movement in France in the twentieth century, an admission which no antagonist of Japanese surrealism, if one could be said to exist, would feel impelled to make. Such manifestations in Japan reflected little more than a sensitivity toward European fashion, and that only on the part of a small minority. Yokomitsu's modernism, although obviously sharing some of that superficiality, produced a literature which even if not outstandingly good is at least real. Yokomitsu's prose *is* Japanese modernism of the 1920s, the only literary modernism of that period in Japanese which can be read with an interest that goes beyond mild curiosity. That is his historical importance.

Yokomitsu's father was a civil works engineering contractor who worked under contract from the government principally in the building of railways. His speciality was tunnels. For Yokomitsu in later life, his father, who died in 1922, came to represent the Fukuzawa Yukichi "enlightenment" Meiji tradition, the idea that European civilization should be taken over *en bloc* as far as industrial techniques were concerned, which process would then automatically give rise to a superior Japanese culture. As Yokomitsu wrote in his final novel, *Ryoshu* [Travel sadness; i.e., an intense, tragic form of homesickness], he seemed to feel that as long as one built tunnels, the required "culture" would appear quite naturally out through those tunnels. It was an optimism toward life that Yokomitsu himself did not share, not merely out of the normal processes of reaction toward one's father and the past that he represents, but because his life was so deprived and tragic.

Not born at home but at one of the numerous places where the family was obliged to live because the father's place of work changed so frequently, he never truly had a place that he could call his. The longest period of his childhood was spent in Ueno (Tsuge) in Mie Prefecture, which is about midway between Kyoto and Nagoya, the birthplace of his mother (and that of the great poet Matsuo Basho, and it is claimed, although not demonstrated, that Yokomitsu is a relation of the poet on his mother's side). However, Yokomitsu is known to have changed his primary school ten times (three times in one year), his father was often away on work (three long periods in Korea among other periods of absence), and for a considerable time when he was nine his mother was ill in hospital, and he lived first with his elder sister and then as a serving boy in the temple of an uncle. In her reminiscences of him, his elder sister lays great emphasis on the misery of these periods of solitude, although Yokomitsu himself wrote of them in later life as ones happily free from adult interference. But Ueno seems to have had no happy associations for him, those being nearly all tied up with his relationship to his sister, in particular to the area around Lake Biwa, where she lived her early married life and in that period when Yokomitsu was in his late teens (see the story " 'Love' ").

From his second year at secondary school (his fourteenth year onward), he lived apart from his family in lodgings, and his reminiscences of that period show how alienated he was from the world about him; although I would not wish to give an image of him at this time as an introverted, tragic, crippled figure, since indeed, in appearance at least, he was almost the opposite, being the school's star baseball player, a member of the judo club, an adept at public speaking, and with no particular interest in literature. Two pieces of writing remain from his schooldays, both in the school magazine; stylistically they are experimental in a way quite remarkable for a country boy of that time, but this very oddness would seem to imply that he was not particularly engaged in what he was doing but merely being clever.

He went to Waseda University in Tokyo in the spring of 1916, but left again in autumn to return home (a home which finally he had, in Yamashina, a village to the east of Kyoto at that time and now a suburb), and he did not go back to Waseda until 1918, a break of a year and a half. The reason for this is not quite certain; the financial position of his father (not permanently employed by the government but only working on a series of contracts, he varied from being often quite well off to being desperately short of money) may have had something to do with it, although it seems more likely that this was the result of a nervous breakdown. His married sister was now living within walking distance at Otsu on the shores of Lake Biwa, and during this period he became committed to the idea of being a writer and began to write in earnest.

On returning to Waseda he made friends with Nakayama Gishu (a writer who did not appear upon the literary scene until his late thirties, by which time Yokomitsu was an established figure), and Kojima Tsutomu (a proletarian writer who died at the age of thirty-three, and mentioned here because his younger sister became Yokomitsu's first wife), both first-year students like Yokomitsu and both two years younger than he. His love affair with Kojima Kimiko probably began in the next year, when she would have been only thirteen, resulted in marriage in 1923 (when she was seventeen and he was twenty-five), and ended in her death from consumption in 1926 at the age of twenty.

Yokomitsu's father died in Korea in 1922, leaving him penniless. This desperate period in his life was succeeded in May 1923 by his finally appearing on the literary scene with his short novel *Nichirin* [The sun in heaven] and the short story "Hae" [The fly], an appearance due to the good opinion of Kikuchi Kan and Akutagawa Ryunosuke. Kikuchi Kan, a new-style literary figure of great power in the 1920s and 1930s (whose existence excited the scorn of Nagai Kafu; see *Kafu the Scribbler* in Bibliographical Note), had brought out a new magazine, *Bungei shunju* [Literary annals], from January 1923, and Yokomitsu became one of his promising new writers. Another of his young men was Kawabata Yasunari, who became a lifelong friend of Yokomitsu at this time.

In June 1923 Yokomitsu must have felt that he had made it sufficiently to make marriage a possibility, and he informed his mother that he was going to marry Kimiko, to which she objected violently because she was busily engaged in her own arrangements over this matter. Before this squabble had been resolved, the great earthquake took place in

September, and later that year Yokomitsu was living with mother and wife in two small rooms in Tokyo. The year 1924 saw the publication of Yokomitsu's first collection of stories, and also of *Nichirin* in book form. In October the first number of *Bungei jidai* [Literary age], the magazine of the new, modernist literature, appeared, with both Yokomitsu and Kawabata on its editorial board. It had been preceded by *Bungei sensen* [Literary front], a magazine devoted to another literary possibility of the time, proletarian literature.

The old, stable literary world of the Taisho period disintegrated in the late twenties as the needs of a larger (and to a certain extent, mass) audience were recognized by new publishers. Stages in this disintegration can now be seen as the earthquake, one of the effects of which was to encourage change, particularly in the performing arts (German expressionist drama in translation, for example), owing to the vacum created by wholesale destruction, and then inevitably a whole series of doubts and scepticisms about the previous roles of the various arts that took the form, among others, of the appearance of the two magazines above; the suicide of Akutagawa in 1927, which seemed to many to indicate that the image of the writer he represented was played out; and the appearance of popular magazines, low-priced paperbacks, and so on, as the decade moved into the thirties.

A great deal of the rumpus caused by *Bungei jidai* can be put down to the fact that it was merely one part of this process, the old guard objecting to the signs of a takeover by brash young men, and it is customary for Japanese literary critics to consider the "Shinkankakuha" (the name the *Bungei jidai* writers took upon themselves since they had been labelled thus by their one friendly critic) as little more than a piece of literary politics that produced virtually nothing of literary value or even true literary historical importance. Odagiri Susumu (see Bibliographical Note) has demonstrated how little of newness the magazine had to offer compared with other eccentricities two or three years earlier.

The "Shinkankakuha" was, indeed, not a literary movement in the same sense that, say, French surrealism was. It was merely that a group of young, although already established, writers set up their own magazine with the aid of a new publisher who was prepared to pay as handsomely as the big magazines for contributions. The word "Shinkankakuha" is awkward to translate (the standard translation of "Neo-Sensualist group" is quite inadequate) since literally it means "New Sensation group," which sounds too weird to be usable, "shin" meaning "new" and "kankaku" meaning "sensation" in the restricted meaning, unlike the English word, of "feeling" or "sense impression" (Western philosophical terms had come into vogue at the time). Since the title was created by a journalist and merely taken over by the group, it would seem foolish to give great weight to it; instead one should consider it only as a name, in the way that one does not worry about whether metaphysical poetry is "really metaphysical."

It is, however, a fact that the idea of a "literature of sensations" (language presenting experience as directly experienced and not as mediated by the mind or the sensibility or the emotions) had been in the air for a few years, and the few manifesto statements of the group do tend to stress this word, although their main stress is little more than a vague longing for the new. Yokomitsu's own contribution to the theory of this group is almost unintelligible, but various remarks about "ripping off the exterior of objects to reveal the thing-in-itself" seem to show, as well as a young man's pleasure in polemic, a view of literature as being concerned with symbolic statements rather than as any rigorous description of "pure sensation." Probably the only member of the group deeply committed to the idea of a new literature was Yokomitsu, for other members of the magazine were soon disturbed by the bad reputation he was getting them all, two or three defected to proleratian literature, and even Kawabata Yasunari, enthusiastic enough at the start, can be seen now as involved in no really deep sense; and after a year the magazine, although it did not fold up for another two years, became merely one which published mainly younger writers who had no particular theory of literature in common.

One reason for this early demise of the group was that its presiding genius, Yokomitsu, was concerned with other things. Early in 1925 his mother had died, and by early summer of that year his wife had taken to her bed with the consumption that was to kill her in the following year. In October 1925 they moved to Hayama, on the sea coast just east of Kamakura, and Yokomitsu nursed her virtually single-handed (in February 1926 the servant girl disappeared) until she died on 24 June 1926 at the age of twenty. After a quarrel with his mother-in-law, who had suggested he marry the younger daughter (who, like Kimiko and her brother and elder sister, also died of consumption), Yokomitsu left her house, to which he had gone immediately after Kimiko died, and lived for a while in the company offices of *Bungei shunju*, where he wrote "Spring Riding in a Carriage," which was a considerable success when published in August of that year. In February 1927 he married again (arranged for him by Kikuchi Kan), in the same month that "Ideas of a Flower Garden," the work that virtually marks the end of his "shinkankaku" period, was published. A son was born in November of the same year.

This year of 1927 saw little creative production by Yokomitsu, but did see the beginnings of his transformation into a powerful literary figure. During 1927–28 he wrote a number of articles attacking the theory of proletarian literature, although by now he appeared to be the only remaining writer with any faith in the "shinkankaku" literature, which he put forward as the one viable alternative. In 1928 proletarian literature dominated the literary scene, and Yokomitsu himself was in considerable sympathy with Marxism, claiming that his objection to proletarian literature was that, unlike "shinkankaku" literature, it was not genuinely dialectical materialist, since it was committed to an outmoded idea of realism. That kind of statement can be taken with the large pinch of salt it deserves, but the "dialectical materialist" aspect of Yokomitsu's writing of this period can be seen in one of his few works already translated into English, "Silent Ranks," translated by John Bester (see Bibliographical Note).

In April 1928 Yokomitsu went to China, spending only one month in Shanghai before cutting short a trip which he had intended to be longer and more varied. The upshot of this was his first long novel, *Shanghai*, which is about a subject that one would expect to find in a proletarian novel (the May 30th Movement of 1925), and was presumably meant to show that a "shinkankaku" treatment of reality creates literary truth in a way that a class-obsessed, committed literature cannot. However, what it really demonstrated is that the jumpy, impressionistic style which is never fully maintained even in a short story cannot be more than a willed excrescence in a long novel, and in effect the novel is a gradual farewell to that style. The truth was that stylistically (perhaps more than stylistically) he had reached a dead end, which was then shown in the fact that with the publication of "Tori" [The bird] early in 1930, and more particularly with that of "The Machine" in September of the same year, his style showed a dramatic change. The dramatic nature of this change has tended to be exaggerated by literary historians, but it is undeniable that a change did take place. The reasons for this are complex; the failure of *Shanghai* (most of it written and published in 1928–29), the defeat of himself and his party in a debate with the proletarian critics over "formalism" (does form control content, or vice versa) during 1928–29, and the common assumption of literary history that he was "influenced" by Joyce and Proust and thus hurriedly created the "new psychological novel."

Certainly Yokomitsu had moved away from the "shinkankaku" concern with fragmented outer reality back to the ramifications of the inner life, but the involved, complex form this takes in "The Machine" is not what one finds in his next long novel, *Shin'en* [The garden of sleep], the first half of which was serialized in November and December of 1930 and which is stylistically very ordinary indeed. The fact that this was serialized in a newspaper, as was another novel in 1931 (that year also saw another novel serialized in a magazine called the *Ladies Companion*), shows only too clearly that rather than writing the "new psychological novel," he was in fact writing the "new popular novel." It was "new" because it was being written for a new audience for the popular novel, an audience that was moving away, at least in part, from the older historical tale toward something concerned with the modern world, or with their image of what the modern world might be, and it was now large enough no ensure that, for example, a translation of Gide's *La porte étroite* sold more copies than the old-style historical novel did.

In 1935 an article by Yokomitsu, "Junsuishosetsuron" [A theory of the pure novel], stated quite openly that serious literature could survive only if it appropriated to itself those elements which had been relegated to the pages of popular fiction (such as "accident" and "sentimentality"), arguing that serious literature had reached its present state of impasse, in which little of interest had appeared during the past ten years, by condemning the fictional to the pages of the popular novel while concerning itself only with a diarylike record of the events of the author's own life. This kind of critique of the I-novel had become a commonplace at the time, and Yokomitsu's article is not a very competent piece of work (one critic's dismissal of it as "pathetic confusion" is probably not too harsh), and it contributes little to that central debate in modern Japanese literature about what "realism" ought to be, and why Japanese realism became what it did; but it certainly does demonstrate, as he himself said, what had been happening to Yokomitsu as a writer since *Shanghai*. Some truly sensitive critics, to whom one is obliged to listen, such as Kawabata Yasunari and Shinoda Hajime, hold some of these long novels of the 1930s in high esteem, and it will appear, justifiably perhaps, as arrogant on my part to dismiss them as of almost no value (with the possible exception of *Monsho* [The family crest] of 1934); and all I can offer by way of apology is the fact that other Japanese critics, such as Hirano Ken and Hinuma Rintaro, would also seem to think that Yokomitsu's real life as a writer ended in 1927 with "Ideas of a Flower Garden."

In 1936 Yokomitsu, now a leading figure in the literary world, made the required trip to Europe, nominally to cover the Berlin Olympic Games but principally to undergo the endurance test of European life, and most of his six months there he spent in Paris. While in Paris he published in Japan a monthly journal, which aroused some consternation since he wrote down how limited and unpleasant his experience there was, going against the normal expectation that a more cheerful and positive account is called for. Life abroad as contrasted with the superiority, for a Japanese, of life at home was the theme of a short story ("Chubo nikki" [Kitchen diary]) published later that year, and also of his long novel *Ryoshu* [Travel sadness], which began serialization in 1937, was broken off, and then resumed at various periods over the next ten years but still remained incomplete at his death in 1947.

It has been maintained (see Jun Eto, for example, in Bibliographical Note) that the novel represents a rejection of the West on Yokomitsu's part, a process which can be linked up with Japanese "fascism." Indeed, after the war Yokomitsu was cited, not officially, as a form of war criminal by a group of young leftish writers on account of this novel; but it is difficult to accept this thesis, since Yokomitsu seems in no way to have "accepted" the West, thus "rejection" can hardly be the appropriate term. And if one considers that at least half the novel was written during the war on a theme of so explosive a nature as the contrasts between East and West, then the book is remarkable for the lack of any spite shown toward his country's enemies, with whom, indeed, it deals very little. Since 1930 Yokomitsu had been concerned with the simple-minded idiot's as a possible life of virtue, in contrast to the self-conscious intellectual whose ability to live has been paralysed through his entanglement with imported ideas, and it is this theme and its variations which run through his long novels. But Yokomitsu's interest in writers such as Gide and Valéry never altered, and the concerns of *Ryoshu* are no more than a continuation of earlier ones, although they become more ideologically pointed since they take the form of debate among the main characters of the novel, rather than being shown only in the sorts of things the characters do and the sorts of people that they are; that is, to use the apposite jargon, they are written into, even imposed upon, the main characters, not merely embodied in them.

Certainly Yokomitsu patriotically supported the war, although he wrote no propaganda for it, but it is difficult to see on what grounds that can be condemned; and admittedly the defeat left him brokenhearted. Toward the end of the war he escaped with his family to a small village on the Japan Sea coast, and he wrote a long journal about his experience there ("Yoru no kutsu" [Night shoes]), which describes the life of the Japanese farmer, something he felt as a constant that would prevail in the degradation of the defeat. It is a fine piece of work, but it received no acclaim when published since the positives it stressed, the complex of ideas and attitudes which can be grouped under the phrase "Oriental nothingness," were out of favour, as was Yokomitsu himself.

The privations of his life in the country and of his life back in Tokyo, where he returned late in 1945, made him seriously ill. He was too innocent, according to his sons' report, to make use of the black market, both he and his wife believing it to be the name of some actual shop they were unable to locate. In early summer of 1946 he vomited blood, collapsed, and took to his bed apparently half paralysed. He feared it might be consumption, and his doctor mistakenly diagnosed it as the cerebral anaemia that had killed his parents, probably not a mistake of much importance since he placed all his faith in homely cures, such as massage, moxa, and the "bee treatment," which entails doses of stinging in order to bring a rush of blood to the throat that then has beneficial effects on the head (there is a moving poem of his about the little black heap of corpses that were dying, as he thought, to give him life).

Finally in September 1947 Kawabata Yasunari managed to persuade him to see a real doctor at Tokyo University, and on learning that he did not have cerebral anaemia he cheered up enough to write "Smile," his last completed work and perhaps the finest short story to come out of the defeat. He was working on some childhood reminiscences when he had another fainting fit on 14 December, complaining of severe pains in his stomach, which were diagnosed as an ulcer. This turned into acute peritonitis, and he died on 30 December 1947 in his fiftieth year. His last recorded words were, "I want to ride in an aeroplane." His funeral took place on 3 January 1948, the very moving funeral oration being given by Kawabata Yasunari.

Despite the coolness of the postwar literary world, Yokomitsu's writings found a wide reading public in those early years; a public which now no longer reads him, and during the twenty-five years since his death, he has received little critical attention. Although he still has a fairly important place in literary history, he is seen mainly as an indication of how modernist literature failed in Japan, and also of the difficulties that Japanese authors have in writing true fictions. Since his death two collected works have been published, one in 1948–51, a projected twenty-six volumes that folded up on the twenty-third, and a completed twelve-volume one in 1955–56. Both are inadequate, indeed slovenly, compilations, and it is an indication of the lowness of Yokomitsu's reputation that no publisher seems prepared to bring out a proper collected works, presumably because he is judged as no longer read, despite the fact that scholars exist now who could do it well. Just how low this reputation is could be seen very clearly in 1972 in the various publications that appeared on the death of Kawabata Yasunari. The names of the two writers have been linked together since the early days of *Bungei jidai* in 1924, but the majority of the limited number of comments made on Yokomitsu in this latest context were disparaging, to the effect that the modernism of the 1920s had been a blind alley, and that young readers today would find his high reputation of the 1930s unintelligible, being fortunately spared that hypothetical state of bewilderment by the fact that they did not read him.

The high reputation of the thirties was based upon the long novels, and as such it was bound to fall. However, even if, as I believe, those novels are unsuccessful, at least they are the failures of a genuinely talented writer, and have an interest about them which one will not discover all that easily in the bulk of the literature produced since the war. It is also possible to feel that Yokomitsu's thirty years of dedication to literature did end up mostly as wasted effort, a point made even by his friend and supporter Nakayama Gishu. But Nakayama felt there was enough of value in the short stories to maintain a place in Japanese literature if their value were properly recognized, and it is in the same belief that the present selection has been made.

During the twenties Yokomitsu tried to make Japanese literature take a new direction, to exploit the possibilities of the new literary language in a way it had not yet been (and eventually was not, or could not be) exploited. It is this attempt that seems to me of particular interest, and in making this selection I have tried to choose works that demonstrate what that attempt was, and have thus not made a selection of what could be judged as unquestionably the best works only, since that would have meant including works that are not really relevant to that attempt. I have also ignored two or three works that tend to be included in Japanese one-volume selections ("Naporeon to tamushi" [Napoleon and the ringworm] and "Hae" [The fly] are examples) since they are in that satirical genre which I find repulsively childish to read and thus impossible to translate. I record this here as the blind spot many Japanese readers might consider it to be.

However, this selection is not eccentric. In the cases of " 'Love,' " "The Child Who Was Laughed At," "The Pale Captain," "The Depths of the Town," and "The Carriage," I have chosen works of which the author himself had a high opinion. "The Machine" and "Spring Riding in a Carriage" are the two best known of his short stories, and the selection of "Ideas of a Flower Garden" and "Smile" can be justified on similar grounds. "After Picking Up a Blue Stone" was chosen for its relevance to "The Pale Captain" and "The Depths of the Town," and also because I like it. Perhaps the one work that does require some form of apologia is "The Defeated Husband," the longest work in this selection. When Kawabata Yasunari published an early draft of this work, "Kanashimi no daika" [The price of unhappiness] in 1955, he referred to "The Defeated Husband" as an unfortunate and botched rewrite of it, and a number of people agreed with him. The reasons for giving it here are, first, that of length, in that it is one-third of the earlier version; second, that as only a partial rewriting it does show very clearly what "shinkankaku" literature is, even if it does not perhaps show it at its best; third, because the material it writes about is so important; and finally, because it does not seem to me as "botched" a rewrite as all that.

Love

3 Love

He was reading a book when his mother came upstairs holding a tape measure.

"Are you going to go on wearing that kimono?"

"It's still wearable, isn't it?"

He looked down at his kimono.

"Why?" he asked, since his mother went on inspecting him.

"I was thinking of using it for baby's nappies," she replied.

"Baby's nappies? Whose baby?"

"Your sister's going to have a baby," his mother said, looking, although he could not think why, exactly as she always did.

The thought of something like that happening to his sister made him flush. But he was pleased by the news.

"Is that right?"

"Well, you don't want that kimono anymore. I could make you a new one and then take that one to bits."

"She's really going to have a baby?"

His mother went downstairs without replying. That annoyed him slightly. Still a smile slipped through his annoyance and floated over it. It was useless even attempting to scowl.

He had only the one sister. She was older than he and had married six years ago. She didn't have a child yet.

On a fine day he went over the hills to his sister's house. He felt too awkward to ask about the baby, so he only occasionally looked at her waist when he thought he wouldn't be noticed. Still he couldn't see any difference there. The only thing was that his sister seemed very lively and cheerful. They went up the hill, found some moss to sit on, and sat with their legs outstretched. The lake was right below them. There was a rust-coloured sail quite still, one dot on the horizon. The sound of wood being sawed came up to them from the deep valley below.

"I'll just get a wild rose and then we'll go back. They'll be in flower quite soon." She got up and climbed in the direction of the wood. He stretched out by himself and lay looking up at the sky. It was a long time since they had been together here like this. He loved his sister.

"This one really takes some pulling." He heard his sister's voice somewhere behind him. He looked round and there she was trying to pull up an azalea bush by the roots, her elbows squeezed into her sides and leaning back heavily from the waist. He thought of the baby dangerously there inside her and jumped up.

"Stop it!"

He ran over, brushed her aside, and tried pulling up the azalea himself. The roots were very firmly set.

"Takes some pulling, I told you. Two of us can probably do it, though." And she went to lay hold of the bush again.

"Come on. Let's go."

He took her hand and they began to walk back to where they had been. She looked wistfully behind her.

"And it's just about to flower, too. That's the best kind of azalea, the one with the sticky leaves. Gosh, I'm exhausted."

He looked at her stomach again and remembered how she had stood pulling at that azalea, as if her elbows would be crushing the baby. At least that was how it looked to him, but how could he be sure about anything? He was too shy to ask her. Things had now reached a point where he simply could not.

She discovered another azalea nearby.

"Look. Now that one does look easy to pull up."

"Oh, forget about it, for heaven's sake!" he said.

"But we almost never come here. It would be such a waste to go back with nothing, not even one."

"Home!" he said.

"You're going home?" she said, looking at his face.

"Come on now," he said, and laughed.

He said nothing else and began to walk slightly ahead of her. He was deeply worried about the child within her. He didn't feel like playing about any more.

"How's your. . . . I mean, do you feel hungry or anything?" he suddenly asked her out of the preposterous notion that if she said she did feel hungry, then that would indicate some state of emptiness within her stomach, and that would be related to the degree to which her elbows had squeezed the child out of place. But she said only that she didn't feel hungry. Of course one couldn't accept an answer of that kind as any sort of evidence.

"My stomach hurts a bit," he said. "I suppose there wasn't anything wrong with what we had for lunch? How about you?"

She looked at him with a little pucker of the forehead and said, "There's nothing wrong with me. Does it hurt you bad?"

If it didn't hurt, then the child was all right. And it didn't hurt. He was beginning to feel a certain sense of relief when he recalled that the sensations of the parent and the child are totally separate from each other. The very fact that her stomach was not in pain could imply that the child was. She must see a doctor; there was nothing else for it. However, to get her to do that he would have to talk to her about what was worrying him, and that was what his awkwardness would not allow him to do. Even if it was in formal marriage, there was still that indelicacy, that act out of which the child was born and that in which it was born, and they would both be aware of it and of each other's awareness if they talked about the baby, and it was that feeling that he did not want. So he kept quiet, and she did also.

After a while she asked, "Does it still hurt?"

"It's all right now."

"There's a chemist's just at the bottom of the hill. Or if you'd like the doctor?"

"I'm better now."

"But it would be wiser to have it looked at, wouldn't it?"

Now it was she who was recommending the doctor to him. He pretended not to hear and tramped on down the hill.

In April he was in Tokyo. The news that a baby girl had been born came from his sister's husband in May.

"She's done it, then," he thought, and the anxiety he had felt up to now, the anxiety he could tell no one about, all of it became absurd and laughable.

"I'm an uncle now, by God."

He felt he had grown as a person. There was no doubt about it.

In June he went back home. As soon as he arrived at his sister's house, he went in without saying anything. His feet were dirty so he crawled on his knees, keeping his feet off the floor, toward the inner room where his niece seemed to be asleep. He saw something round beneath a yellow eider-down.

"That's her. Tiny little thing."

He grinned and hung over the child, feeling himself draping hugely like a mosquito net.

"Here. She looks like me."

It was a mystery to him. Then he laughed and remembered that, well, it wasn't his child.

"Another person. Someone else in the world."

He wanted to offer praise somewhere. This one is on my side, this one really is.

His sister came in smiling and radiant from the veranda.

"What train did you get here on? The two o'clock?"

"She looks like me. Look, doesn't she?"

Her sister looked down at the baby, flushing slightly. She let down her rolled-up sleeves.

"Well, she does, doesn't she? What's her name?"

"She's called Yuki."

"Yuki?"

"The 'Yuki' in Yukimura."

"The one meaning 'happiness'?"

"That's it. That one."

"That one. I'd got a name all worked out for her. Did you just pick it out of the dictionary?"

"The something or other Chinese-Japanese one. I said we should leave it to you, but your brother wouldn't have it. You don't like the name? There's something wrong with it?"

"She's a lovely baby. A real beauty: after all, she looks like me."

"Does she indeed. You know, when I take her down to the bath all the girls there make a terrible fuss over her. How did you get a lovely little thing like this, they all say."

"She's great. You'll have your hands full with her, though."

He smiled at his sister, and then felt suddenly displeased

with his own experienced-man-of-the-world manner. He went to the well to wash his feet. And then because he felt tired he lay down close by the side of his niece. When his sister wasn't looking he played with the baby, pulling its fingers, squeezing its nose. He couldn't get off to sleep.

He dreamed that he heard a baby crying a long way off, and he woke up. By his side lay his niece waving her hands about as if she were trying to undo a tangle of string. She was crying.

He remembered how he had read a very realistic description of the death of a baby in a novel by a famous author, and that baby had cried in exactly the same way as this. He felt worried and called his sister, but she wasn't there. Then he picked the child up and began swaying it from side to side and rocking it, and it stopped crying.

He tried to put it down to sleep but it only started crying again. He picked it up once more. And it stopped crying. He tried the same thing patiently four times, and then got tired of the whole thing and yawned hugely with all his might. His niece's stomach heaved as she cried.

It began to get on his nerves. The baby went on persistently crying.

"Cry then! Go on! Cry!"

He glared at her malevolently, but in the centre of hi loathing was an unbearable sense of the child. He put his arm under the baby's yellow pillow and raised her head, and she stopped crying immediately. Still, he had no intention of picking her up again. He smiled at her and softly withdrew his arm, whereupon she set up howling with all the strength of her body and much louder than before.

He thought he would try seeing if he could work the same trick on her again, when it occurred to him that this was probably the first time in its life that the child had been deliberately deceived by somebody.

(And that somebody was her uncle.)

If you considered it like that, then what he had done had not been something trivial for her. He picked her up again. He went on holding the child out of a sense of guilt until his sister came back and nursed it.

The next day he went over the hills to his home.

"I thought you were supposed to be coming home yesterday. I got your favourite dinner ready for you and it was all spoiled."

His mother poured water into the foot bowl for him.

"I arrived yesterday all right, but I went over to sis's and slept in the same room as the nipper. She's got a cute little face, that one has."

"But that navel of her's is so big, you know. Why, it's so big I'm worried that just a little rub and it'll start bleeding. I'm sure it will. You didn't notice anything wrong?"

"Well, I don't know, it's not all that big, is it?"

He washed his feet and remembered a story by a woman novelist called *The Navel Cord*, and a scene where she described blood coming out of an infant's navel and it dying, and that gave him something else to worry about.

"Do children die of things like that?"

"They certainly do."

"She's not going to die, is she?"

His mother made no reply.

"But that sort of thing just mends, doesn't it, mother? You know, don't you, mother?"

"Well, I sent your sister a copper coin wrapped in cotton and told her to keep it on top of the navel, but I don't know if she's done that yet. You didn't notice?"

"I didn't look."

"You wouldn't. The kid only has to strain a bit and that navel starts rumbling away just like your stomach. Is your stomach getting any better?"

Although he'd finished washing his feet, he went on sitting on the step, staring at the water in the bowl. After a while he said again, "She won't die, then will she?"

"Who's to know? I wish I could get you to do something about your hair. Your face would look thinner."

His mother knitted her brows slightly and then went round the back to throw the bowl of water away. He felt a deep gloom spreading through him.

"Die! Die indeed!" he said, and having first lost balance with this outburst, he then got to his feet with great energy.

Yukiko's navel gradually grew firm. When he'd first looked at it, the skin over the stomach seemed barely to stretch that far, being then twisted and stuffed into the hole. When the child cried, the navel popped out and the whole stomach looked like a grotesque helmet with the bobble navel at the top rumbling away. It was certainly a disturbing and restless navel, suggesting that the very contents of the stomach might shortly be exposed to view. And yet his sister seemed quite unconcerned by it all. He even noticed that there were times when the copper piece was not in its right place. He had read in one of his books the remarks of a doctor who said that that very kind of navel could be an absolute killer, and interlarded with a few skilful fictions of his own, he gave this threatening information to his sister.

"Is that right, then?" she said, and gave a little laugh.

"In its death pangs. Look at it."

And she gave the baby a little pop on its navel.

"You fool," he said, half smiling and half glaring at her.

Then she gave a few more little pats on the navel and said, "Go on. Try putting your finger in."

He felt like toying with the baby so he pressed the tip of his forefinger slightly on the head of the navel. There was no resistance and the finger disappeared as far as the first joint. God only knew how far it would reach to if he went on pressing.

"No thanks," he said, and withdrew his hand.

That particular worry did not occupy him for long. One day his sister told him happily that the baby had begun to smile. Maybe some external stimulus was causing it, for it appeared so suddenly, like bubbles on the surface of the water immediately vanishing back to stillness. But it was a wonderful smile; you saw it and you knew that the smile was the most precious of all things that ornament human life.

One early evening he was walking along the railway embankment looking for some chickweed to give the chickens. A small boy kicking a stone was coming in his direction. He remembered seeing a black curtain over the entrance to the boy's house, and he asked him who had died. The boy didn't reply.

"Who's died, I said."

"Baby."

"A baby? What did it die of?"

The boy hung his head shamefacedly and started as if to run away. He quickly caught hold of him by the wrist.

"What's wrong with you? Come on, say something, there's a good lad."

However, the boy wouldn't say anything but just screwed up his mouth and tried to shake the hand off. He looked severely at the boy, then let go of the hand. The boy did not, however, run away, but wandered down to the railway line and sat astraddle one of the rails. He himself just squatted on the grass, not looking in the direction of the boy.

"Shall I tell you, shall I?" the boy said.

"All right, go on, tell me. What did it die of?"

The boy was silent for a while, scraping some of the rust off the rail with a piece of broken glass.

"No, I don't want to," he said.

He now looked fixedly at the boy but said nothing. Then the boy said, " Mum killed it with her breast."

"With her breast? How?"

"Well, she was having a nap and she killed it."

He couldn't make head or tail of this so he simply continued looking at the boy's face. Then for no intelligible reason a bewildered look came over the boy's face, he looked up at him for a moment, then suddenly ran off in the opposite direction.

A little while after, he learned from one of the neighbours that the boy's mother had been sleeping with her baby, and her breast had blocked up the baby's nose and thus smothered it. He had never heard of a baby dying like that before. But of course that could happen, if you just thought a bit about it. He began immediately to start worrying about his sister.

The next day he went to her house and started talking about this very subject.

"Of course a baby could die like that. Happens quite often, in fact," his sister said.

"You know about that sort of thing?"

"How do you think I'd manage if I didn't know at least that much? You think I'm some kind of overgrown child. There's not much I don't know, let me tell you that."

She said this with an air of triumph, and then laughed. He felt somewhat relieved. But then soon afterwards she started talking about a neighbour's child born on almost the same day as Yukiko who had died of pneumonia only three days before, and of the baby of a friend of her husband who had caught pneumonia too and the doctor had simply said there was nothing to be done about it.

My God, something else, he thought. Clearly just to go on living and getting bigger was a remarkably difficult achievement. The thought depressed him no end.

Two or three days later he set off for Tokyo. Before leaving he called in at his sister's house and learned that the baby of the friend had finally died. The news upset him. He stood on the veranda. He could hear the bell from the neighbouring house where they were holding a memorial service for their own dead baby. A cool night in early autumn.

Then a child's voice was heard singing a children's song, and the rhythmic beat of the bell suddenly quickened to keep time with it.

"You silly little fool!" A voice, presumably the mother's, began scolding the child.

That made him laugh. He could hear his sister laughing too, somewhere in the darkness.

The next spring vacation he arrived at his sister's house and there was the baby sitting on his mother's lap with a sheet of newspaper in its hands that it tore across two, three times.

"Hey, what are you up to!"

He put the package with the toy he had brought in it on the table, and then sat down round it with his mother and sister. His mother undid the package and took out a celluloid doll.

"Oh look, Yuki, look what your big brother's brought you."

"He's not big brother, is he? He's uncle, isn't he?" his sister said to the baby.

"Oh, he's uncle then, isn't he, and he's brought such a lovely weeny present for you from such a long long way away. Look, isn't it nice!"

The mother showed the present, and the baby looked at it, then at his mother's face, then at the doll again, and again back to his mother's face for some time, and then finally stretched out its hand slowly in the direction of the doll.

"Look at her face!" his sister said, and smiled. He then produced another toy, this one a monkey's head made of rubber, and held it right in front of her nose.

"Look here, Yuki. Here's a monkey this time."

His sister gave the monkey's head a push with her fingers and out popped a red tongue like a long thin bag. Yukiko's eyes glistened and she started away from it, but her head was held against his mother's chest so all she could do was close her eyes and turn her face away. Everyone laughed, but he was feeling tired and simply grimaced to himself.

"She's grown," he said.

"She's grown? Mother, has she grown?"

"Well, of course she has. They do."

"She must have, then. I haven't noticed, but then I'm always with her," his sister said happily.

His father was in Kyushu, and a message came from him telling his mother to come as quickly as she could. His mother didn't want to leave her grandchild's side, but she at last made up her mind to go.

She leaned her head out of the train window. They were all lined up to see her off, his sister's husband, his sister, Yukiko with her head sticking out over his sister's shoulder, and himself. None of them knew when they would all be able to be together again after this.

The train started to move.

"Byebye, Yuki, byebye. Come back soon. Byebye."

His mother had eyes only for the baby. He kept waiting for her to look in his direction.

His sister twisted her shoulders so as to bring the baby strapped on her back to the front. The baby opened its mouth and gaped after the moving train.

"Byebye, Yuki. Yuki, byebye. Come back soon. Byebye."

His mother never once looked at him. When the train had disappeared from sight, he separated from his sister and brother-in-law and hurried through the ticket barrier and outside. Her grandchild's more important than her son. The thought troubled him all day.

When the vacation was over he went back to Tokyo. The day before he left, a printed circular arrived at his sister's house advising that vaccinations would shortly be held for all children born in the previous year. His sister and brother-in-law decided they would rather have it done by the family doctor, but he felt they would be better off not having it done at all, if that were possible. He felt it would somehow dirty the child.

After about two weeks a letter arrived at his place from his sister saying that Yukiko had had her vaccination and that since then, for five days, her temperature had not gone down, and she was worried about it. He knew that vaccination could lead to a minor bout of fever, but surely it shouldn't last for five days. He became convinced that it must have developed into some other illness. What his sister wrote only fed his imagination but did nothing to contain it. So he wrote back for more news, asking for as speedy a reply as possible, but four days passed and no answer came. Every time he went back to his lodgings, he asked the girl if there was a letter for him. While he was out he would imagine an answer had come and hurry back. After a week there was still no reply. He started to feel angry.

"Damn it, then. Let anything happen!" He tried to bully himself into that state of mind, but he had an unceasing sense of menace in his life, and he remained like that for another week, at the end of which a letter from his sister came. It was a clumsy scrawl, all blots and crossings-out.

"Yukiko's vaccination developed into erysipelas, but it took only the arm so her life was spared." That was all that was written.

He had a picture of Yukiko with one amputated arm

rolling over and over on the floor like a broken toy. An objectless rage rose within him. He took up his pen and wrote a postcard to his sister.

"It's because Yukiko was given into the care of someone as careless as you that this crime has been committed."

While he was writing he wept. When he tried to dip his pen into the inkpot, it wouldn't go in properly.

He took the postcard and went out. It's happened at last. What had been hanging over him for days had now taken on its clear and unmistakable shape. If only it could be his enemy; if only he could fight with it to the death. He felt an unknown violence boiling within him, but there was nothing he could expend it on. He was walking down a dark lane, and he thought of Yukiko grown up with this perpetual source of misery that was now hers. The thought made him stop in the dark.

"I'll marry her, then."

The idea came to him and he started working out the difference in their ages. Then he began to compare his own intelligence and ability with those of others.

"Come on, there's nothing all that wrong with me. I'll make her happy all right. I'll make her much more happy than anyone else could. It's settled."

He started walking again. Then he kept seeing pictures of his niece, a celluloid doll with its arm off, and the tears came again.

"A crime. A stupid, mad thing to do. Damned criminal thing to do."

He tripped and stumbled over a stone.

"Oh, shit!" he swore aloud.

The delivery boy from the noodle shop was coming toward him with plates piled on top of a tray on his head. He was aware of himself approaching the boy and glaring at him full of the brutal desire to smash all those plates down. The boy grinned at him with his eyes. The eyes had some kind of discharge in them.

"Hello," the boy said, and raised one leg in greeting.

He walked past, ignoring him. After a few paces he started to imagine the fatuous look on the boy's face as he had all his plates knocked flying, and he burst out laughing at the thought. He went on laughing and started to stagger and roll about the street like a drunkard. He wanted to drink. He wanted to get drunk.

It would soon be the summer vacation, but he didn't want to go home. He couldn't face the sight of his niece with only one arm. He wrote about his feelings to his father, who immediately replied that there must have been some misunderstanding since Yukiko had not lost an arm and there was nothing for him to be concerned about at all. By chance on the same day another letter arrived, this time from his brother-in-law. The poison had affected only the arm, not spreading to the rest of the body, and thus she had been able to survive. She was now as healthy as before, and crawling all over the place.

He picked up his pen and started writing an angry letter to his sister saying there was a limit to how badly people were permitted to write, when he felt all the strength drain from his body and he stopped halfway through. He had a wonderfully empty sensation of pure indolence, and he stared at the white azalea in the garden. After a while he decided he would lash out and have something really good to eat that day.

He went out but he only felt restless and confused. It was a feeling like being out of step, as if what other people called one he called two. It was as if he were making some kind of blunder.

The vacation came, and he went straightaway to his sister's place. Yukiko was by herself, clinging on the wooden frame of the lattice door leading into the front room, rattling it backward and forward. She was more than a year old now.

"Yuki. Here I am. I'm back."

He sat down heavily on the step in front of her. His niece looked afraid and clambered one step away from him.

He decided that it must be his long hair that frightened her, so he pulled his cap firmly down over his head to hide it and then crept forward a little.

"Come on. Come on, then."

The little girl began to get flustered and moved another two or three steps away, then looked round at him.

"Here, what's wrong?"

He suddenly got up and made a grab at her. She clung on to the door and, to his surprise, burst out crying. She cried just like a cicada that is being knocked down from a tree. He had no idea what to do with her.

Nearly all the work that should have been done during the vacation came to nothing from looking after Yukiko. Of course no one had asked him to do anything; it was a role he had taken on himself. And despite all that, Yukiko just would not take to him. He contorted his face in numerous ways to make her laugh, he gave her too many sweets, and then, having decided that she must be in the right mood, he would say cautiously to her: "Come on then, love, come on, love, it's all right," and take her by the hand. Immediately she would begin snivelling and take her hand away. Every time he had the same feeling of letdown, of solitude. He began to be afraid that the child was aware of some ugliness in him, that she directly sensed it in him like a bad smell.

"I know I'm no good for anything, but I really like you, I really do." He wanted to tell her that and hold her, and he had to restrain himself, but sometimes he couldn't help himself and he would try to take hold of her.

Once he forced his niece onto his lap. At first she just wriggled to get away and snivelled. Despite that, he started to hold her tighter and closer to him, and so she burst out crying. She would stop crying if he let her go, he knew, and so it was not serious and he decided not to let her go, whereupon the crying changed into long-drawn-out sobs. He pushed her away from him. She crawled away quickly to some distance as if fleeing from something truly horrible, and then knelt down on her little naked legs, sitting back upon her heels in a very grown-up manner, and continued crying. He gave a sudden motion with his body as if to tell her he was going to try to get her again, and she cried even louder and hastily drew herself further away.

(What is it in me she hates so much? And why am I such a fool as to dote on her like this?)

Then he wrote in a letter to a friend: "The end result of

our dealings with the swindler known as love is inevitably squalid. The reason for this is that we calculate what is due to us, our own payoff. And that's something we have no choice in, something we are bound to do. We don't know why we have to calculate like this, but we do it. And moreover, right in the centre of our incomprehensible, weird calculating nature, Love squats, the cashier at its till. That's it, wouldn't you say?"

However that might be, he was still obliged to spend all day and every day looking after Yukiko without ever being able to touch her. This kind of task began to get on his nerves and wear him out. The trouble was that his sister trusted him with the baby and was able to get on with all the household chores that wouldn't have got done any other way, so he couldn't just leave the child and ignore it. If he let his attention wander from the child for a moment and became absorbed in a book, then off she would go in search of her mother, edging along the wall in a very dangerous-looking way toward the veranda or the step, muttering "Baah, baah" to herself as she tried to peer into the neighbouring garden, which she could not yet manage to do. He would then bring her back into the centre of the room despite her howls. She would go off again. This happened countless times every day. If he was with Yukiko be could neither play with her nor get any work done at all. He just had to sit in a room where he could see the child, feeling irritated and bored and that was all. Sometimes he could stand it no longer and would caper around the room shouting and dancing about the child until his breath gave out. Then Yukiko would let forth a stream of incomprehensible sounds in obvious good humour. He would collapse onto his back with a theatrical gasp of weariness, and the child would roll over by his side in exactly the same way, gasping "Aaah" as well. But he had only to brush her with his hand and she would purse up her mouth as if she were going to cry and get up.

"Come on, love, it's all right, love, come on, love." He was reduced to just saying that, and watching her.

When he left his sister's he imagined that he would not go back.

But the next summer he did go back. There was no one in when he arrived so he lay down in the living room and read a book. After a while his sister came in and let the child down off her back. He felt a sudden spurt of happiness within him.

"Well, then. Now who's here, then? Who's that?"

His sister pointed at him, but the child only screwed up her face and began edging backward away from him, throwing out her arms as she almost fell down the step.

"Watch out," said his sister, and took hold of the child.

"Have you forgotten me? I'm your uncle."

Yukiko laid her hand on her mother's shoulder and looked at him with some signs of recognition.

"You are a forgetful little thing. He's your uncle."

"Uncle." Yukiko imitated the sound of her mother.

That made him feel horribly shy and he just grinned. Yukiko turned right away from him, hiding and rubbing her face in her mother's lapels.

He sometimes thought about the nature of the emotion Yukiko aroused in him. There were even times when he quite seriously thought that he had actually fallen in love with her. His one obsession was to really hold her in his arms for just once, even if for once only, and for her to truly allow him to do so. If he demanded more than that, then it was that she would permit him to hold her whenever he so desired. He took a lot of pains over this, but his reward, his "payoff," was the same frigid one as in the summer of the previous year. There were more and more days when he positively hated Yukiko.

"Why won't Yukiko let me hold her?" he asked his sister.

"I expect it's because you're too rough with her."

He was sure that wasn't it. But Yukiko did let herself be held quite nicely by other men, even men she hardly knew, so long as it wasn't her uncle, so perhaps his roughness was the reason. Whatever it was, the person Yukiko disliked most was her uncle, and the person her uncle liked most was Yukiko.

"I'm sick of looking after Yukiko. I don't want you to go on thinking that as long as I'm with her she's all right. Particularly with someone like me, who the more he's trusted, the nicer he becomes. I'm sick of being nice. It gets on my nerves being nice. I've had my lot of it."

Despite this preamble, however, his sister went on with her work and entrusted him with the child. Being trusted, he was trustworthy: he moaned about it but he looked after Yukiko. He restrained his desire to touch her, twisted his face and stood on his head to make her laugh, the complete fool, and then began to despise himself for being so. When she responded and laughed, he got carried away by what he was doing, his face all red, and became truly involved in imitating a dog, or a man stepping on the pedals as he cycled uphill. Then halfway through he would feel a hatred for what he was doing and stop. Then Yukiko would go on shaking her head and treading on the pedals and making the ringing sound of the bell with her tongue, running around the room by herself. For this child her uncle was simply an object, like the wall.

"Watch this one, then," he murmured to himself, looking at Yukiko.

The Child Who Was Laughed At

23 The Child Who Was Laughed At

The family used to discuss Kichi after dinner every night, debating what sort of person he ought to become. They were doing it again now. Kichi was cooking the bran porridge for the cows. There was a bubbly froth coming out from one of the twigs of firewood, and that intrigued him.

"Well, I reckon we'd better send him off to Osaka. If he can stick it out for fifteen years, they'll give him a share of the business, and he'll be able to make money hand over fist."

That was what his father suggested, but his mother replied: "He can't go to Osaka. That's out. They say the water's real bad there. What's the point of making a lot of money if you're going to die early?"

"Let him be a farmer, then, a farmer," his brother said.

"Kichi's clever with his hands. He ought to go to Shigaraki and become a potter. They say there's no trade like that one for making money."

That was his smart sister butting in.

"That's it. That's a good idea," father said. Only his mother said nothing in response.

Kichi noticed the big glass bottle of sake glittering on the dark shelf above the sink. He went out into the yard. He raised the bottle, put it to his mouth, and tipped it up. After a while a drop of sake rolled over his tongue. Kichi slurped it around his mouth, then tried again, but this time there was no luck. He put his nose inside the bottle.

"Are you at it again!" his mother shouted, and glared at him.

Kichi gave a foolish laugh and wiped his nose and mouth with his sleeve.

"He ought to be working down at the pub," his sister said, and his father and brother burst out laughing.

That night Kichi had a dream. He was in a pitch dark and endless plain, and a huge face, with a grin split from ear to ear, was laughing at him. The face was something like that of the lion in the lion dance he had seen somewhere one New Year, but when it laughed at Kichi its nostrils moved and twitched like those of a real person. Kichi tried with all his might to run away, but his legs were weak under him, and all he could do was stand there in the road with the sweat running off him. And all the time the face was coming nearer, but it did nothing to him, just went on forever merely smirking and grinning. Kichi didn't know what it was laughing about, but he did understand that it was laughing at him, that it was making a fool of him.

Next day he sat up on his mattress and stared at the faint light on the wall. He was still sweating, just as he had done for so long last night.

That day he got told off by the teacher at school three times. The first time was during the arithmetic class when they were doing improper fractions and had to turn them into mixed numbers, and Kichi was unable to answer when asked about the quantity of numerations involved.

"Just as I thought. You've been gaping out of the window ever since the period started."

The teacher was cross.

The second time was during writing practice. Kichi's writing paper had nothing on it resembling any writing of any sort, but there were three faces, looking something like the guardian dogs at the shrine gate and also something like human faces. The line of the mouths was painfully exaggerated, and because of being drawn and redrawn over and over there was no more than a black mess.

The third time was when school ended and the children were going home. They all took up their things, bowed to the teacher, and left. But Kichi was called back, scolded, and told to do it again properly.

He ran home, took a razor wrapped in oil paper out of the chest of drawers, and went off to the shed, where no one could see him, and started sharpening it. When he'd done it, he walked around the outside of the house looking among the piled-up wood. Then he went back into the yard and felt the pestle used for pounding rice. Then he wandered round to the scullery again and turned the chopping board over and thought about it; and then suddenly he ran off to the well and looked up at the well bucket.

"That's it. That's just right."

There was a log of heavy zelkova wood that acted as a weight for the bucket, and he took that away and attached a stone in its place. He made the wood into a wide, oblong shape about four inches thick, and then took it, a pencil, and the razor, and went up into the attic.

The next day, then the next, and every day for some time after that, Kichi would do the same thing.

A month passed. It was April and Kichi left school. Still he went on sharpening the razor and going up into the attic, his face a little pale now. And still the family would take up from time to time the question of what kind of job he ought to have, but the discussion never got anywhere.

One day after lunch his father felt his face, then took out his razor. Kichi was sipping his tea.

"Who the hell's been cutting my razor about?"

Father held the blade up to the light to scrutinize it, then took two cuts at a piece of paper. The blade dragged slightly. Father's face became severe.

"Who's been slashing this razor to pieces?"

Father rolled up his sleeve to bare his arm, and tried the razor on it.

"Useless," he said.

Kichi held a mouthful of tea in his mouth for a long time and said nothing.

"Kichi was sharpening it a little while ago," his sister said.

"Kichi! What have you been up to?"

Kichi gulped down the tea. He didn't say anything.

"Well? What have you been up to?"

It seemed that Kichi wasn't ever going to reply.

"I know. Kichi's always up there in the attic. I bet he's been doing something up there," his sister said, and went out into the yard.

"You keep out of it," the silent Kichi at last burst out.

"Given yourself away now," his sister said, and climbed up the ladder suspended from the outer rafters. Kichi dashed barefoot into the yard and started shaking the ladder.

"Stop it, Kichi. You're scaring me, doing that."

His sister had contracted her shoulders in fear and just looked at him for a little, then pursed up her mouth and made a gesture as if to spit at him.

"Kichi!" his father bawled at him.

After a while his sister's voice could be heard coming from the attic.

"Oh look, he's been making a mask up here."

Kichi waited for her to bring the mask down, then jumped her. She pushed him away and speedily handed the mask over to her father. Father held it up almost reverently for a while and looked at it in silence.

"It's a fine piece of work, this is."

He stared at it in silence again.

"Yes. This is a fine piece of work."

The mask looked down at his father, leering at him, mocking him.

That night his father and mother lay in the back room talking about it.

"Kichi can be a clog maker." His father came out with that first. His mother said nothing.

"We can take out the front wall from that shed by the road, and make a shop out of it. There's not one clog maker in the whole village," he added.

His mother, who had been keeping silent in an anxious sort of way up to now, said, "That'll do, then. The boy's not strong, and I wouldn't want him to go a long way away."

So Kichi became a clog maker. The mask he had made laughed down from the lintel above the door of his shop. Naturally nobody knew what it might be laughing about.

Kichi spent the next twenty-five years fumbling about making clogs beneath that mask. He remained poor. Naturally his father and mother died.

One day Kichi looked up at the mask. He hadn't done so for a long time. The mask leered down at him from the lintel, making a fool out of him. It made him angry. Then it made him sad. Then it made him angry again.

"It's all your fault. You turned me into a clog maker."

He dragged the mask down, swung his hatchet, and smashed it in two. He took the broken mask in his hand, looking at it in the same way he would look every day at the wooden base of a clog. Then it struck him what a fine pair of clogs this would make. Then his face softened and took on its usual vacant expression.

The Defeated Husband

31 The Defeated Husband

I

The wind went on blowing in the dark. Outside you heard the fence swaying in the wind. Bundles of stacked-up firewood sometimes rattled and tapped at the long windows. Even so, his wife could not be talked out of going back home. He said no more about it. As they both went out, her trailing hair was suddenly caught up by the wind and blown sideways to cling to her face.

"Come in here if you want."

He opened his cloak for her as a gesture of reconciliation.

"It's all right," she said.

"All right, then."

Another slap in the face. A solitary girl stumbled across the plank bridge over the ditch. From above the tall fence the glare of an arc light cut down to where they walked. His wife's face was pale and sullen beneath the hair that flickered across it.

"Let me in," she said after a while.

He had already thrust love aside. He did not reply but again he opened his cloak. Suddenly a car with no lights flew past like a spear.

They turned the corner and descended the slope. There was no one about. Somewhere there was the high shriek of a whistle. That means bad luck, he thought. His wife was trembling slightly. There was the dance of newly leaved branches and scraps of straw on the rise, dust blown up and away in the wind, and nothing more.

"You'll hurry back?"

"Yes."

Branches were being beaten down onto the fence. The lights of the town flashed out. They reached the end of the rise where the town was forced down under the sounding storm. There was a wooden bridge with one of its cross-beams swaying loose.

Below the bridge, below the stone embankment, the always turbid water raged.

"This will do here," his wife said.

He stopped. He wanted to part here too. He would go and

see the lady in the bookshop. He would go and see the lady in that bookshop he always went to.

'Well then."

She stood in front of him for a while looking up at his face. He avoided her eyes and looked toward the street corner ahead.

"I'm off now."

"All right."

She made no effort to smile at him and went away. The edge of her shawl and a corner of her sleeve fluttered as if about to fly away. In a few minutes she had crossed the bridge and disappeared into the next street. But he still stood there. It would be better if his wife did not see that he was off to the lady in the bookshop. The door blind of a deserted street stall flapped and beat. In the empty lot on the street corner there was a vast mound of dust and rubbish. On top of this mound a pole had been planted askew, and a piece of sodden cloth waved at its tip. Then the figure of his wife, who should have been totally gone by now, suddenly peered out from the corner of the street and glanced in his direction. He couldn't think it was because she regretted leaving him and had come back for one final glance. He leaned on the rail and looked back again. He could still see her face there at the street corner, as if she were lying in wait for someone, a child playing hide-and-seek. He felt a fear start within him. She had been lying about going home. She must be going to meet someone else. He himself had been pretending to see her home but in fact he had been going to the bookshop. He had been playing hide-and-seek with her as she now played it with him, peeking back to make sure where the person after her might be. He turned round and went in the direction of his own home.

"An irony, by God, an irony."

II

His frustration at not having seen the lady in the bookshop turned into a vicious anger against himself. There was a piece of paper fastened on the wall of the room in front of him, something he'd written on a day when the two of them were happy.

And love is various
In loveliness and Ah
In varying delights.

He ripped down the yellowing piece of paper. He felt like inflicting something really painful upon himself, writing something truly poisonous in place of that. Still, he did not. He would go and see the lady in the bookshop. He knew that she was in love with him. Or, anyway, to imagine that she was would be the best plan. He had first met her three years ago. He had been standing in front of the bookshelves when he realized he had dropped a book somewhere that he needed for the next period. He gave a little cry of surprise.

"Is anything the matter?" she had asked him, hesitating as she was about to sit down. That was how she first came to know him.

He took out his watch and looked at the time. It was eight o'clock. This was the time he always went to she shop, stood there a little, said nothing to her, then came home. He felt the pulse in his wrist. He drew the collar of his cloak closer about his neck and went out again into the wind.

III

The bookseller and his wife were sitting on either side of the stove in the shop.

"Hasn't *The Lightning* come out yet?" he asked.

Neither of them said anything. Only the wife went red and looked into her lap.

Something's up, he thought.

"It hasn't come out yet, *The Lightning*?"

The husband simply held the poker tight in his hand and looked outside as if he hadn't heard anything.

"Yes, it's not appeared yet," the wife said.

The wind was beating against the glass doors at the front of the shop. The poker in the husband's hand trembled.

"When will it be out, then, *The Lightning*?"

The woman avoided his eyes, moved her mouth slightly, but said nothing.

"It'll be out soon, will it?"

"Yes," she replied in a low voice. She's afraid of that

husband of hers.

He said goodnight and left. As he went out, he felt a momentary wish to go back and talk to the man who was so annoyed with him, tell him that his wife wasn't in love with anyone else although someone else was in love with his wife. He wanted to say that for her sake; anyway, he wouldn't go there again. He couldn't go there again. He stopped by the side of the road. He had no right to be annoyed with anybody. Then he suddenly remembered a girl back home in the country called Kanko. Surely she at least had been truly in love with him? And he with her once. But they had said nothing whatsoever to each other about it and drifted apart.

He thrust his shoulder firmly against the revolving door of a wayside café. From the opening, the sound of a serenade played on the gramophone leaped out at him.

"Good evening, sir. What a dreadful wind."

A waitress approached and began wiping the marble top of the table. Curtains were flapping up in the wind. He stabbed at the menu with his finger.

"Yes. Cocoa?"

He was thinking about whom he was really most in love with. In some corner of his heart to which there was no doorway, something whispered that it was his wife. But if it was his wife, Tatsuko who betrayed him, then that only made him that much more lonely.

IV

He got home late that night. When he arrived his wife was there before him, and she had gone to sleep. He stood and looked at her sleeping face.

"I love you, and you don't love me. So I don't want to love you. You're the one who's making me behave like this."

He almost succumbed to the desire to embrace her. But what about her? Her face appeared more beautiful than usual. He suddenly wanted to kick her.

She opened her eyes all of a sudden and called his name.

He didn't reply.

"Halfway there I decided not to go and came home."

"You came straight back?"

"Yes. The wind was so awful."

Then she closed her eyes again.

You met someone, I know, he wanted to say. But that was what he ought to be saying to himself. So he said nothing and went into his own room.

After a while the door slid open and she called him.

He said nothing but looked up.

"Aren't you coming to bed?"

"Shouldn't you be in bed yourself?"

He began stuffing his pipe with tobacco.

"What are you thinking about?"

He didn't reply.

"I know what you're thinking about."

He looked from her face down to her feet as if investigating her good looks.

"You mustn't look at me like that. I don't like it."

She came close to him and leaned her warm body heavily against him.

"Oh, let's go to bed now. Let's."

He remained sullen and obstinate.

She laid her cheek against his head and gently swayed it to and fro. He let himself be swayed. He realized she was offering a compensation for her private actions that evening.

"Stop it," he said.

She suddenly let go of him and moved away. Then she went back to her own room and slammed the door.

V

In the marketplace the figs and grapes had disappeared from the greengrocers' stalls. Persimmons in new boxes were lined up in their stead. The shadows in the streets fell in new directions, and it became cold. He wasted almost the whole day in aimless walking. He no longer went to the bookshop. He drooped, like a summer leaf that feels the cold. Then one fine day he came home from his walk and found a letter addressed to his wife fallen face upward in the hallway. Thinking nothing in particular, he reached to pick it up. Suddenly something passed through his mind. He snatched his hand away and stared down at the letter.

"I'll bet it's from a man."

Suspicion flickered up at him from the unknown handwriting on the envelope, and as it deepened he did not feel like turning it over to see the sender's name.

He went into his study. She was out, as he had expected. When he'd been overtaken by similar doubts in the past, he was in the habit of remembering other, earlier times when he had suspected and been mistaken. Doubting oneself was a fruitful method of repressing the pain of real doubt. And yet, since in most cases there was always at least some truth behind his suspicions, this introspective clarification of his own state of mind really only meant causing himself double labour.

After a while she came home. He waited for her to say something herself about the letter. But she didn't come into his room, but only kept up a continual clatter with the handles of the chest of drawers. He felt he couldn't put up with this any longer, and called her.

"Oh, are you back?" She slid the door open a little and peeped in. "I'll have the dinner ready soon," she said considerately.

This very considerateness on her part only strengthened his suspicions.

"There was a letter for you, wasn't there?"

"Yes."

"Who from?"

"A friend."

"Of mine?"

"No, mine."

"Where've you been?"

"I went to get some stock. And you know there was something really funny. You know the dry cleaner's, the one with the blue curtains, you know? Well, there was a blind man with a towel tied round his head, and he was. . . ."

"You're lying."

"No, honest. And he was. . . ."

"I'm talking about the letter. All you can talk is lies."

"But it's true, it's from a friend. Shall I show it to you?"

"What sort of friends have you got, then?"

"Well, I do have friends."

"Show it."

He put out his hand. She pouted like a child and said, "I don't want to." Then she made to go into the next room.

He stood up. She started walking quickly away as if to escape, although she looked round at him slightly.

"I've torn it up. There were all sorts of naughty things written in it," she said with a playful little smirk.

He didn't pursue it further. She was now sitting slumped beside the stove, staring pointedly away from him and pouting. He stood stock-still in the centre of the room and stared at her with her silly swollen cheeks. Then suddenly he felt the strength drain out of his body.

My God, look at that. And that's my wife. He gaped at her as if he lacked the power to close his mouth, looking coldly at her composure.

I've had enough.

He went quickly out through the front door.

He tramped along with his head down. High heels kicking up the hem of a skirt. The scattering of horses' hooves. Thick car tires turning in the dust. Then a bicycle crashed sideways on a curve halfway up the hill.

Who was the man? But at this point who cared who the man was. He decided to leave his wife. And the way he had dragged after her, trailed after her up to now, dirtying himself, a dirty tin can dragging after her. His rage went against himself. Still, it would be unbearable to go on feeling like this. He must do something. Drink perhaps? No, drink was no good.

Then he was suddenly aware of himself going in the direction of the bookshop. He felt there was nowhere else he could go that would be of any help to him, the way he felt now. So go then. It would do him good to see her, and there was no chance of it making relations between her and her husband any worse than they were now. The further he got from his own house, the more cheerful he became. The evening light lay in the turbid air. Night stalls were being lowered from their carts. A trailing cinema poster flapped colour over a chalk-white ticket office. A woman with an apron crossed busily before him. On the enormous chopping board of a poultry shop, naked birds hung down their dangling heads. The cook rolled up his sleeves. A carving knife flashed out sharply in the evening light. The streets were coming back to life again. He didn't want to go to the bookshop until it was quite dark. Because what he was most afraid of was being seen by her husband. He then noticed himself standing in front of a draper's show window. What was he looking at? He had no idea. Then he was aware that it was just that in the days when they'd been happy he had this habit of looking for cloth of exactly the right pattern to suit his wife, days when he would walk along endlessly like this, looking; and the habit had remained and now just reappeared. With a look of bitter displeasure he started walking again.

VI

He waited for dark, and then approached the bookshop. He passed speedily along the brightly lit road in front of the shop, then had a quick, careful look inside to see if the man was in or not. The wife was sitting alone, staring vacantly at some unmoving point outside. He ducked his head before she noticed him and passed by. Then he regretted that he hadn't had the courage to intercept her gaze until she recognized him. Why hadn't he? He went on a little farther and looked back. Then her head appeared in the doorway of the shop, as if she'd seen him and come running out. So he wheeled round and went on hurriedly in the same direction again. He could not understand what it was in him that made him behave like this. He could so clearly sense her looking in his direction but he didn't know whether to turn round or not, and then he also started to wonder why she had come running out when she saw him. Perhaps it was just to tell him that the book, *The Lightning*, which he had ordered, had come out. He turned in her direction. She was still standing there looking in his. He automatically began to lower his head in greeting, but he was put off by someone passing by and immediately straightened up again; and once more turning and looking fixedly before him, he walked on. But suppose it was just that she wanted to let him know that the book had come? He really ought to go back. But then he imagined turning round and the desolate feeling if she were not still standing there, and the desire to turn back left. Then he thought of the darkness waiting for him when he arrived back home.

"I can't stand that any more," he thought.

His pace slackened.

"I'll go to the bookshop. She's in love with me, isn't she? Then what am I hanging about here for?"

He tried to urge himself on like this, but then the miserable face of the husband appeared in his mind's eye, and his courage failed. Because his own unchaste wife tormented him, he was trying to get rid of that misery by imposing the identical suffering upon somebody else. Obviously that was unforgivable. But he was sick to death of thinking about these things. All it led to was misery. He wanted to slash through these entangling emotions with one blow. He wanted to force some insane courage into himself, so he cried out: "Then let people who will, suffer. Let them suffer."

He was going back to the bookshop; but his legs did not move.

"Let's go," he said, but he was still standing still.

"Come on."

He started walking back toward the bookshop. She was no longer in front of the shop. Still, as he got nearer the bookshop, he felt a weird power inside him. A savage and energetic forward march.

He barged into the shop feeling that he might well fall over. The lady had her hand out giving a customer his change. When the customer had gone, she noticed him. But she immediately sat down by the stove, gazing silently into her lap.

He stood where he was and looked straight at her. She went on looking down with her pale face, still saying nothing. He felt tears welling up in his eyes.

"I shan't be coming any more," he said after a while.

She raised her head for the first time. He sensed her eyes glistening also.

"I'm sorry," she said softly, bowing her head slightly.

"I was thinking of going back home."

As he said so, her eyes rounded in what almost seemed panic.

"But you'll be coming back?"

"Is your husband at home?"

"No, but you will be coming back?"

"I'm not sure. I feel I've done wrong by your husband."

"No, that's not so. It's nothing at all really. But is there something wrong at home?"

"Nothing in particular. Is your husband at home?"

As he said so, he was aware that his mouth said nothing of what he actually felt.

"Excuse me, then." He suddenly bowed his head and started to leave.

She looked at him with a little gasp of surprise, but made no reply.

He went out the front door.

As he got farther away from the bookshop, his state of excitement left him. Would he really not go there again? Would he really go back to his home in the country? As he thought about it, he began to think for the first time that he really would go there no more, and would in fact go home. It wasn't just because he had announced to her that he would do so, but rather because the thought that such things were possible had suddenly risen up within him. This was something apart from the mere fact that he had told her, although the very fact that he had done so meant that he now knew he had driven a very powerful nail into his desire to see her again.

"No, I certainly won't go back there. Even supposing she were in love with me and I with her, what sort of reason would that be, what sort of excuse for taking her? None at all."

Then what would be a reason for taking her? That he still did not know. Only he thought of all those cases of people who had used that as the one reason, and he felt that one ought not to ignore in one's calculations the misery that sort of thing led to. He wanted to take up once more some truly serious and honourable attitude toward these things. Men are calculating animals. Calculating means the setting of things in order; it implies the idea of progression, of movement forward. A passion that does not calculate, does not work things out, is a form of wager, a gamble. Since the fate of any wager must always be uncertain, he decided that it must be considered as a wrong action. And yet, behind all this, he could sense his desire to meet the woman again. But recalling how clearly she had shown her affection for him, if he went there again what kind of wretchedness would that mean for her husband? It did not bear thinking about. Then what could he do? The thing was just to leave everything and go off back home to the country. Kanko was there.

He took some pains, on going home that night, not to look at his wife. Up to now, whenever he'd had the experience of hating his wife, just to look at her face would weaken that feeling and the resolve that went with it.

He sat at his desk and looked at the doctorate he had recently been working on. The title of his thesis on genetics was "Some Determining Principles and Lines of Mutation in Sexless Generative Organisms." Then a letter flopped on top of a probability curve tracing the relationship between the incidence of protoplasm within the chlorophyll of duckweed and the effect of sunlight. He looked round and his wife was standing there. She was glaring at him viciously in obvious ill humour.

"What's this?" he said, picking up the letter.

"Look and see."

She went back to her own room. He looked at the letter and saw it was an old one he had written to her some time ago.

Once more you ask me of my love for you.
Then I reply 'you love me not'.
My love is in my anger towards you.
Then since you do not know my heart
Weep bitterly, but weep.
Since I love you, I must be dumb and still.
There is no need for you to question me.
Even this still, dumb heart must love you.
Then let us grow old so.
If you but understand there is no sorrow.
We wrong our hearts to ever bid them stir.
My heart, be like the silent well at dawn.

He took this old love letter of his and hurled it away from him.

VII

From the next day onward he was waiting until he should feel a definite impulse to return home. But since his wife never mentioned the idea of separation, he felt incapable of bringing up the subject. Certainly his natural lack of ability to make decisions would have contributed to this, but more than that, there was still a considerable part of him that did not want this separation from his wife to take place. And not only that. There were trivial reasons, like the bookshop being near and so he could always be off to see the woman there if he felt like it, and others, and these kept him with Tatsuko although always ready to take flight. While he was living in this state, Mishima arrived in Tokyo from his home in the country. As soon as he arrived at the station, Mishima came straight over to his place, complete with heavy luggage. They had been friends ever since they'd been at school together.

"Still another year to go?" he asked.

"One more year," Mishima replied.

Mishima had entered the university late, and he'd been called up for military service while still a student. Thus he had to complete another year of residence in order to graduate.

"I've lost all interest in life recently. It didn't use to be like that, though," he said to Mishima.

"That's hardly the way to be going on with things as they are now, is it?"

"No way to be going on at all. Not at all."

"What are you working on at the moment?" Mishima asked.

"I've been dabbling in biology a bit. Still, I've lost interest. I found the study of mutation, unexpected and sudden biological change, pretty absorbing, but since nothing of that kind seems likely to happen to me. . . . That's what I need—total change of personality."

"Sudden mutation?"

"That's right. It's all right to dream about, but since one can't change, one loses interest. If one's going to dream, one's better off with astronomy. These are one hundred and thirty thousand different worlds. Imagine those one hundred and thirty thousand different suns. Now there's something interesting, you know, working things out from that. I suppose you don't have astronomy in the army?"

"No baby yet?"

"No, not yet."

"While you're working out about those one hundred and thirty thousand suns, it would be amusing to produce whole swarms of kids."

"Come off it, you fool."

"I'm serious. At least it'd be better than the army."

"I'm not with you there. Give me the army."

"You try eating the stinking food, then."

"Valiant exploits and all that."

"What do you mean, 'valiant'? What 'exploits'?"

"No, I mean just being in that sort of mood, you know. The great thing about being a soldier is that you're always being made to do things by someone else—don't have to do anything on your own, which must be quite a relief."

"You have very extraordinary ideas about the place, I can see."

"Maybe. Still, even though I've been alive for some time now, every time I thought that now I really had got myself free, well, even at the best it wasn't much to write home about. Probably the very fact of still expecting to become free means one's still only a babe in arms really."

"So you're a babe in arms?" Mishima said.

"You don't think so?"

"Hardly."

Mishima smiled as if he found it all slightly ridiculous.

After a while his wife came in carrying some vegetables.

"Why, Mishima," she cried, standing there as if astounded.

"Sorry to have barged in like this again."

"You have become horribly brown and sunburnt."

"I must have. You wouldn't know any speedy method of turning white again?"

"You should smear brown sugar all over your face."

"But that would only make me more brown and horrible, wouldn't it?"

"Where are you at the moment?"

"Here."

"Don't be so clever."

"No, really. I came here straight from the station."

"Oh dear, I've said the wrong thing," his wife said, and formally welcomed Mishima there. "I must apologize for not having written or anything. It really is very good to see you, and looking so well, too."

"I'm the one to apologize for not writing," said Mishima, and bowed his head slightly.

"You never used to like living in lodgings, did you?" he said to Mishima.

"I hated it."

"You still feel you can afford not to like it, even after your army experiences?"

"Even more so after that."

"But why, then, don't you stay with us?" his wife said.

"Yes, sure, we've got a spare room. Of course in your case we'd expect a pretty fat rent."

"Please do stay," his wife added.

"If it's not going to put you out too much, I'd be very glad to," Mishima said.

"I'm used to it. My husband puts me out all the time."

"So there'd be a double imposition."

"Oh, I never thought of it like that," his wife said.

He didn't look at his wife's face. However, in the exaggerated tone of surprise in her voice, he felt that her expression must have something provocative, something flirtatious in it, and he felt a coldness in his heart. Then he was angry with himself because he still felt threatened by the idea of some revenge, any revenge, that his wife might be thinking of taking upon him.

"You know you won't find lodgings at this time of year. Don't you think you'd do best to stay here? That's all right, then? She'll probably give you some pretty tasteless stuff to eat, though."

He felt pleased at the thought that these words of his would have gone against her designs, her expectations, and also at the easy way with which they had come quite unimpeded from his mouth.

VIII

A dry, dusty wind blew for two days, and then ceased a while. His wife was cleaning his room. He sat on the low windowsill and looked at the suburban streets. A stagecoach was returning to the country, its horses shaking their heads. The quietly hanging carriage curtain was blown open. The face of a woman appeared. There was a smile upon her face, a slightly cynical one as if she had just cleverly deceived somebody.

"Look at this dust." Tatsuko spoke from behind him.

He went to glance at her face, then stopped. He realized he had looked at her only once all morning.

"You really oughtn't to sit there. You'll get smothered in dust."

He didn't reply. He understood she was trying to get him to look at her

The swishing sound of her broom stopped. He was counting the leaves of one of the potted plants on the windowsill.

"Isn't the dust awful. Just look."

"Shut up, can't you?" he said loudly, and glared at her.

She compressed her lips tight. Then when he looked in the other direction, she stopped her cleaning and went off to the kitchen.

He was preparing himself for some kind of revenge from her, since it was bound to come sometime. He started to think about what form it might take. However, since she'd no doubt already got it all worked out, something of the most melodramatic nature, then let it come. Thinking like that calmed him down. He watched a small boy holding a bicycle with one hand and banging a clog with the other against the stump of a hackberry tree.

After a while Mishima came into his room.

"I'm just going as far as K for a while. It's about a room I asked about there," Mishima said.

"The wind's stopped just right for you. When the wind's really bad, you'd be surprised how many people go smack up against the horses' faces."

"Whatever for? Oh, because they can't see? The dust is really foul, isn't it."

"Once, when was it? Anyway, sheets of corrugated iron got caught up on the telephone wires, dried sardines got blown out of the kitchen and bowled along all down the road, birds were being blown all over the place. God, that was a laugh."

"That must have been great."

"It was."

"Sardines bowling down the street." Mishima laughed.

"But it doesn't do to be amused by things like that, you know."

"Anyway, it's funny. There's nothing I can get for you while I'm out, I suppose?"

"Not sure. Well, anything you like, I guess."

"Are you going out, Mishima?" Tatsuko called out gaily from the kitchen. Then she opened the door and came in rubbing her mouth with a towel.

"Where are you going?"

"Just down to K for a bit."

Tatsuko narrowed her eyes as she looked at Mishima, then spoke in a low voice husky no doubt with passion: "Oh, but you won't be late?"—crestfallen, gloom and despair visible in the depressed tilt of her head.

"Very well, I shall come back early today."

"Oh, will you really? I know you."

"Place your trust in me, at least a little."

"Right, I trust you. So don't disappoint me, will you? Hurry back."

Now he could see her revenge was beginning, but he also found his normal jovial remarks still coming forth from himself, an effort on his part presumably to ride her punches.

"Have a cup of tea before you go. Put the kettle on, Tatsuko, will you?" he said.

"Oh, he doesn't want to waste time drinking tea. Hurry off now and come back all the sooner, is what I say. You will, won't you?"

"I wouldn't mind a cup of tea," Mishima said.

"Well, I shan't let you have any. You can have one if you don't go. You won't go, will you?"

"What am I supposed to do now?" said Mishima, leaving in a great hurry.

"What? You're going? I suppose you're just going to drop in somewhere for a quick one again?"

Tatsuko crossed her arms coyly in front of her, and trotted after Mishima as if she were seeing off her husband.

Now that he was alone, his face became bitter.

"Goodbye, then. Hurry back home. It's so lonely here all by myself."

He heard her friendly voice coming from the doorway. So I'm a total stranger, am I?

A little after, she came back into his room. He was very calmly pouring hot water into the teapot, and he looked up at her.

"Do you want some tea?"

"Yes. Thanks."

She stood quietly by the window, avoiding his face.

—It's all over between us, I know, but that's all right by me, is what he felt he read in the lines of her back, lines and pages in a book that had given him so much pleasure and pain. Then she began singing a song quietly to herself as she still went on looking outside. It was a lullaby. He felt a terrible uprush of anger at her calmness. He felt like throwing the teapot in his hand at her. Immediately his anger submerged into the midst of a depressed, unmoving loneliness.

IX

It would soon be nightfall. He was weary of waiting for night to fall. When it got dark, he wanted to go to the bookshop he hadn't visited for so long. He had been looking forward to it since morning. He opened wide the curtains of his study and let the evening sun full into the room. He saw the curve of a vegetable garden and the pasture beyond it. Dappled cows were standing in yellow grass. A young milkman shouldering milk buckets passed outside the wall along his bookcase. The red dome of a church caught the sun far off and glittered among the low trees of a wood. He suddenly began thinking about his aged mother.

"Are you coming to the bath?"

Tatsuko spoke from the next room. He did not reply. She opened the door of his room. She was holding a small metal bowl.

"Aren't you coming?"

"No."

"I'm going anyway. All right?"

She went toward the front door without waiting for a reply. Then she turned round again.

"I suppose Mishima hasn't come back yet?"

He really hated her now.

"I suppose he'll have dropped in somewhere. And there's all that rice needs eating up."

Then he heard the sound of her slipping on her clogs.

"Keep your eye on the cooker, won't you? I've already put the rice on. Don't forget."

The face that she should be using the short period of time while dinner was cooking to go to the bath showed not that she was having wifely thoughts about him, but instead that she was dreaming about Mishima coming back.

"She's the enemy now."

What he most feared was the beauty of his wife after she had taken her bath. He felt he would have been able to love his wife better if only she had been less beautiful. He was straining to understand these feelings of his that always wanted to cling to and twine about his wife, to try to see them as simple objects clearly diffused in light, transparent to the view. The vegetable garden, the pasture, the dome, the herd of dappled cows, the wood, the evening mist like drifting smoke above the roof of the farmhouse. The backs of the cows began to move inside their shed. The lightning conductor on the dome let forth one last glitter of light in the air. Below, the wood was silent. He reflected that at this very moment, somewhere and everywhere, many people must be dying.

X

Mishima came back with an exhausted look in his eyes.

"Ah well, things are not going as I'd thought," Mishima said, and stretched out by his side.

"How was it?"

"There's someone ahead of me, it seems. Won't know till tomorrow apparently."

As he looked at Mishima's face, he began to feel a slight sense of fear. The fact is there had been times when the voice of an errand boy at the back door could be full of menace. Then walking the streets he would see men who seemed to be searching for something, his eyes would meet theirs, and he would feel a weight pressing down on his heart, because those men would be looking here and there searching for Tatsuko, who was not by his side. Sometimes he would wake up in the middle of the night. Then the ticking of the pendulum of the grandfather clock became the footsteps of some mysterious man who had crept into the room to take Tatsuko.

I've got to really watch out now. Tatsuko's after me. She's going to kill me.

Mishima was tired and had nothing to say. He was finding it more and more insufferable to have to be near to Mishima like this. Then he noticed something bright; it was his wife's dress cast loosely, carelessly over the back of the clotheshorse. He could feel the scent of her body clinging to it. He wanted to crush down the spurt of lust he felt within himself, so he let the focus of his eyes move slightly away. The incense burner on the floor looked like a carved lion in the evening light that filtered through the curtains. The hanging heads of dahlias drooped on top of the bookcase. The pattern of the carpet and the shadows thrown by his piles of specimens lying on the floor were reflected in the slanting mirror suspended from the wooden doorpost.

His wife returned from the bath. He noticed that as she stood in the doorway to his room her eyes glided in the direction of Mishima.

"You have got back nice and early. A bit too early for my liking. The dinner's not ready yet and I'm sure you must be absolutely starving," she said to Mishima.

"Not at all. Since I'm fed every day with your tasteless concoctions, I took the liberty to try elsewhere today."

"Well, what a thing to say."

"Do you enjoy Nara pickles? I bought some at the place I went to."

"You mean *you* enjoyed Nara pickles. Why don't you say what you mean? And fancy going all out of your way like that just to eat Nara pickles. I know I wouldn't."

"You seem incapable of grasping my meaning."

"Why?"

"I was asking if you enjoyed Nara pickles since I have bought some for you in the belief that you did and you do."

"I fear I have no desire to eat Nara pickles."

"Then what do you like?"

"I like babies."

"In that case, it seems you will need to be a little more patient."

Tatsuko gave a burst of surprise and doubled up with laughter. He didn't like the way Mishima perked up like this when he saw his wife.

"Don't you know what babies are?" Tatsuko asked.

"Let me remind you, madam, that I am a university student with all knowledges at my fingertips."

Tatsuko had stopped laughing but now burst out again as if she couldn't help herself.

"What is the joke? Certainly the antithesis of babies and Nara pickles is somewhat eccentric, but. . . ."

"Babies are sweets, you know."

Mishima was silent for a while, and then said: "I was aware of that all along, of course." Then he began sniggering himself.

"You didn't know. You are funny."

"I did know."

"You did not. And how should a man who delights in Nara pickles be acquainted with babies?"

"What on earth are these babies?"

"There you are. You see."

"They have hands, they have feet. . . ."

"They do not. They're all belly. And they have a currant instead of a belly button. But they're awfully nice when you're a bit tight. A sight better than your Nara pickles."

"We have had enough, I feel."

"You a university student with all knowledges at your fingertips."

"Look, she's your wife, for heaven's sake. Tell her off."

But he sat there in silence, smiling slightly and puffing away at a cigarette as if bored with the whole thing. His wife seemed to have decided that she had sufficiently displayed her after-bath charms, since she suddenly went off in a great bustle into the kitchen.

"Oh, my God, the rice is all burnt now. What's the point of asking you to do anything? Look at it. What am I supposed to do now?"

Gathering from the plangent tone of her voice as she said this, he felt just how much true pleasure and total satisfaction being able to tell him off in that theatrical way must be giving her.

He thought he would welcome what was going to happen between Mishima and his wife. He'd got to the stage where having to look and speak in this lying way before a friend was becoming quite unbearable. He felt like destroying himself to cure this weird sickness that he had. He thought how contemptible he was with his perpetual fears about his wife's chastity, his obsession with preserving it at all costs, this continual watchfulness, the thought of an existence consisting entirely of precautions; all this in him he wanted to smear over, rub out with the realization of that event which he supremely feared.

XI

When he left the house it was already dark outside. He began to walk at once in the direction of the bookshop. A little girl with perfectly normal legs was limping hurriedly along imitating a cripple. After her came a truck racing along jammed tight with policemen. The load of policemen stood silently protruding above the cab like black stamens. A car followed after them. There was a girl inside who was tired. The wooden bridge shook as the vehicles passed over. He came to the main road and turned right. Several trams flew by shaking their human bundles to the rear. The crammed flesh ricocheted inside the square trams. Whirlpools of sickly fragrant lust, bounding and leaping.

He thought about himself in terms of being a man going to see another man's wife. His pace slackened. Even if he had reasons for it, even if he had no desire to go the whole way with her, it was still undoubtedly a form of dissipation.

Then within the depths of his being he felt a single power

that had been sleeping within him spring suddenly into life.

"I'll go home now, straightaway. I'll see Kanko."

He went to the tram stop to take the tram to the station. It came. He pushed aside a great many people and got on the tram first. He was suddenly aware that now at this moment he was deciding his own fate for himself. Within the fierce coldness of his heart, waves of pure tragic despair beat upon the shore. All the joy of his past relationship with his wife appeared now arrayed in splendour.

He looked round at all the people about him. He wanted to discover someone beautiful there, something to cling to. But as he considered the wild course he was pursuing, racing toward disaster at breakneck speed, he felt even more the desire to whip up his willpower faster and faster.

When he arrived at the station, he checked his watch against the timetable. There was enough time until the train left to think about his wife and the woman in the bookshop until his old uncertainties would return. There was thirty minutes, and anything could happen in that time. He realized that the most vital thing was to get his ticket bought. Then he chose the busiest part of the huge station and walked up and down, up and down. It would be dangerous to sit down on a bench, for that would invite the past back into his mind. The great thing was to take this opportunity to think about the future in purely optimistic terms, and to get his mind working upon subjects that would stimulate those cheerful imaginations in the most fruitful way. Beneath the huge dome supported by stone pillars, the gay and various crowds of people rippled and swayed. The electric light was spread above them like an umbrella. The metal lights on the walls glinted through breaks in the waves of people. And then, wrapped in the crowd far off, between the pillars he seemed to catch a glimpse of something uncertainly peach-coloured that flickered out at him for a moment. He tried to look at it with attention. But this peach-coloured existence had already been swallowed up in the waves of people, and he could see it no more. Yet he had sensed that it was something of surpassing beauty. He walked in that direction. He passed through the pillars and stood before the entrance to a room with arched doors. But there was nothing remarkable there.

He stood undecided a moment, not knowing which way to go, when a girl of fourteen or fifteen with a paper umbrella emerged from the shadow of the green cushions, and together with her father she approached him. This is she, he thought; this is undoubtedly she. The truth is that she was the most beautiful girl he had ever seen. Peach is the colour of young girls, the impression they give. And her cheeks were peach-coloured and beautiful. He began to follow slowly after her. She was waiting with her father at the platform entrance behind the other people. He imagined to himself the good fortune of getting on the same train with her. If that were so, then he knew he'd be able to take that train back home. People were being allowed onto the platform, and the crowd surged forward. When it was his turn to pass through the gate, he handed over his ticket, looking at the same time at the figure of the girl, who was running down the platform with her father. Then he followed the girl as far as the entrance into the third carriage from the end. But the girl didn't get on the train. She was standing with her father beneath a window. She must have come to see somebody else off. He felt all the strength drain out of his body, and he seemed to lose the energy to search for a seat. And yet in order to enjoy at least the semblance of being the recipient of her affections, he chose the seat by the window in front of which she was standing. Her father was talking through the window to a fat lady who sat in the seat facing him. The girl stood beside her father, holding her umbrella as if she were playing a clarinet and twirling round and round on one leg. There was no trace at all in her of that vulgarity of mind which is the awareness of one's own beauty. And he thought that no matter for how long and by how many people she might be praised, she would probably preserve this pure simplicity always, which was surely not some baseless, sentimental reflection, since in every motion that she made, in each gesture, appeared the deep lineaments of true modesty and womanly gentleness.

He felt himself totally entranced. He was astounded at the deep sway that beauty held over him. And he thought that if he could only show this girl to all those many young husbands like himself who were tormented by their wives, they would undoubtedly receive the strength and stimulus that would allow them to act and pay their wives back in kind.

The departure bell rang and echoed. The girl clasped her hands together and looked at the distant steam engine, and "Oh, it's going, it's going, it's going," she cried out, and began to shuffle her feet.

XII

The fence around his home was covered in bright, red ivy. The number of chickens in the shed at the back had increased. The water wheel turned in the small brook, which was covered over with grass. He heard people talking in a calm and leisurely way among the trees. He just told his mother that he had come home because he felt like a change. But really would his wife and Mishima do the thing he most feared? He trusted Mishima implicitly but the fear was always there in his head, and he remained constantly on edge even after he'd arrived home. He had tried to get far away from everything like this, but still he was mystified why it should be only his wife, Tatsuko, of everyone in his past, whom he alone felt as a true presence in his mind. While living with her he had never been able to see what was truly good in her, but now they were apart it was those aspects of her that appeared to him as representative of what she essentially was. What in fact had she done to him? He started to think that she had only behaved in the normal way that normal wives do behave. Wasn't it, then, that all his sufferings arose from his own debased character, and that he had himself created the sources of all his various griefs, sought them out himself, pushed himself into misery, sunk himself into melancholy? If that were so, then how stupid he had been to return home like this. And yet if he were to spend just one or two days like this, reminiscing about his wife, and then tamely go back to her, how meaningless would become all that vigour and resolution that had been required to take this step, and how difficult it would be to live with himself after that. He began once again very carefully going over in his memory all the details of her faithlessness, collecting them together, dragging them all up. The figure of the unchaste wife suddenly appeared again.

I won't be going back for some time yet, he thought.

He wanted to see Kanko as soon as possible to drive the image of Tatsuko out of his mind. Since the night he'd returned, he would often go upstairs at odd moments and look in the direction of Kanko's house. And yet, for some reason, the shutters on the upstairs windows of her house were always closed. On the evening of the third day he was again looking in the direction of her house. Then he saw Kanko herself walking down the narrow lane toward his house. She seemed to have put on a little weight since he had seen her last. Her white, rather long face, framed in luxuriant black hair, had not lost its former air of pellucid sadness. He drew his head back slightly from the window. But he felt no different at all toward her. From a sense of loved attachment to the past they shared, he moved his face forward again to the window. Then she chanced to see him. Her face turned pale. As if struck, she lowered her face, and hiding her tightly compressed mouth behind her sleeve, she passed by.

He decided she must know that he had a wife. After a while Kanko returned from wherever she had been, passing by with her head still lowered, returning home. When she had disappeared from sight beneath the branches of a plum tree whose leaves had fallen, he still for a long time did not move from where he was. Then he was aware that of the shutters on the upstairs of the house that should have been closed, two were now open. As he looked at them, a third was also slid open. Then Kanko appeared between the shutters. She strained forward slightly to slide the final shutter home, then stayed where she was, smoothing back her hair and looking at the distant mountains. She did not once even glance in his direction. He waited for her to look his way. But then she closed the paper screen windows and disappeared inside the room. He thought she would appear again, leaning on the low balcony railing as she had done, and he waited. But she never came out. In the past she had used the act of opening the shutters as a method of showing, conveniently avoiding the eyes of others, her love for him.

XIII

From the following day onward, Kanko would pass twice in front of his house each day. At first whenever he heard her footsteps he would try to watch her without her being able to see him. Still, given the fact that he had only just left a wife so suddenly like that, this method of approach could hardly be very satisfying. If he had the chance, he wanted to tell Kanko that he had left Tatsuko. In the afternoons he went to the village bath. To get there he had to pass Kanko's house. When he arrived at the bath there was never even one customer, male or female, in the place. However, about the second or third day he noticed there was one other person, who bathed in the ladies' section. Then one day as he was crouching down to scoop up a bowl of water, he saw the reflection of the person in the ladies' section, since it was separated from the men's section by only an incomplete partition; and what he saw reflected was the top half of Kanko's naked body there on the still surface of the water in the square, granite frame of the pool. So the customer who came early to the ladies' bath was Kanko. Being fearful of breaking her reflected image, he just stood there with his bowl in his hand. He was intrigued by the idea that even though they were in different sections of the bath, partitioned off from each other like this, she could still be observed. She seemed to be unaware of the fact that he could see her from next door. The sun entered the dark bath room from a few narrow skylights in the roof, falling in bars of light. In that light Kanko was innocently powdering her nose and cheeks with a puff. Then she folded both arms about her neck and began vigorously powdering her shoulders, then she crouched to scoop up some water. The naked upper half of her body broke up into a complex white stitchwork as the surface of the water started to sway. He waited until the water would stop swaying. Then he became aware that she must have got out of the water next door. He himself hurriedly got out in pursuit of her, and put on his clothes. Just as he was slipping on his clogs, Kanko was standing by the entrance with one hand on the door, looking back in his direction. By that glance of hers he could tell that she had been well aware that the man who also took his bath early was himself. He followed her outside. She was walking along one side of the road, holding her body a little stiffly with her metal bowl cupped in her arms. He wanted somewhere and somehow to let her know, even if only very briefly, that he and Tatsuko had parted. Then the end of her sleeve caught on a low bamboo fence by the wayside. The metal bowl popped out of her arms and rolled in the road, making a considerable clatter. She went red in the face and began to pick up her toilet and makeup things, which had scattered all over the road. He realized how embarrassing this must be to her, so he promptly retraced his steps. Unhappily he had no idea where he should retrace his steps to. Consequently he marched once more into the deserted public bath. The young girl attendant welcomed him back, but he merely took one look around and went out again. Kanko had by now picked up her bowl and was walking toward her home.

That evening at dusk a mist rose over the fields. He stood on the veranda, cupped his hands behind his head, and looked into the far mist. One could not distinguish the shapes of people. Lanterns, blurred in the mist, moved swaying along the bank of the canal. He felt he would like to go out now into the fields by himself and walk relaxed and free within that mist. Then he heard the sound of footsteps passing in front of the house. He was sure it must be Kanko by the strong sharp sound they made, as if the wearer were dragging her feet slightly. He went outside. The footsteps came to a halt in the narrow lane between his house and the next. He went toward that point. Kanko, with her sleeves crossed over her breast, was looking fixedly toward him. Through the fence tangled in ivy, the light of the lantern there in the garden was bathed in mist. He went up to Kanko, then stopped. His heart seemed to be an emptiness somewhere. Kanko said nothing. He was hoping to feel some sort of excitement. But he felt almost nothing. He noticed how the light from the garden slanted across her knees then faded away. Then Kanko seemed suddenly to slip away from him back toward her own house. He walked away in the opposite direction, toward the canal. He trembled as he felt the cold air upon his skin. Why had he remained silent like that? He felt depressed by himself. This coldness in his attitude toward Kanko did not mean that he was turning cold toward her. It simply meant that his having loved another woman since made him feel guilty, thus constricting and restraining his feelings toward her. He went up onto one of the embankments that held in the canal. He felt a small elation within his loneliness. The mist drifted and circled over the fields he was now looking down upon. A boat was being pulled along the canal, beating out waves with its hull. He began walking along the embankment. The turf was wet with dew. The scent of trees drifted up from the woods below.

XIV

From then on, this silent form of mild dissipation with Kanko's reflection in the bath became his chief source of pleasure each day. When he thought about his wife, he decided that since he trusted Mishima he wasn't much concerned about either returning or not returning. It did strike him that he really ought at least write to Mishima telling him what he had done and where he was, but since there was no telling when he might feel like returning—he might even go back tomorrow—he did not get around to it. He was aware of himself moving gradually closer to Kanko. He also felt how Kanko's presence was cancelling out his sense of regret at not being able to meet the lady in the bookshop again, and those little spurts of fear that up to now he had sometimes felt at the thought of Tatsuko's paying him back for everything, they also were growing less and less powerful. That pleased him most of all. Especially now that Tatsuko was not with him. In fact, in some ways he regretted her absence. He would have liked to have shown her Kanko's beauty, and then let her be a secret onlooker as Kanko began to fall in love with him. However, he had no particular desire to take any action himself toward Kanko. What he wanted was that she should fall most deeply in love with him. So in such reflections he was able to pass two weeks quite happily. But beyond the mild sport in the bath, relations between himself and Kanko made no progress whatsoever.

After he had been at home exactly a fortnight, a letter arrived for him from Mishima. It was very brief: "Why don't you come back? If you have gone back home and this reaches you, please come back as quick as you can, for my sake. I won't go into any details, but things are dangerous for me here."

When he had finished reading, all his achieved calm immediately started to vanish. Certainly he had sufficiently foreseen what was written there. But now that what he had foreseen had quite plainly become true, he felt quite differently about it from the way he had when he had merely foreseen it. For the first time he felt real fear. Everything he had thought about his wife had turned out to be a series of misconceptions. It was as if a regret about which nothing could ever be done had raised itself and now stood irremovably blocking his path. All the objections he had ever felt toward his wife were now blown away, and all he felt was the simple and enormous desire to return to her. But how worthless he now seemed to himself after all the resolutions which were shaken so quickly and easily just like that. Yet even so, when he thought about that version of himself who prided himself on his own willpower, concerned himself with preserving his self-respect, and for which reasons tossed his wife to a friend, he found that powerful version considerably more worthless than this weak one who wanted to rush back to his wife's side. He had completely forgotten about Kanko. As his desire to meet his wife again grew stronger, she seemed to become more and more virtuous and innocently beautiful, and at the same time thinking of his dalliance with Kanko, albeit it was only a mild curiosity in another woman of the rebound variety, he began to feel ashamed of the way he had behaved, ashamed before Tatsuko's goodness. When he'd been living with his wife, the feelings of guilt which came after one of these bouts of lecherous thoughts about other women (thoughts themselves that arose as a form of revenge against his wife), these in their turn would be soon wiped out by the next piece of objectionable behaviour on his wife's part. That was the norm. But being solitary like this, there was no way of expelling the self-reproach from his breast. In particular, given this situation, how strong these feelings of self-reproach had to be. Certainly he had a good hunt in his mind to recall those unchaste portions of her existence, which he could hardly forget anyway. But the odd thing was that now these aspects of her character had quickly grown to have even a beauty about them, become some splendid adornment of hers, and he felt the full power of her attractiveness therein. Then he began to wonder how he had ever been able to find the strength of mind to cast away this pearl of a wife, and he tried to reawaken within himself that bold willpower he had once possessed. But it was all quite hopeless. He was like a horse that feels the spur, the spur only, straining his head always toward that one goal, forward and forward finally to collapse at his wife's side. Since his own desires had been frustrated so these two weeks, it was as pure woman that he recalled her most, that gentle softness of hers, the way her sensuality would suddenly flame out in all the magnificence of the longings of the flesh. Of course she was his, since she was his wife. Since she was his wife, then certainly she was his. Up to this moment he had never truly felt the wonderful gentleness, closeness, and depth for him of the word "wife." To think that she was flesh of his flesh, a union decreed by fate, gave him a piercing sense of delight, a lovely warm sweetness in the heart. He had been wrong to criticize her. He felt that instinctively now as one withdraws the hand from that which should never be touched.

Thus that night he boarded the train to return to his wife, in the same excited and flustered state in which he had left her for home. He decided that when he met Mishima he would tell him everything that had happened to him, all that had passed through his mind during these weeks. Then he would make things up with Tatsuko, fall in love again; for he would be as generous as he knew to be; he would repress those things in his character that clashed with hers. He felt a loathing toward the way he had been living up until now. He decided to stop accepting monetary support from his mother. If he could manage to do that, they would be able, the two of them, he and his wife, to lead a completely new and different kind of life. But of course it was always possible that Tatsuko was now so inclined toward Mishima that she would not want to accept this love that he offered. In that case, perhaps he had been in too much of a hurry to take this train, and not given the whole question proper consideration. Ever since he'd read Mishima's letter, he felt confident that once he returned he could win her back. He sometimes tried to imagine the feelings of his wife and Mishima toward each other, what they had been, what they were now, how they had changed. Still, the very fact that Mishima had written a letter like that meant undoubtedly that the event he most feared had not yet taken place. Certainly that he should judge things in this way indicated the degree to which his faith in Mishima was influential in his judgements, although one could not overlook how much that had been encouraged by his desire to believe that what he feared most would happen in fact would not.

XV

At dawn he got down from the train. He hadn't slept but his head was quite clear. Since it was cold he took a ricksha from the station to the suburb where he lived. The doors of the houses were still closed. He got down from the ricksha in front of his house and knocked softly on the door. Then he called out twice, but there was no answer. He remembered the loose habit Tatsuko had of going to bed without locking the front door properly, and so he tried opening it from the outside. It slid open. As he entered the house, he felt a slight nervousness as if he were entering somebody else's house. He went up from the hallway into the living room, then slid open the door to the inner room. Tatsuko and Mishima were sleeping side by side in just the way his fears had imagined it to him. Momentarily he felt that confusion which comes from intruding upon someone's privacy. Then immediately his heart went cold. His thighs began to tremble. At the same time, he was shaken by a terrible explosive rage toward Mishima, and he felt his teeth grating against each other. Then his wrath turned aside from Mishima and Tatsuko and suddenly struck at that something unintelligible within himself that had condemned him to be like this, had made a complete fool out of him like this.

Right. Persecute me as much as you like. But I'll never give into you, you'll see.

Then he restrained this attack upon whatever it was within himself, since it was tempting him to turn his attention away from those two upon whom it should have been fixed; and so he sat by their bedside and looked intently upon his wife's sleeping face. The pain within him grew. He could no longer prevent the convulsions of his mouth. Then he felt himself at peace again, as if he were sitting now absorbed in the presence of some unintelligible marvel, some enormous mystery. He felt that he was in fact able to contain and endure the pain that all this had aroused in him, and feeling so his normal calm returned to him.

I've done it at last, he thought, and with this thought his wife here before him who had enthralled him for so long had become this thing she was now, a low vulgar animal who had nothing at all to do with him.

I have won through, then. I have won.

He felt a deep and powerful joy. He went to stand up. It was then that Tatsuko first opened her eyes. For a moment in the vagueness of sleep she returned his gaze with open eyes. Then a sudden sorrow passed over her face. He said nothing to her. She hid her head under the bedclothes and did not move.

He stood up and left. Life was gradually coming back into the streets. A number of carts piled high with large white radishes were moving toward the noise and bustle of the town.

A crowd of young men pulling an empty cart and shouting out their energetic cries ran vigorously past him. Sparrows, boisterously chirping together, chased each other above the high buildings, which now caught the rays of the sun. He felt his heart full of a piercing sense of joy, of life.

"It's wonderful, wonderful," he shouted.

Tears began to flow from his eyes. He felt like running along the road until his strength gave out. A free unfettered delight was flooding the whole world of his consciousness. He crossed the road and made his way straight into a wood. Branches broken off from the trees littered the ground at his feet. A man led a donkey among the trees and tied it up to one of them. The dew fell from the leaves. The lightning conductor glittered high and far in the sky.

Knowing he had been betrayed by his wife, why should he feel this near-hysterical cheerfulness? He did not understand this himself. He suspected that perhaps he was starting to go insane. But he was also aware of how brilliantly clear his mind was. He raced through the wood and then down toward the pasture. As he did so, his feelings of joy suddenly all concentrated within his breast and crumpled emptily there. All the dirty pleasures his wife's contaminated body enjoyed appeared unendingly before him. He stopped rock-still. He thought of someone else doing to his wife the things he had done, and his teeth clenched and grated together again. A numbing, wintry sadness and cold seized his heart. He felt his body was going to collapse on the road. When he felt that he could go no farther, he suddenly turned and went back toward his house. He wanted to make himself suffer more, to see what he could take. He wanted to crush his wife's body against his, inside his, that body of hers that was the source of all his misery.

"I'll torture myself, torture myself to death."

He ran ferociously back through the wood, then out of the wood onto the road. He raced off the road into his house. When he pulled back the door into the inner room, Tatsuko was sitting on top of the bedclothes adjusting her sleeves. Mishima got halfway out of bed, placed his hand across his furrowed brow, but said nothing.

"Is there nothing to eat?" he said.

"You did go back home, then?" Mishima said with an awkward little smile; then his face darkened again and he looked away.

His wife wasn't saying anything. He went off into the kitchen and opened the lid of the bin.

"Not a thing. And I'm hungry. I'm hungry."

"I'll make you something," his wife said.

"God, it's cold in here. Can't go on like this without a fire."

He started clumsily breaking up the charcoal in the charcoal box.

"That's all right, I'll do it," his wife said, and came close to him. He ignored her and started throwing bits of charcoal into the range, when the warm odour of his wife crouching by his side struck him. His stomach was rumbling, in such pain that he felt it might split open. He took out some matches and lit the ring, and began fanning away beneath it with a fan. He fanned violently, making a loud flapping sound, something with which to drive everything out of his head. He tried to be aware of himself in the act of working. He was concentrating only on what had to be done next. First there was the rice to be washed. Then boil the water, make the soup, after that wash the dishes, sweep the house, give everything a good wipe, rake the garden, and then, and then; always thinking, going on thinking; but even if there was no end to this labour, even if it continued all one's life, yet sometimes one must rest, and in that space back would come the pain, the misery, and one would be destroyed by it.

His wife had stood quietly and awkwardly by his side for a while, but then she had gone back to the bed and sat there with her head bowed. Mishima was just sitting on the floor of the living room with an annoyed look on his face, staring all the time at his two hands clenched together.

The charcoal began to crackle as it caught fire, and he forgot his anger while he fanned crazily away. But then the absurdity of what he was doing came to him. He threw the fan away and stepped up into the living room. As he did so, Mishima stood up. Mishima looked hard at him for a moment but said nothing, and then went outside dressed as he was.

He couldn't work out what Mishima had to be angry about. Anyway, he had no desire to think about what it might be. He went to his wife, who lay face down on the bed.

"I used to love you," he said.

She stayed silent.

"I'm going."

He started to walk toward the door.

"Wait. Please wait," she said hurriedly, and clung to one of his legs.

"Let go, for Christ's sake," he said, and kicked her away.

She rolled over, stood up, and looked angrily at him with tears in her eyes.

"Don't you understand, you made me mad? Leaving me all that time like that. I was angry with you."

She buried her face in the bedclothes again. For a moment he felt sorry for her.

"Do you know I thought I wanted you to bear my child."

He said that in one breath, then went out the front. He heard his wife suddenly break into loud, high-pitched sobs. He stopped for a moment at the door, listening to her crying, before he went out into the street. At the corner of the lane, Mishima was standing looking in the other direction. He came up behind Mishima and just stopped. Mishima hadn't noticed him.

"I'm going back home again," he said to Mishima from behind.

Mishima turned round toward him. There was a thin thread of blood coming out of the corner of his mouth. They stood in front of each other for a time but not looking each other in the face. He felt he couldn't look at Mishima's face. If he did look, he felt he would be merely inciting the appearance of something dreadful. Yet even if it was for this reason that he did not look, still the truth was that Mishima had become nothing to him, an irrelevance like a stone by the side of the road. What was he standing here like this for? He started to move off when Mishima suddenly said: "Let me have Tatsuko, please."

He merely grunted his assent and went on walking. Only he felt all the time that there must be somewhere he could reach an end to all this. There was something funny about his legs; they weren't moving properly. Sometimes he stopped to try to control them. After he'd gone some way, he found that again he was going toward the bookshop. Just the place he ought not to be going. I must not go, he shouted out within himself to drive away this weakness, but there was nothing else for him. He was useless now. Somehow if he did not go to her, he would most likely break down; if he were to walk on like this with nowhere to go, there was no saying what he might not do to himself. If only Kanko or someone were here. When he had seen Mishima and Tatsuko together, immediately he had wanted Kanko so desperately. But Kanko was too far from him; she could be no support to him in this broken state of mind. The bookshop came in sight. He couldn't care less if the man were there or not. He couldn't wait for things anymore. He stumbled into the garden of the shop. Nobody was about. There was a pleasant smell of breakfast cooking, which made him yearn for the past, for those days when his own home had been happy. He felt a gentle joy at having touched upon where the perfection of life might be. He wanted to lower his head to the ground and apologize to her husband. He stood there dreaming like that in the garden for a while, when suddenly the lady herself appeared, wiping her hands busily with a white cloth; and she saw him. She seemed to give a jerk of surprise.

"What are you doing so early?"

He could not reply.

"You didn't stay away long, then? You did go back home?"

He looked at her face in silence, but he felt perhaps he was crying, so he turned aside.

"Is something the matter?" she asked in a low voice.

"I think, I think it's all over with me."

He said that, and immediately disliked what he had said. He had wanted to say something cheerful.

"What time is it now?" he asked hurriedly, as a mundane corrective to what he had just said.

"I imagine it must be about seven o'clock."

"Oh, is it? About seven? Have I got thinner?"

She merely looked at him in surprise.

"I think I've got thinner. When I can't sleep, you see, I get thin right away."

"Don't you feel very well?"

"Is your husband still asleep?"

She blinked a little as she looked at him.

"I was at home until yesterday. I've just arrived first thing this morning. But I think I'll probably be going back again."

"You mean now?"

"Yes. I'm going back now."

"Back to the country?"

"Yes. I'm a country boy so I don't take things to heart much. You know, sort of carefree."

"Is something wrong?"

"What?"

Her face had clouded over as if she were sorry for him.

"Is something wrong? Has something happened?"

"Well, it's a bit difficult. I can't really talk about it. Would you give my regards to your husband? I don't suppose I'll be intruding upon you here again."

"But please do come to see us again. We'd like you to. You'll soon be coming back again, I expect?"

"Well, anyway, I'm going now. Goodbye."

He bowed his head politely.

"Oh, you mustn't rush away like that."

"Well, you see. . . ."

"Just stay a little longer."

With his back now turned toward her, he bowed again and went out. She stood at the door watching him go, forgetting to say goodbye.

He did not look back. That had probably extended his life for another hour, and now he must think of what he could do to get him through the agony of pain that was sure to come soon. If only he could see Kanko. And yet he thought of his frigidity toward her, and of how he now began to cling to her because his wife and the woman in the bookshop were no longer available, and he felt how truly contemptible he was. But he simply wanted someone to talk to; he wanted to tell Kanko everything. But to get free of the suffering received from one woman, why did he have to need yet another woman? Because he understood that this was a necessity for him, his heart died within him.

Why am I like this? When am I going to stop being like this?

He wanted to grow old very quickly, to become an old man. He was weeping openly again. And yet he had shut the heavy door of the past, closed it securely with his own hands. Because he could feel this, he could also sense a small flicker of light somewhere deep within him. This was something quite new that he could feel. His whole life lay spread out before him, moving strongly, eagerly, and free.

"I'm free at last. I'm free. Free."

He walked with quick ungainly strides toward the station. He walked energetically, his body leaning forward. He mingled with people whose breath was white in the morning air as they entered briskly through the open gates of a factory. Crowded trams clanged through the confusion of mist and morning sunlight. The horns of passing motorcars splintered delicately about him. Amid the glittering metal and white smoke, people stepped out gaily. He raised his head. There in his path before him a huge building thrust itself sharply into the sky.

After Picking Up a Blue Stone

I was walking along in Tokyo in broad daylight flourishing my towel. Then I fell over. I had tripped over a stone. Blood was coming out from my shin. I picked up the small, pale blue stone that had cut my shin and went into the bath. As I poured the water over my naked body I had a continuous feeling of anger toward the world.

I left the bath and went straight over to K's house. The shadow of her house seemed to have something oppressively blue about it. K was sitting in a corner of her silent room powdering her face.

"I'm going back home after this," I suddenly said to her back.

"What's up?"

She turned round in surprise and looked at my face. I was still standing up. I didn't reply.

"You mean to Kobe?"

"Uh."

"Why?" K asked again.

I had no idea why I felt I wanted to go back to Kobe. It was just that suddenly, after I'd picked up that stone, I had got the mysterious feeling that I should simply go back there, nothing more. My big sister lived in Kobe.

"But you wouldn't feel like going home for no reason at all."

"Still, I don't have a reason. I just somehow feel like going home, that's all."

"You are strange." She looked hard into my face as if she were looking for something there.

"Anyway, I'm going tonight. I'll come straight back."

She hadn't finished powdering herself, but she didn't go on with it. We both said nothing. Only the mirror shone bright.

"It looks odd, I know, but there's absolutely nothing for you to feel suspicious about," I said after a while.

Somehow, although I thought I was calm enough, I was a bundle of nerves. And yet I had no idea what I was being nervous about.

I said goodbye to her and went outside. The streets were bright under the glittering sun, and as always swarming with people. Despite that, the voices of the town seemed to be softened, subdued. In the centre of that quietness my mind only was restless.

I boarded the train that night with a toy for little Mah in Kobe. In my sister's house in Kobe, Mah was making a fuss about something up on the landing.

I was tired so as soon as I arrived I went to bed, ate a banana, then went off to sleep. I woke up during the night. Mah had got her legs stretched over my body.

When I got up the next morning I started to write a letter to K. While I was doing so a telegram arrived from Korea. My sister took it and we read it together. It said that father had had a sudden stroke and died.

"What are we going to do now? What are we going to do?" My sister burst out crying.

I imagined that it probably must be true. I passed the telegram back to my sister and went on writing my letter.

"I got here and then simply went to bed, and all I've done is sleep. I've just heard that father's suddenly died. I shall go over to Korea straightaway. I loved my father very deeply."

I finished writing and then ate a whole bunch of rich, purple grapes. I couldn't think of any other way of letting myself go. I understood that what had been disturbing me since yesterday was this. I began to feel weirdly at peace within myself. I was aware of myself entering some extreme region of coldness.

Late that afternoon I took a train to get to Korea. I travelled by myself. Mother would be by herself in Korea.

A girl with fat legs stopped eating a banana halfway and stared at me, her knees thrown wide open. That was because I was crying. The more I raised my head and looked at the scenery outside the window, the more the tears came. And yet I didn't feel at all unhappy.

I got off that train, crossed the sea to Korea, then got on another train. A Japanese man stretched out his hand toward a Korean he didn't know at his side, and said: "Yobo."

The Korean then placed a box of matches into the palm of the Japanese, who was rolling a cigarette between his lips. The Japanese looked aside and took the matches in silence.

Seoul was all yellow. I got off the train and was looking at the face of a very pretty Japanese girl when someone pulled at my sleeve. I looked round and it was mother. I said nothing and neither did she. We went out into the yellow square in front of the station. Mother looked up at the sky with her worn-out, tired face, and so did I. An aeroplane was flying overhead.

"Is the house a long way from here?"

"A long way," mother said.

After we'd walked a pretty long way, we turned a corner and there was a house with "In Mourning" written on its glass door. There's someone died there as well, I thought, and I walked on past the house.

"We're here," my mother said from behind.

"This is it?"

I followed mother into the house that had "In Mourning" written on it, a house that seemed to be made entirely of glass. There was no one in, and flies swarmed in the faint light as in a stable.

"You've had the funeral?" I asked after father for the first time.

"Uh." That was all she replied.

Still wrapped in a piece of silk cloth, a six-inch-square box with his remains in it was on the plain table.

"That it?" I pointed.

"That's right," mother said.

"Is that what he's turned into." I laughed and picked up the box and handled it a bit.

Mother got out a fan.

"The place is rotten with flies," she said. There was a persistent smell of carbolic.

"That's carbolic, isn't it, that stink?"

"It stinks all right. They've got dysentery next door, and someone, I don't know who, splashed the stuff all round here."

"Gets on your nerves."

"Stinks the place out," mother said.

After a while she produced a gold watch and chain.

"Your father thought very highly of this. You can have it."

"It's gold, isn't it?" I put it down gingerly.

"You hungry?"

"Yes."

"There's nothing much here." She went to the cupboard and brought out some fishpaste.

We sat at the table and started to eat. Then the grief welled up within me. I wanted to spit the food out of my mouth so I threw down my chopsticks and went to the lavatory. I started to sob, long, drawn-out. I supported myself with my right hand, stared at the wall, and held my breath. Smaller sobs escaped through my nostrils. When the feeling in my stomach had quieted down, I went back to mother and picked up my chopsticks. The same thing happened again. This time I ran outside into the road. I ran noiselessly sobbing in the middle of the twilit road. The pale road trembled through my tears. I turned off the main road into a filthy back alley. A Chinese and a Korean were hitting each other in the narrow lane. The Korean was struck in the face by a stone and knocked down into a rubbish heap by the side of the lane. His legs stuck up and his face was red. A lot of Koreans were silently looking on, towels tied round their heads. And then, "Dad's dead. Dad's dead," someone started singing, over and over, in the middle of my head.

Father had left nothing, no money. I wrote a letter to K from Korea.

"I've found out that I've no money, so we can't get married," was the gist of it.

I made a point of not letting her know this address. If I were expecting a reply, I'd be in a continual state of anxiety waiting for it.

The man in the house next door had dysentery and was dying. There were two children, an elder daughter and a son, and creditors kept coming every day. I was one of those creditors. I didn't make any demands, and yet if they didn't pay back the money that father had lent them, we wouldn't have our passage back home. I didn't have the heart to go and get the money back. The trouble was, however, that a mob of people all totally unknown to me, who'd been trying to get money back from the house next door, would then come over to our place.

"How much money have they got in that house? What other kinds of valuables? Where's the most likely place the money's going to come from? How much property do they have back home? How much money have you lent to them? Do you think there's any chance of getting your money back?" And so on.

One of them seemed to think I was in the same class as himself, and came and suggested: "There's a pistol worth ninety there, you know. You can have that, and I'll have that Awataguchi sword they've got."

Another one seemed to be after the lady of the house. Although he was a creditor of theirs, he once even left a present of some dress material at our house with instructions to hand it over to the lady when she returned from the hospital. These creditors also seemed mysteriously well informed on the progress of the sick man. I didn't even know the man next door, or his wife. According to my mother, the wife used to be the maid of the house and the two children were by a former wife. Then the husband and wife didn't know of the sudden death of my father. The crowd of creditors, who were simply waiting for the illness of the man next door to reach its appropriate conclusion and thus pushing their various claims in advance, would drift round to our place and start chatting away, when they would suddenly grasp that father had died only a matter of days ago. Every one of them who came would give his cry of astonishment, gaze round the room for a bit, and then the colour would visibly drain out of their faces. One of them sat without saying a word, then suddenly jumped up, said he was frightened now of merely being alive, and went away.

The fact is that father had apparently been in perfectly good health, when he suddenly collapsed and died within less than half an hour. For these crooked moneylenders, so far removed in Korea from the places in which they had grown up, nothing was more terrifying than being presented with the fact of sudden death.

Besides the house next door, five places had debts owing to us that I had to get back. This was the first time I'd been to Korea, and there was really nobody there that I knew. I gave up the idea of the house next door, and thought first of all I would have a go at those other five. The longer we stayed here would only mean more and more useless expense. If we had to wait ages here instead of going back home, simply in order to get the money paid back, the upshot would be that even if we got all of the money back eventually, it would by then have already been spent anyhow. Obviously if I made that point honestly and openly to the persons in question, they would make every effort to put off the day of repayment. Then there was the question of place. I could see that my adversaries would be pretty confident that if they got away once, I wouldn't find it so easy to meet up with them again. Also I was no good at bargaining. I tended to feel that if you honestly told someone all the facts as they were and they still wouldn't pay up, then that was that, they could stuff it and I could do without it. So I went to all five places. Well, three of them expressed sympathy with out position and agreed to return the money before the stipulated expiry date. Yet not one of them expressed any sympathy over my father's death. The only real sympathy they expressed was not with that death, but with themselves and the sad consequences it was having with them in that they were being rushed and badgered in this way, and they showed their displeasure very openly.

I heard from the hospital that the man next door was now dangerously ill and not expected to live. Of the six places that owed us money, the next-door house owed us most. In fact, if we could only get the money out of next door, then the other five really didn't matter all that much. Still, that being granted, the fact was that the affairs of the house next door were in as sinking a condition as our own. Well, those who have sunk choose other sinking objects to sink in order to pop up from their own sunken state; and presumably there are people who extol that state of mind as appropriate to the splendid life-and-death struggle in which we are all involved, and maybe they are right to do so. And I was still only a university student. I was still independent, so probably I could have got by without sinking the house next door with all hands on board. And yet how were mother and I to get by tomorrow, and the next day, and the day after? And

I was a creditor. The house next door was being besieged by plenty of other creditors besides me. If their father died, the two who were going to catch it straightaway would be those two children next door. I suppose you could say that after all their mother would sell herself to that man who was after her. But the two children belonged to their father. It was pretty obvious that she could hardly be thinking of doing that and also dragging the two children along with her, at least if she was thinking in terms of being still a true mother to them. How could she be thinking in such terms? And then how had I come to think of myself in terms of being a creditor, someone with the right to take money off people? Where had that come from? After all, just because I was the son of somebody who had lent somebody else money, and because he had died and left me badly off, I was trying to get that money back. That was all it was, and I was coming to think that just that reason conferred no rights of any kind upon me. Then I started to think that with regard to those households where everybody was alive and well, even in those cases I had no right to press for repayment, either. I was reaching a point where I could no longer see the distinction between lending people money and giving people money. It was perfectly clear that once you gave your money to somebody else, it became somebody else's money. It was certainly very arguable that the act of demanding it back was actually extremely ridiculous. The fact was that the distinction between given money and lent money was a question of the two parties involved, of how they both felt about the matter; and since that was so, where had I, the mere son of the man who'd lent the money and thus with no emotional right to demand that such money be returned, where had I gained the qualification to turn myself into a fully fledged, dunning creditor? All my ideas about money were being chronically confused by these direct, felt experiences of it. The concept of something borrowed now had only a kind of feebleness, in fact a kind of craftiness, about it, and there was no doubt that the reason I was trying to get the money back as fast as I possibly could was an attempt to convince myself that the concept was a perfectly honest one after all, one with absolutely nothing cunning or wrong about it. And yet, in purely formal terms, so long as the person who had borrowed the money made no attempt to give it back, he surely was the one being crafty, and as long as his formal craftiness persisted, it was from this craftiness of his that my formal qualification to be similarly crafty was created. Realizing this, I decided for the first time that I must launch an attack, as father's representative, upon this craftiness that existed in all those other crafty people. If they wouldn't pay up, then the fact that money had been lent to them would be a moral exposure of their craftiness, and that alone would be my reason for pressing them, for it was they who would be in the wrong. Still, I would have to leave the people next door alone; that could not be helped.

I had never seen the next-door woman come back from the hospital. When the two children came home from school, they would announce the fact to my mother by calling out a greeting from the back door. Sometimes the two of them would gaze at me from their back gate, two very identical faces both blankly looking at me. Then it would strike me that I was a creditor of theirs, someone after their money, which was really very funny when you thought about it. At such times when they were feeling friendly toward me like that, I wanted to take on a really devilish expression and scare the life out of them by shouting, "Hey, get out of it!" Sometimes the two of them in the house by themselves would do the housework together, besides indulging in the various naughtinesses they were always up to.

Once the girl abruptly said: "I know something that I really hate."

Her little brother immediately chimed in: "I know something that I really hate too."

This thing that was supremely hateful to both of them was their mother, something they did not have to mention to each other in so many words, since they were both aware of each other's feelings on the matter. If they could talk like that about their mother, it was pretty clear that she could never have showed them any kind of affection. According to my mother, the man next door was constantly having rows with his wife over the children. Since the husband was now dying, some other man had taken the opportunity to make advances to the wife. And in her case, since her husband had children and creditors to provide for, there was no money for her at all. However, unlike our situation, when and if the husband died his pension would still go on being paid to his older child, his daughter. But even those payments would come to an end when the daughter reached the age of twenty, and there were only another three years or so until she did. After three years the boy could perhaps start making his way in the world. But he'd still be only thirteen, and what can you do at the age of thirteen? Anyway, those creditors would soon start eating their share of that three-year pension.

As far as our household was concerned, I would soon have to start making my way in the world too; I would have to perform. I decided that my first performance, my first display of talent, would be that of getting the money from next door. My old mother was already dreaming of the huge rewards she was soon going to reap from the status conferred upon me by my lengthy student life. But I was privately looking at the colour of the sky and observing the long, sloping shadows cast by the trees. While observing the colour of the sky and the shadows of the trees in this way, and reflecting upon the psychological implications of myself as a roving, dashing creditor, wondering whether this new phenomenon might not, and to what degree, skilfully manipulate my debtors into some semblance of motion, into these reflections intruded my mother.

"You know, when your father died I did think it was lucky that he upped and died so quick like that. If he'd gone on and on like next door, and with no money coming in, I don't know what I should have done."

I suppose if one is going to say something like that, it's as well to come right out with it. If that is to be the last word on forty years of married life, of togetherness as husband and wife, then by God I could become an intrepid dunner all right. No doubt mother's faith in her son's powerful extortionist talents had led her into praying for her husband's speedy death. Still, the man next door didn't need to oblige anybody by dropping dead at this precise moment. Admittedly, the wife had this man making advances to her and in that respect she would clearly appreciate her husband's death; but there was always another aspect of the matter for her to take into account, which was that when he died those creditors would soon be able to lay hands on the daughter's pension.

One night mother and I went to the house of a creditor upon whom we'd already served notice. It was in a sunken back street, all dark. I waited outside and listened to mother's negotiating within. As soon as she came out I realized that the creditor had skilfully given her the brush-off.

"They say he's not in," mother said.

The man worked in the Governor General's office in some minor capacity and had lodgings in this boardinghouse. The next night we both went back there. The old lady appeared and said he was in. This time I took over from mother and went inside. Then the landlady of the place took over from the old lady and stopped me in the entrance hall.

"We *thought* he was in, but in fact he's not," she said. She'd nipped out a bit too quick for my liking.

"But look here, we came last night and you said he'd be in tonight, didn't you?" I said.

"Yes, that's right, but he's not in," the lady repeated.

I guessed that this particular debtor had decided that his only opponent was my mother, and so he could do what he liked with her. Clearly he knew nothing about my presence. He must have given instructions to the landlady to say that he wasn't in whenever my mother called, and so get rid of her that way. The crooked impudence of the man was starting to get my back up.

"I think he's in," I said, upon which someone inside somewhere said "Idiot!" in a loud voice. That made me really angry.

"Who's an idiot?" I shouted back.

A man of about thirty-five or thirty-six burst out into the entrance hall from somewhere and stood before me.

"If we say he's not in, what do you mean by saying he's

in, eh? You are insulting me. You are hurling mud at me and at my house. You'll apologize. Come on, apologize!" he said, working himself up into a fine frenzy.

I knew that he'd seen what a pale, skinny specimen I was, and so he despised me and thought he could squash me with this display of power. And then he was obliged to bawl at people in order to gain the confidence of his numerous boarders. Still, I had a certain confidence in myself. I knew that even if three men like the one in front of me had a concerted go at me, I could still keep my own end up with a bit of nimble sparring and dodging. At least they wouldn't be able to down me. I'd had experience of that in the past, so when this object suddenly and ferociously appeared in that way I wasn't scared of him. I could feel the old violent fighting spirit tightening itself within me. During this time a considerable number of his boarders had come out into the hallway and were standing about. I was damned if I'd give in now.

"You tell me to apologize. You talk about apologizing. All right then, you'd better apologize. I've done all that politeness required of me by the mere fact of coming here. I've done plenty."

"Politeness! You're told someone's not in and then you insist he is. Very polite indeed! Call that politeness? You are casting aspersions against my establishment. Do you expect me to take that lying down? I must speak up, on behalf of *all* my guests!" And he kept on saying the same stuff, to which I responded with similarly ill-regulated expostulation.

Finally he said: "Right. You say he's in. Then come in and see."

"By your leave," I said, and slipped off my wooden clogs. His guests opened a path for me through their midst. The lady led the way along a dark corridor into the far recesses of the house. Walking behind her, I thought that it wasn't exactly out of the question that somebody might jump me, so I strained all my senses into the surrounding darkness as I walked. Then we came to a dead end where there was a narrow staircase. We went upstairs, and she opened a sliding door and I could see a small room.

"This is his room," the lady informed me.

Of course I'd been perfectly well aware from the start that my debtor would hardly have been lolling about there like a fool. Anyway, I didn't know if this was his room or not, besides which I had no way of knowing who was or who was not the debtor in question. There was a rifle standing in the narrow alcove. The landlady rubbed her hands in her apron and looked at me unconcernedly. She was a plump, pretty young woman. I felt like asking her if she was happy in her work.

Having now fully demonstrated that my debtor was indeed not there, she had, however, at least as far as I could see, no look of irony upon her face.

"Of course, I don't know that this is his room, do I?"

"Yes, there's that," she said.

"I don't even know the man, either. However, my apologies for all this trouble," I said, and started to go downstairs, at which point the landlord whom I'd had the row with was mounting them.

"Was he in?" he asked in a quiet tone different from before.

"After all that, who expected him to be?" I said.

"Look, I saw red because you were so damn rude. I keep a boardinghouse. I can't afford to take that kind of lip from anyone."

"That's all right. I've spent all my time in Tokyo boardinghouses. I'm used to it. Something like that's not going to bother me."

"But why should I say someone wasn't in if they were?"

"Look, it's not you. I thought he was in. I said so. I don't suppose you follow me."

We continued this kind of conversation at the top of the stairs for a bit, when a voice boomed up from below.

"What's going on, eh? What's up?"

A forty-year-old man came ponderously up the stairs. Despite its being summer, he had on a quilted jacket with his hands slipped beneath it out of sight.

"It's all over. It's all worked out," I said, standing directly in front of him.

"I said what's up. I've been listening. There's a lot of

things I don't quite catch on to," he said, his eyes looking below mine.

I got ready for a fight. At which point my mother came up from below, caught sight of the lady of the house, and bowed to her.

"My, what a terrible lot of bother the boy is causing. He's such an ignorant child, kicking up a dreadful fuss like this and turning the whole place upside down. I really must apologize for this preposterous behaviour on his part."

"Oh, but I must really take much of the blame, since of course we did say he would be, and if only he were, and it's so unfortunate that he never seems to be, after you've taken all the trouble to come all this way." The lady smiled at my mother, and then they went through the ritual of a few polite phrases. This friendly exchange on the part of the two women suddenly relaxed a great deal of the tension upstairs. There would be no fight. So I took that opportunity to go downstairs and out the front. I knew that my desire to protect my mother had got mixed up with the feelings created by my father's death, and had thus taken this violent, barbaric form. Even outside I was still trembling with the impulse to fight with my bare fists until I dropped.

After a while mother came out. Mother followed me home but made no comment on what had happened. I said nothing either. Nothing had worked out as I had feebly imagined it would. Truly the road back home for a defeated dunner in a foreign land is a sad, wretched one. We left the back streets and entered under the bright lights of a main road.

"Shall we go back on the tenth?" mother suddenly said. That was in five days' time.

"Can we get it all together by then?"

"I don't know, but if we stay here any longer we're going to find it hard just to pay the rent."

"I guess so. Hope the sea calms down a bit."

"It won't bother me if it doesn't," mother said.

We started to get our belongings together that night. I got bored eventually with the fiddling business, opened the box with father's remains in it, and tried tapping the bones. The bones made a sound like bits of unglazed pottery, and some white powder flew off them. Was that my father making that noise and giving off that white limelike dust? I could see that neither as true nor as comic. Father clinked in the palm of my hand. It was ridiculous. Why couldn't I accept that father had been in one form and had now taken another, these bones? Why couldn't I feel that? But this just wasn't father, it wasn't him. All this was something clinking away in my hand. After all the truth of father's death was in that mother had told me of it. If one were to mourn over that form of truth, then these bones could just as well be those of a horse. Perhaps I ought to think of them as the bones of a horse. If I were to force myself into thinking of these bones as father, it would be like being shown a totally different person and believing that that was indeed him. But in such a case I would be obliged to say that it was not so. The father I had known, the father I had seen with my own eyes, was not these bones; nor was he some other man. If I were to call these bones father, what would happen to my real father? I said the word "father," and straightaway his image came into my mind.

"How could that father be this? This is lime, lime."

I took a handful of the bones and tossed them back one by one into the box. The grief I had felt at having to acknowledge these bones as father was departing from me gradually. In the same way that life is only what the five senses experience, so death did not exist unless experienced by those same senses. All I had seen with my own eyes of father's death was no more than the oppressiveness that had suddenly appeared in mine and mother's daily life as a consequence of it. I had become a creditor. I threatened my debtors. If that alone were true, then life itself was no more than a question of various material alterations that sometimes took place. Thus K and I could not get married now because of one of these material happenings. This had not yet hurt me, this fact, because of the grief over father's death, but I knew it was soon going to come, a deep and cruel anguish.

One day when we had almost finished the packing a beggar died by the side of our house. He had fallen face downward in a muddy pool left by the rain. A policeman came, and when he lifted up the beggar's face it had left its imprint deep and clear in the mud. But the living unrestrainedly walked by, ignorantly trampling in what remained of him with mud-covered boots.

The lady next door came back from the hospital for a short while. I wasn't at home at the time. According to mother, she had heard of the death of my father and come straight back from the hospital, and she had taken up the question of the repayment of the money they owed without my mother even mentioning it.

"Still, they haven't got any money, have they?" I said.

"They don't have any money, so she said we were to please take the sword and the pistol and sell them," mother said.

Of all the places we had lent money to, only the next-door house, despite the fact that it had borrowed most, had been lent the money without any formal paper transactions. We had no proof of the debts, and so what was one to make of the fact that these people, by way of the wife, should have taken up the question of repayment without any pressure being applied from our side? One couldn't say merely that it was because the man next door was an honest man. It seemed to me that it showed how cleanly, how decently my father had lent the money. The husband was dying under a foreign sky, and despite that, they wanted to pay back money they didn't even have. It would have been strange for us not to have been given deep pleasure by that. In contrast, that official in the boardinghouse had received the smallest of loans, and yet he spent all his time dodging us. Actually, we hadn't got a receipt from him either, and being a civil servant, in the police department at that, he was the one who knew best how to make use of the absence of such paper proof, and also how to condemn to oblivion any ideas of moral obligation that might be connected with the concept of debt. Right to the end he kept on skilfully eluding us. Next after him was an official who worked in the Legislation Bureau. Notwithstanding the fact that he lived in a splendid house and told numerous servants what to do, he kept putting the day of repayment off a little, then off again. Then there was a businessman who paid up on the stipulated date all right, but managed to look remarkably nasty about it while so doing. He paid back clean, crisp banknotes, accompanied by mean, grubby words. Considering all our creditors, the only one who gave us a sense of decency in our dealings with them was the unfortunate house next door with its illness. Mother described the man next door as a retired captain of pale, unhealthy complexion who suffered with his nerves. He was hardly the sort of person who would make a go of things in Korea. He had, I suppose, come to Korea not essentially to succeed but in order to be driven into failure; and when one thought of him and his nervous disposition, then the conflict between his children and their stepmother, it was hard to see how the number of buns produced in his shop could ever have reached any respectable figure. Mother said that once during his absence she had seen his wife seated in a chair with another man, in the same chair and merrily smoking the same cigarette.

As the reward for my dunning labours, I got hold of one thousand five hundred yen. That came to two-thirds of the money to which we were entitled, although the truth is that I had never calculated on getting even that much. If father hadn't died, people would never have paid back the money so fast, which was something. However, as far as the people next door were concerned, I decided it would be too much trouble getting their pistol and sword through Japanese Customs, so I told them to sell them when and where they could and send the money on to me, and I left it at that.

The sea was rough the day we went back. I held father's remains in my arms, and the two of us, mother and me, crossed the wild sea. We arrived at the mainland, at Shimonoseki, then took another boat across the smaller straits to the island of Kyushu in the rain. Father's home village was in Kyushu and we had to pay a visit to the temple there. It was the first time I had been to Kyushu. Looking at father's village from the coach as we neared, it seemed to be buried in ears of corn. A great many girl cousins I had never met were living there, all seemingly of marriageable age. They appeared less given over to sorrow about my father's death than to pleased curiosity on meeting a relation who was a student in the big city. I liked to walk the lanes, the fields, the hills, wherever I went my body almost totally hidden in those waving ears of corn and rice, and with the wind brushing wave after wave of the tall grasses against my face. My girl cousins would pursue me on my walks, tracking me from among the grasses. After only two days there a letter came from my sister's place in Kobe. Her only daughter, little Mah, had caught dysentery, and the doctor said there was nothing to be done about it. Mother and I immediately left for Kobe. The girl cousins came to see us off, and one of them cried as we left, burying her face among the ears of rice and weeping.

When we reached Kobe, my sister had come back by herself from the hospital and was standing by the entrance to the dark scullery.

"How is she?" I asked.

"She's got no chance," my sister said briefly and calmly.

I said nothing. Mother just stopped where she was on the step up into the house and said nothing either. Disasters were contending with each other to see which should come out top. The whole damned business was too much. I felt like starting some sort of riot myself.

Sister didn't ask anything after her dead father. She wouldn't look at my face, as if she were angry with us. I walked across the still-unlit town at dusk to the hospital. An impudent-looking nurse was squatting in front of the hospital smoking a cigarette. When I entered, she followed me in. Another nurse was sitting, pale and unmoving, by Mah's bedside. Mah looked at my face silently. Her gaze was piercing and not what one expects in someone who is ill.

"She's not going to die," I thought.

And then suddenly she said in a loud voice: "Uncle gave me a banana." I had given her some bananas when I'd come down from Tokyo.

"Does it hurt?" I asked her.

She kept her mouth firmly shut this time. I looked at the temperature chart and noticed that for a week it had been fluctuating wildly around the 103 mark. After a while her father came in from the corridor holding a fan.

"How are things?" I asked.

"Hard to say, but she seems to be holding her own," my brother-in-law replied; and then: "You must be pretty well worn-out. I meant to go across myself, got all ready in fact, and then this little blighter suddenly catches it. Haven't slept for three nights." He laughed.

"She's going to get better," I said.

"Maybe. The doctor said she wouldn't, and if she doesn't then she doesn't, I suppose. Just have to see how things work out."

"But she looks fine, doesn't she?"

"She's looked all right all the time. It's a funny sort of illness. Everyone who's caught it this year's been just like her."

"Is there that much of it going around?"

"Going around and to spare. Plenty over to wipe your arse on. Every room in the hospital is full up with people, and they've all got the same thing. The kid in the next bed died last night. Dropping dead like flies. Since we've been here, how many have died in this place?" he said, and looked up at the ceiling as if he were calculating the number.

"Six," the nurse by the side of the bed said.

Six! In this tiny place! Wherever I went there was death. I felt that my body was some form of organism that scattered death all around it.

"Someone was dying of dysentery in the house next door in Korea," I said.

"Here." My brother-in-law turned to the nurse. "That's a good one. What do you make of that? And his dad's just died over there as well. He's just got back."

"Just before I left, a beggar died at the side of our house," I said.

Although little Mah had been condemned to death, she lay on the bed with her eyes wide open listening to our speculations on the matter. When I looked at the life that shone in her eyes, I felt that those eyes alone would be enough to cast off the death being forcibly wrapped around her. She would kick it aside, run away. But as I looked toward the dark corridor I felt true fear. Death was silently looking in from the doorway, that insane, indiscriminate, and merciless power that ravaged this place.

After a week Mah had got somewhat better. We also heard that the man next door in Korea had died. I was glad I hadn't gone after them about the money; glad they hadn't grown to hate me. And I also discovered that all the money I had laboriously dunned out of people, every penny I'd collected, would have to be handed over to my sister's husband. My creditor was my sister's husband. Practically all the money that my father had sent to me over the past two years had been in fact provided by my sister's husband. The creditor in Korea became the debtor on his return to Japan. In the same way that I had been compelled into being the creditor of the man next door despite the fact that he was dying, so my brother-in-law was being compelled into being mine despite the fact that my father had died. And in the same way that my father's death had inevitably transformed me into next-door's creditor, so this new creditor, my brother-in-law, had been as inevitably created by the dangerous illness of his child. He was a low-grade civil servant, and the whole of my school expenses he had been paying out of his scant savings. The fact is that the whole of his savings would quite soon have disappeared because of me. I didn't see any point in going over the matter with my mother, so I simply gave him the gold watch and all the money I'd collected in Korea, left mother with them for the time being, and went back to Tokyo. I realized it was exactly a month since the day I tripped over that pale blue stone in the road and cut my shin. When I'd picked up that stone, father had been dying in Korea. I wondered where that stone was lying now. I started looking for work, but since I was well aware that one didn't find work all that easily, I started pawning father's expensive silk clothes. I also pawned his gold spectacles. They had to be weighed, revolving slowly on the pan of the pawnshop scales, and father's eyes still seemed to be in them.

An old friend of mine returned to Tokyo from Shanghai at that time and came to see me. Because he came, some other friends pushed their way noisily in as well. One of them played the violin (always the same tune, "La Paloma"); another was a socialist who kept blowing froth from the Third International into my face; another was an expressionist actor; another was a great cinema enthusiast. I was always with at least one of them. Not only that, but they also took me places: concerts, expressionist plays, films, socialist meetings. There was absolutely no letup in this mad whirl. It was also a form of life totally irrelevant to my needs, since I never in fact knew where the next meal was coming from. But the first friend soon went back to Shanghai, and the others then stopped coming. At last I was quietly on my own, and then all the physical and mental exhaustion of the past month hit me at once. The grief over father's death for the first time possessed me as a slow realization. I had to use whatever moments of respite I could gain from that for wandering around looking for work. I had no money whatsoever; it had all gone. I could afford only one meal a day. Once out walking I saw some labourers sitting by a hole they were digging in the road, laughing and eating their lunch. There was one piece of salmon perched on top of the rice one of them was eating, and it looked to me like a rose.

One of those days I made up my mind to go and see K. She had grown quite magnificently plump. She seemed really pleased that I had managed to get back safe and sound.

"I wondered what on earth was up with you after getting a letter like that."

"But it had to be written."

"You really must never write like that to me again. I felt you were so far, so far away."

"Well, I was actually over on the continent."

She ignored that witty remark. As far as I could see, she was using the fact of my being penniless as a particularly relevant stage in the furtherance of our love affair. Certainly she was very tender toward me, and some of her pleasure in me began to affect me, too.

"You didn't send your address with your letter, so I didn't know where to reply."

"I didn't want you to. I didn't want the worry of wondering what sort of reply you'd write. I was having a particularly rough time then."

"What a nasty thing to say."

"If I wasn't nasty some of the time you wouldn't know what to do."

She didn't reply; in fact she said nothing more. She obviously wasn't going to forgive me for that, perhaps almost hated me for it.

That evening a letter arrived at my place from her. She wrote how much she hated me for thinking that she was the kind of girl whose affections would change over money. It was what I thought she would write. That woman next door had been hoping for the death of her husband, who would leave her no pennies, because of a man. And now my K said that she wanted to be my wife, me penniless with a mother to support, and she with her whole life before her.

"I don't care in the least what sort of thing should happen to you or what you might become. Please don't mention the word 'money' again. I hate it when you talk like that. All that grieves me, truly grieves me, is that your father, who would have been my father also, should have died."

I wasn't able to consider the letter as absolute untruth. Only it struck me that she was so obsessed with the idea of bearing my child, before that early death of mine which she so clearly foresaw, that she was getting all ready for this childbirth now; and I found this painfully touching, more painful than touching. Still, I decided I would welcome this resolve of hers. Why? Because I hate cleverness, I hate cynicism, I hate irony.

One day about a week later a letter arrived from Kobe. It said that Mah was gradually recovering from her illness. It also said that mother had suddenly been confined to bed suffering from physical and mental exhaustion. Here was something else to shake me. There was somewhere within me a desire, even if only a faint one, that mother should die. It wasn't because she had now become a burden to me, but because it seemed to me that the idea that the effect of father's death might extend so far as to take mother's life was a rather beautiful one. Mother had wanted father to die quickly; it pleased me that that early death should hasten her own. There was a rightness about it. I had been secretly outraged by mother's feelings toward father's death. I wanted her to die in order to silence that sense of outrage within me, and the fact that a son should wish such a thing for his mother would seem to be an indication of how inevitably unforgivable such feelings on the part of a wife must be, no matter how serious might have been the reasons for her holding them. There must be countless wives who do not love their husbands; but that lack of love toward the father will always provoke fierce hatred toward the mother in the son.

I decided that if mother's condition deteriorated I would go back to Kobe. However, even if I did I wanted to make sure I had found a job first. Then it was my own head that started to go wrong. If I looked at a newspaper, my head would gradually begin to slip forward and my eyesight would become blurred. If I concentrated hard with my eyes, the print would seem to float about the page and the words collide with each other. To get news about my mother's illness I had to write letters to my sister, but in the third letter I tried to write I found I couldn't hold the pen properly. I shut my eyes and scribbled the words on the page. God knows what I wrote, since if I considered what I was writing I couldn't even manage three words. I was finished; I wanted to give the whole damn lot up. What sort of job could I get now? What the hell was I fit for? Nothing. Still, I couldn't tell my sister any of this. It would be too much for her to bear, with my mother as she was and then finding out the state I was in. All I did was walk the streets every day, wandering about up on the hills where the sun was. The swirling, rising dust of the town no longer bothered me. The only solaces I had were the popular songs I could hear drifting faintly from a gramophone in one corner of the town, and the whole prospect of the city as it lay shining and glittering in the sun, spread out before me and looking like a shattered pomegranate. But the pleasure of listening to the songs on the gramophone was soon denied me. I found myself trying to listen and then my head began to hurt. One day I went in fear and trembling to a doctor acquaintance of mine and had him examine me.

"I could suggest a nice, peaceful convalescence, but even with six years of that you wouldn't get any better."

I didn't know what to say to that, so he went on: "Look, when you're walking along a street, for example, I suppose you think about what direction you ought to take."

"Sure."

"That's it. That's what's wrong. That's what you shouldn't be doing."

I might just as well be killed straight off, then. On the way home I went back to the place where I had picked up the blue stone. In the sunken back streets, which were like the depths of some gorge, a group of children were larking about mimicking a blind masseur. I quietly picked up a black stone and then went home. My mind responded to nothing anymore. I was forbidden to think about anything. Was that it? If I looked at colours my head hurt. If I listened to music my head hurt. When I got back to my dark room and lay down, the only things that came into my mind were various methods of avoiding suicide. I collected everything that had a blade, then threw the whole lot as far as I could out of the window into the darkness. I blessed my good luck in not having brought back with me from Korea that pistol that had been offered to me as security. I was turning into an animal that did nothing but wander about, halting in front of greengrocers', dawdling by the windows of flower shops, sniffing the fresh, green odours they gave off. The only places I had of rest and refuge in my wandering of the streets were the quiet flower shops or the marketplace with its stalls piled high with fruit, or the hills where the sky looked clean and the streets of the town could look even healthy. Or I would be walking past a spacious garden and the scent of fragrant olive would overtake me like an enchantment, and a lightness would rise up within me, and there would be slight stirrings of hope, a sense of something about to flower; all of which, after it had gone, would only leave me that much deeper in despair than before.

I sometimes went to see K. But I couldn't tell her about

this state of mind which I might fall into at any moment of the day. I had this fear that persisted with me that in the same way that my father had been destroyed by my mother so I was also fated to be destroyed by K. Still, I could walk about freely and unaided, and I suppose I appeared to everybody as normal and healthy. Finally my whole existence was becoming one complete and perfect lie. However, I decided that I would make sure that no one knew about this shattered state of my mind, that I would drift along, an inflated bag of lies. I could always keep on deceiving everybody like this, and thus I didn't see why I should ever be a source of inconvenience to anybody at any time. I could consider myself fortunate, I suppose, in that I still possessed the ability to eat. And yet, although I could rely upon my healthy intestines to handle this question of eating (their ability was beyond question), it was a matter of deep chagrin to me that I couldn't in fact earn one penny with my own hands, since I was only an inflated bag of lies drifting the streets, and what form of drifting would waft into my hands the necessary comestibles? My possessions were already limited to a pair of originally high (although now totally broken-down) wooden clogs, and my bedding. Still, I endeavoured to keep cool and collected over this. Gradually things ceased to hurt or upset me; I felt a coldness growing within me, and gradually it gave me strength.

And then one day money suddenly turned up: forty yen. This money came from no other source than that unfortunate house in Korea which once during my dunning days I had attempted to sink. They said they'd sold the pistol. The prospective sinker sinks himself, and those whom he attempted to sink rescue their sinker from his own shipwreck. With that money in my hands I could remain undisturbed in my lying life for at least two months.

"The pistol's been sold, by God, the pistol!"

Yet why should they have taken all that trouble to help me?

"There's always somebody somewhere sweating his guts out trying to be honest and good."

And yet even with just the little experience I had of some aspects of life, I had reached the point where I could begin to understand that that statement was indeed true, a clear and definite truth which I now felt.

"The pistol's been sold, by God, the pistol!"

All that day, whenever I thought about the pistol, I felt like shouting that out in the middle of the street from pure joy. That had more meaning than picking up a black stone instead of a blue one, not only in that it was a calmer, luckier feeling, but also in that it was more powerfully felt, beating upward from the real depths of my being.

The Pale Captain

Father suddenly died. I crossed the straits, eating bananas for four days, and arrived at an unknown town. Mother was in a weird, triangular house that was all glass windows, on a street corner, sitting solitary like a table doing nothing.

"Well?"

"He's dead."

That he certainly was. From that day on, my life as a creditor, my dunning life, began.

"Pay up. Dad's dead."

"Hand it over. Dad's dead."

That was how the dun chorus went.

First, I parleyed with a local law official, a mechanic at the steel works, a secretary at the County Council, and the owner of a watchmaker's. Yet money never dances to a clumsy dun chorus. Then I ignored the demands of decency and started having a go at the house next door, my weakest opponent. He was a retired captain. Now I learned he was ill with dysentery, and dying. His two children, a boy and an older girl, were in the dark kitchen baking buns for the shop in silence. I was sick of dancing for money.

Every morning the bell of the donkey tinkled coolly as it passed by. At the crossroads a mounted policeman glared at a Korean who had glittering eyes.

I wrote a letter to my girl I had left behind.

"We won't be able to get married. I've found out that father left no money. So of course I don't have any. I've even got to find the boat fare back somewhere. Don't say you love me. It's the money I must have, and don't have, the money that tears us apart."

When I got upset, I took the remains of father out of their box.

"Is this dad? How can dad be like this? This is only lime."

I picked father's bones up one by one and tossed them back into the box. Father made a cheerful, jingling sound. I remembered wrestling with him and throwing him down.

Outside, a Chinese and a Korean were hitting each other. The Korean was pushed and fell in some rubbish. One leg stuck up and he howled pathetically.

The captain next door went into the hospital, and his daughter came to our house bringing a sword with no hilt as security.

"It's all right. Don't bother."

"But you ought to have. . . ."

"Don't bother. It's all right," I said.

From the next day onward she would often steal carefully and silently out the back way and peek in at us.

By the side of a huge heap of rubbish in the junk yard across the narrow lane, a group of Koreans were unconcernedly messing about giving themselves shots of morphine. One of them was crowned with a shapeless top hat. Another had an umbrella with all its ribs sticking out. Another was a cripple; he had on those odd sandals that cripples wear.

"What's that lot over there?"

"Those, my boy, are beggars and thieves," mother said.

The faces of the beggars and thieves were like smashed tiles. You never saw them smile no matter when you looked at them. They merely hung around, smoking, injecting. Sometimes they would fight among themselves with their expressionless, dull faces.

Top Hat was a considerable fop. He took his syringe out of a cloth he kept tied round his thigh. The cripple took his out of a towel he kept tied round his head. As he sat almost buried in the pile of rubbish, his body shook and trembled, like a dog that was dying.

One evening I happened to meet the girl next door in front of that rubbish heap on her way back from the hospital. I stopped, and she stopped too, as if she had something she wanted to say.

"How is your father?" I asked.

She didn't answer but just smiled slightly.

"Is he getting better?"

"No," she said.

The pale street light at the corner shone on her plaited hair. The eyes of the cripple trembled among the junk-yard junk like two flickering jewels.

"How old are you?" I asked her.

"I'm fifteen."

"Mother says you helped us a lot when father died."

"Not really," she said.

"Well, mother's grateful anyhow."

"My mother said today I was to help out at your place."

"That's very kind. I suppose your mother has to spend all her time at the hospital?"

"Yes. Then there's the pistol."

"Pistol? What's all this?"

"Father said I was to give you the pistol."

"Have you got a pistol, then?"

"Yes. This one," she said, and suddenly took a black pistol out of its cloth wrapping.

I took the pistol and balanced it in the palm of my hand. The responsive, heavy feel of it gave that sense of satisfaction that holding a weapon gives.

"This sort of thing's too dangerous for you to have, so I'll look after it for you for a bit."

"All right. Then there's these," the girl said, and handed me some bullets.

It was the first time I had ever had a gun and ammunition.

"Right," I murmured.

From then on, every evening I would enjoy the stealthy pleasure of examining the fierce glint of the barrel under the street light. In a corner of the mountain of rubbish by my side the crippled morphine addict would again be perpetually shaking. Sometimes Top Hat, like a real fop with a stick thrust under one arm, would come home in his worn-out shoes.

"But what about the money?"

Every morning whenever I thought about the money I would feel gloomy and small under the high, blue sky. I would have to give up the university. I would have to provide for mother. I began to worry over the skinniness of my shoulders. Still, the main thing was the fare for the boat. Why did the green waves of the straits look like so many bared teeth? I slipped the pistol inside my lapel and took up my abandoned troubadour dun refrain.

However, the local law official had transformed his telephone into a lie-making machine. The mechanic at the steel works used his rusty steel plates as a shield against creditors. The secretary at the County Council drowned my words with the light scratching of his pen. The owner of the watchmaker's had unshakably persuaded himself that the time of his stopped watches was the correct one. So the only thing that could get me and mother on board a ship and across the straits was the pistol of the pale captain who was dying.

The girl next door would wait for me each evening by the street light at the corner, playing with her plaited hair. One night when I met her there, she started complaining to me about her mother.

"Do you hate your mother all that much?" I asked her.

"Yes. I hate her. I want to go to my real mother," the girl said.

"Then the person you call mother is really your aunt?"

"No, she's not. She's just the maid."

"Well then, where's your real mother?"

"Dead."

"Dead?"

"Father's always having rows with mother about me."

"Then when your father's dead what will you do?"

"I don't know," the girl said.

Even so, when the girl talked about her dying father she didn't look particularly unhappy.

"Do you love your father?"

"No. Not one bit," the girl said.

I couldn't understand, then, what made her so miserable. Whenever I looked at her she was always glumly staring at her feet.

"When are you going back?" the girl asked.

"Quite soon. The sea's rough now, too dangerous to cross."

I seemed to attract the attention of a passing mounted policeman. A pigtailed Chinaman slowly pulling a cart entered the dark lane.

After a while the girl suddenly put both hands to her eyes and burst out crying.

"What are you crying for? Don't cry. You mustn't cry."

I put my arm around her shoulders and led her away out of the light to beside the dark hut of the junk yard. Among the rubbish the usual cripple was shaking with his pale, glittering eyes. My nose caught a whiff of opium.

"Please, you mustn't go, you mustn't go," the girl said.

I watched the cripple in the heap of rubbish with his unmoving face like a dark hole, and wound one of the girl's plaits around my finger.

The next day the girl's mother came hurrying back from the hospital, but she didn't stay long. That evening she went off again to the hospital. I raised a corner of the curtain and watched her go. She came out the back way then went stealthily round to the front part of the house, where it was misty, and began talking in low tones to a man she had kept waiting in front of the junk-yard hut. The man leaned his shoulder against hers, and she flirtatiously edged him away.

I assumed that they must be praying for the death of the pale captain. After they had gone off in the direction of the hospital, the back door of the house opened again. The face of the girl appeared, softly spying after her mother. She ran a little way to the street light, then craned her neck and peered into the mist where her mother had disappeared. Then she turned and began to stare in the direction of our house. Avoiding my mother, I went out to where the girl was.

"How's your father?"

"They say he's got no chance now."

"Then you'd better go, hadn't you?"

The girl said nothing and looked again in the direction her mother had taken.

"Why don't you go tonight, now?"

"I don't want to go."

"Even so, you ought to."

"Mother's just gone, just now."

"She's just gone?"

"She said I needn't live with her after father's dead. I'm glad."

I said no more.

"Father used to beat me a lot. He used to tie me up and hit me with a bamboo stick. It was all mother's fault. Mother, when I got hit, she used to laugh out loud. I hated her so much, I couldn't stand it, so I ran to the police station one night. Then father really got told off because of it."

"But your father didn't hit you because he didn't like you. He was worried about you, so he hit you. Look, you go off to him now. Come on, hurry."

"Perhaps I ought to go for a bit."

"That's right. Off you go."

"Still." The girl didn't move.

"Are you frightened to go by yourself?"

"Will you stay here?"

"Yes, I'll stay. Now you go."

"Then I'll stay here too."

"Then I'm going home."

"No, you mustn't. I don't want you to.

"All right, but you've got to go and see your father."

"I don't want to."

"Then I'm having nothing to do with you."

So she started crying again as she had the night before. I liked to look at her hair as she stood sobbing there, under the pale street light in the misty street. The furtive silhouette of a Chinaman's cart faded away in the mist.

"Look, are you going to the hospital?"

She went on crying, but nodded her head.

"All right, it's this way."

I walked with her past the storehouse in the junk yard. I felt the desire to kiss her full on the lips, there in front of the expressionless face of the cripple trembling among his rubbish.

"Anyway, you mustn't cry. Stop crying," I said.

The girl stopped before me.

"Now look up."

She raised her lowered head straight, but then looked down again. I took her cheeks between my hands, raised her face, and drew her toward me. She raised her hands painfully to my breast and laid them awkwardly there. Then I remembered her mother flirting with her man in the same place. Then the face of the pale captain came before me, as if I could sense his presence there. The thought of kissing the girl was repulsive to me.

"Now hurry up and go to your father. Hurry."

She looked at my face in silence.

"Aren't you going?"

But she went on standing there. I left it at that and went back home. She then walked off dejectedly and slowly in the direction of the street light. I stood and watched her shape as it gradually blurred into the mist.

That night I suddenly wanted to meet my girl back home again. Just like the girl next door, weeping with me even with her father dying, now I, with my father dead, thought only of my girl. She was present to me, clear.

I raised the dunning banner again. I must set that watchmaker's watches going again; I must make them tell the right time. I went off to his shop and finally said: "The only clocks you've got in your shop are ones that don't go. If I'm going to believe what they say, I'll never get home. Stop this farce and hand over the money. Come on, the money."

And he reluctantly paid up half of what was owed. Then I went to the law office.

"My money, please. My money. As long as we can't get home, I shall hold you personally responsible for our expenses here, and all our bills will be sent to you."

Upon which he pleaded with me to give him just one more week. I'm quite hopeless when faced with a pleader. I made a sour expression and went home. When I got there, some other creditor dunning the house next door was in our house talking to mother.

"Well, shall we do this, then? You can have that fine old sword from next door, and I'll have the pistol. That's the proper way to do things, don't you think? That sword is genuine Awataguchi so it must be worth all of two hundred."

"What about the pistol?" I butted in.

"That? Well, let's see. I suppose it would come to around ninety. Of course, one doesn't come across pistols like that nowadays, so it's a little difficult to say, as I'm sure your respected father is well aware, that it's not the sort of thing one comes across nowadays. However, I did once discuss the whole matter with your father, and since the outlook for your neighbour is, well, that he doesn't have long to go, it would seem best if we got together, your father and I, and settled matters, with things as they now stand."

"Father's not here."

"Oh. Has he gone somewhere?"

"He's dead."

"What!" the man cried out.

"He died at the beginning of the month."

"But he was in the best of health the last time I saw him, not so long ago."

"Yes. It was all very sudden."

The man was clearly in a great hurry now to get away, and he glanced vaguely around the room.

"His remains are over there. Those are his remains," my mother said, pointing at the box.

The man's eyes began to grow frightened, and he looked in silence at the box for some time.

"Don't feel much like going on living either," he muttered.

Then he got up and crept as hurriedly as he could out of the house, omitting the usual polite expressions when he left.

Although wife and child were waiting for him to die, the next-door captain didn't seem able to make up his mind to do so.

One morning mother woke me. The crippled beggar who always trembled and shook among the rubbish heap was now lying on his face, dead, in a pool of mud left by the rain. Top Hat was at his side, smoking a cigarette, looking at the cripple's back. The donkey passed to its morning's work coolly ringing its bell.

Then a policeman came with some coolies. The coolies covered the beggar with straw matting, lifted him up, then went away after the policeman. One deep death mask was left clearly imprinted in the mud.

I looked out from our triangular glass house at the beggar's carved death mask. I was wondering who would be the first person to trample on it.

Top Hat sank half of his body into the rubbish heap where the beggar had been, took out his syringe from the band tied round his thigh, and thrust the needle into his arm.

That evening I went down to the street lamp again. I wanted to make the girl next door cry. It was clear to me that she actually enjoyed crying.

The pale street light, with a melancholy about it like flowing water, was just the place for wringing tears out of her eyes.

"Is that, er, lady in your house going. . . ?" inquired the girl, who looked at me and came very close, almost nestling against me.

"How's your father?"

"Is that lady going back to Japan soon?"

"Well, we're certainly going back. If only the sea would hurry up and calm down a bit."

"I want to go back soon too."

"You'll be able to go back very shortly, won't you?"

"But who knows when that's going to be? I don't."

"There's no point in worrying over it. Just be good and patient and you'll be able to go. If your father should die, I'll give you the name of a shop where you can sell that pistol. You'll get enough money for it to pay your passage home."

"But mother would never let me do that."

"Then you'd take it without her knowing, and sell it. Then there's a very valuable sword in your place, you know. You want to hide that as soon as you can. There are plenty of people who've got their eye on that. Don't you hand it over to any of them."

"I want to go back with you," the girl said.

"If you can manage to get yourself ready to leave before I do, then of course you can."

"I wish father would hurry up and die."

"Now look, don't talk like that. I can't stand people who

talk about their parents in that way. Go on, go away," I shouted at her.

Then she burst out crying. I had that little secret thrill of pleasure again. I put my arm around her, then led her on the pilgrimage to the front of the dark hut in the junk yard where on one could see us.

The trembling, shaking beggar was no longer there among the heap of rubbish. Now there was merely a heap of silent waste like a dark wall. I suddenly recalled that death mask of the cripple. Now where was it? I struck a match and searched around in the muddiness at my feet. In the light of the match the wrinkled mud glittered like skin stained with oil and reflected my face. Then in the mud I saw one sunken mask, expressionless like a dog, with its forehead trampled in by someone's boot. I stopped, and remained still. This was it. I dropped my match in my eagerness, then struck another, and gradually moved my face closer to the mask. Within that death mask I discovered my own contorted face. I threw the match down into the mud without thinking. I began to feel all round my own face with my hands. No matter how much I felt my own face, it was the face of the shaking beggar that was there, living, before my eyes, countless trembling faces, weaving before me, clinging and sucking like tentacles. I ran back home and went indoors. Father's remains were staring at me. I took up the box in my arms and shook the bones violently from side to side, rattling them.

"Stop that, will you," mother said. "Listen."

I held the box in my arms and looked at mother for the first time. She was leaning her head in the direction of the house next door, her white hair hanging down her neck, and listening to something. Then she said in a low voice: "That old man next door—he seems to have died."

Mother's face looked to me like a gravestone now.

The Depths of the Town

There was a shoemaker's on the corner. The place was packed with shoes from floor to ceiling. Between the black, closed walls of shoes the head of the shopgirl perpetually drooped down. Next door a watchmaker's with its watches spread out in a dense pattern. Next door to that an egg shop, an old man squatting in a foam of innumerable eggs, a towel tied round his bald head. Next a crockery shop, in the midst of whose frigid hospital whiteness the lady of the place, still young and gay, seemed as if she were about to kick over the columns of plates.

Next a flower shop. The girl was grubbier than the flowers, among which appeared from time to time the rapt, idiot face of some small boy. Next a dressmaker's with headless bodies dangling; and the owner poked a bloodless finger into his ear and sniffed the odour from the café. Next a bookshop, like a suit of armour, opened its mouth. There was a draper's next to the bookshop. Like the dark bottom of the sea, its mountains of muslin, beside which a thin, pregnant woman was sinking, a flatfish with glittering eyes.

Next to that the gate of a girls' school. At three o'clock a multicoloured wave of girls poured out. Next to that was a public bath. Beyond the glass, mermaids were broiled, their fresh naked bodies cast down on wooden slabs. Next a fruit shop. The son kicked the fruit with a foot made powerful by prolonged pedalling. There was a doctor's next door. The heads that hung by its windows seemed always to have a ripeness in their indolence.

Every day he passed those shops in silence, then climbed up to the top of the green hill beyond. The hill was a cone of thick, green grass jostled and contained by the straight line of the main road. Its grass bent softly to the air. He lay in the grass beaten by the light, unmoving, attempting to drink in hopefulness from the hopeful tones of the streets.

He couldn't move. If he moved, the accompanying effort of thought hurt his brain. Because of this he couldn't eat. He had to learn to live in useless glory on this hill. From here one had two choices of vision, and the various objects of the town competed for attention.

On the high ground to the north stood the spacious residences of the well-to-do. There the breeze and sunlight entered at will. A dignitary with his lady rushed his car between the stone gates of his mansion, pondering the gravitational facts of his own body. Then, like a bouquet of flowers, gaudy dancing girls were crammed in and sent away. Then a polished silk hat, then a frock coat like a bird. But he was thinking of nothing.

He looked southward to the bottom of the narrow valley. Here fumes of carbon dioxide built up pressure: what freely entered was only dust blown by the east wind, typhus, factory smoke. Nothing grew here. A collection of tiles and germs and empty bottles, market leftovers, workers, whores, and rats.

What should I think about? he thought.

He needed ten sen. If he had that, he could get through the day without thinking. If he didn't think, he could get well. If he moved, his stomach would feel empty. If his stomach felt empty, ten sen would not be enough. Thus he lay all day, his face grey, like an insect that hopes to acquire protective colouring in the green grass on the hill.

As evening approached he went down from the hill and entered the streets. Sometimes he would be caught up in a crowd of workers, grey black, an avalanche of weariness, and borne along with them. They had been making boots all day standing in a row, and yet they flowed in procession, heads bowed at times as in a funeral, toward the centre of the lower streets.

At times he was drawn along by them in their group hunger to enter silently an eating shop. Meat and rice. The heads of pigs and cows, the skin flayed off, rolled over on the kitchen table like sleeping human heads. The workers lined up in silence between the cramped tables. When the food was slow in coming they beat their rice bowls with their chopsticks. When the place was full of steam their faces reddened, widened, and grew small.

He filled his stomach with cow's head, threw down his ten sen, and went back alone to his backstreet home. He rented a three-mat room. The pillar that propped the roof was splintered and askew. The wall was blackened like the inside of an oven; the rain had drawn a pattern on it like a map, in which the muck of flies was etched in little spots. He leaned his head back against the pillar, kicked aside the torn-up sheets of paper with his foot, and brooded on the glories of suicide. Outside, children were swaying the fence, playing zoo. A blind masseur passed along the narrow lane calling for custom. The children started to creep along one by one behind him mimicking his walk.

He lay down and lay still. From where he lay he could see the broken back wall of the house across the way. Through one chink he could see a pendent female breast. It belonged to a pale, sick woman who lay eternally in the same posture. The one thing he could be certain of seeing when he came home was that immodest breast. The breast had virtually become an intimate of his. He longed just once to see the owner's face. Yet whenever he looked, the breast lay squarely beyond the chink in the wall, fallen, spread out, unmoving. Always seeing it, it was as if the world had become one gigantic breast alone, and twilight was falling. The electric light came on over the mountain breast, drawing extravagant patterns over what had fallen under its own heavy gravity, casting the shadow of a smashed gun turret, face down and out.

When it became dark he went out. The sunken street, a heap of rubbish by day, glittered like a festival. Stalls were set out beneath the low roofs, and heaps of cheap toys and metal objects flickered and shone. He strolled along, looking, breathing in the fresh air, past the stalls lined up by the muddy ditch, toward the vegetable market. Here was the unexpected, a vegetable garden which drank in the acetylene light set greenly on the road at the bottom of the town. The rows of freshly watered vegetables were like a field, a continual source of fresh, green, gentle air that drifted among the passersby with the scent of coolness.

He rejoiced in his own rare lightness of heart and glanced affectionately at the mountains of copper coins that had collected on the straw mats. The jammed heaps of heavy copper possessed a form of elegance, like mysterious towers. He felt the dynamism of their presence, here slumbering at the bottom of the town, as a kind of pin or nail that held together the various conical inclines that were the town itself.

"That's it. And suppose one drew out that pin?"

He imagined the whole town spread out in fragments, and that pleased him, so once again he went and jostled shoulders with people. And yet amid the smell of human bodies he was overwhelmed by an unexpected and unexplained sadness. The misery of momentary life flashed out at him, the sudden cross-section sight of a blunt heavy boat opened to the view. Still one grinned and went on walking. He passed between warehouses full of empty bottles and went home, got into bed as he was, and curled up.

He knew he could make ten sen a day if he sold three magazines. As long as he kept hold of this principle, life would not be terrifying. One day he picked up the coin obtained by selling three magazines and prepared to go out. There in front of the door was a blind old woman he had never seen before, standing dirty, solitary, and barefoot. She held a brush in one hand, bowed severely, and began her spiel. She kept on bowing.

"I'm seventy years old, sir, and my husband's died at the age of seventy, and I had an only son, sir, but he's dead too, sir. The police won't let me beg, sir, so please won't you be so good as to buy one of these brushes? I've got money for myself but the old man's funeral will cost eighteen yen and I don't have a copper toward it, sir. I have to pay thirty-eight sen a night for my lodging, sir, and if I can't pay that I don't know what I shall do. Please be so good as to buy one of these brushes, sir."

He folded the ten sen into her dry palm and went out. He was going to sit in the grass on the green hill.

Whatever he thought about, his head hurt. He stood on the sunlit road. The town spread out with himself as its centre. There was the shoemaker's on the corner. The shopgirl was silent among the shoes. Next to that was the geometrical watchmaker's. Among the innumerable angles of the clocks and watches the moving hands were at three. He stopped in front of the girls' school. A wave of brilliant girls poured from the school gates, glancing at him. A stake washed by the overwhelming sea, he stood and watched. The wave of girls broke into two at his breast. Like a waving field of flowers they flowed serenely on.

Spring Riding in a Carriage

The cold late-autumn wind began to sound among the pine trees on the shore. In a corner of the garden a clump of small dahlias shrank in upon themselves. From the side of the bed where his wife lay he watched a sluggish tortoise moving in the pond. The tortoise swam and the bright shadows that were cast back from the water swayed on the surface of the dry rocks.

"Oh, do look. Isn't the light on the pine trees lovely now."

"You've been looking at the pine trees?"

"Yes."

"I've been looking at the tortoise."

They were returning to silence again.

"You've been lying there all that time and the only thought in your head is that the light on the pine trees is lovely?"

"Yes. But I'm making up my mind not to think about anything."

"It is not in any way feasible that a human being should be able to lie down and not think."

"Well, I do think about things, like wanting to get better and then going down to the well and scrubbing and scrubbing away at all the washing. I think about that so much."

This unforeseen desire on her part made him smile.

"You are certainly a queer one. Making me take all this time and trouble so that you can do the washing. That's great."

"But I remember when I used to be so well. I want to be like that again. You've been an unlucky person, haven't you?"

"Uh," he said.

He thought about those years before they'd married, the four or five years' battle with her family. Then he thought about when they were married, the two years of troubles caught in the middle between wife and mother. Then his mother died, leaving them alone together, and then she had immediately become ill and had taken to her bed, and he remembered that long year of suffering also.

"I see what you mean, anyway. I'd rather like to do the washing myself."

"I wouldn't mind for myself if I died now. But it's you.

I want to give you something back for what you've done, then I'd like to die after that. I worry so much nowadays that I won't be able to. It's only that."

"What are you going to give me, then, if you're going to give me something back?"

"Well, first of all, I'd look after you. . . ."

"And?"

"There're lots of things I'd do."

But he was aware that she was not going to recover now.

"That sort of thing doesn't matter to me, not a bit. But you know, what I would like, I'd like just once to wander around Munich—Munich in the rain. It would have to be raining. I wouldn't want to go otherwise."

"I want to go too. I want to." She started wriggling about on the bed, her stomach plunging and rippling like waves.

"You've been ordered absolute rest and quiet."

"But I don't want it, I don't. I want to walk. Help me get up, please. Please help me up."

"I will not."

"Help me up. I don't care if I do die."

"Nothing will come of dying."

"I don't care. Just help me up."

"Look, keep still, can't you? I'll tell you what you can do. You can spend your whole life over it. Look at the pine trees and that light on them, and think of the one word that describes it perfectly. Just the one, all right?"

She became silent and absorbed. That was one peaceful problem to quiet her with. He stood up trying to think of others.

Out at sea the afternoon waves broke on the rocks and scattered. A boat leaned and rounded the sharp point of the headland. Down on the beach two children sat like scraps of paper, steaming potatoes in their hands, against a background of deep, surging blue.

The waves after waves of suffering that came in upon him had never been something to be evaded. The origin of those waves of suffering, each different in each onslaught, existed in his very flesh, had been there from the beginning. He had decided to taste this suffering as the tongue tastes sugar, to scrutinize it with the total light of his senses. Which would taste best in the end? My body is a scientific flask; the most important thing is absolute clarity.

The dahlias lay tangled and twisted on the ground, pieces of old, dried-up rope. All day the wind blew in from the sea, from the horizon, and it was winter.

Off he went through the swirling sand, twice a day, to buy her the fresh chicken innards that she liked to eat. He would try every poulterer's in the streets on the sea front one after the other, and each time, after an initial glance from the yellow chopping board out into the yard and then back again, he would ask: "Any innards? Innards?"

When he was in luck and the agatelike innards were brought out from the ice, he would stride off heroically back home and arrange them neatly by her bedside.

"This one like a rounded jewel is a pigeon's kidney. This glossy liver came from a domestic duck. And look at this, just like a piece of lip bitten right off. And this green one is, look, an emerald from the jade mountain in far Tibet."

His eloquence inflamed her, and she would writhe exoticly on the bed in her hunger, like a girl waiting for her first kiss. But he would snatch the innards cruelly away from in front of her, and plop them immediately into the saucepan.

She watched the contents of the saucepan through the cagelike bars of her bedstead, smiling as they boiled away.

"Looking at you from here, you really are a weird animal," he said.

"An animal, indeed. Let me remind you that I am still a married lady."

"That's right, a married lady inside a cage who craves for animals' guts. I've always felt that somewhere there's always been this certain amount of cold-bloodedness inside you trying to get out."

"Speak for yourself. You're the one who's so cold and intellectual, so cold-blooded, thinking all the time about ways of getting away from me."

"That's your cage mentality again."

He always had to end things up like that, because she was sensitive to each motion of his face, to every half-shadow that might drift across it, and he needed to baffle and cancel out what she perceived there. Yet also there were times when this kind of response of hers would outwit him, suddenly slip through to where it hurt and completely unbalance him.

"The truth is that, well, I *do* object to sitting here with you. Tuberculosis is hardly a thing to rejoice over, is it?"

There were times when he counterattacked her openly like that.

"Well, is it? Even if I do manage to get away from you, all it consists of is going round and round that garden. There's a rope that always ties me to the bed where you're lying, and all I can do is move along the circumference it draws. What else have I got? What else besides this misery?"

"It's because. . . . It's because you just want to enjoy yourself," she said bitterly.

"Then you yourself don't want to?"

"But you, you want to enjoy yourself with other women."

"All right, that's what you say. But suppose it were true, what then?"

She would always burst into tears at this point. That would shake him, so he would have to retreat the way he had come, very gently taking to pieces the argument he had built.

"But obviously I can't like having to sit by your bed from morning till night. I want you to get well as soon as you can, so I go round and round that same garden all the time, don't I? It's not something exactly up my street."

"But you only do it for yourself. You're not doing it for me, because you don't care a bit about me."

When she pressed in upon him this far, he had finally to yield to her cage mentality. She had to be right; yet was it only for himself that he refused to give any expression to his own misery?

"All right, have it your way. I put up with everything simply for my own sake. But whose fault is it that I've got to put up with all this for my own sake? If you weren't here, do you think I'd want to give this stupid impersonation of life inside a zoo? It's being done for you. How can you be so damn ridiculous as to say it's all for me, irrespective of you?"

When things reached this point, his wife's temperature

would invariably rise to over a hundred. Thus the clarification of an argument obliged him to stay up all night changing the ice in the ice bag for her head, opening it and closing it, over and over.

However, if he were going to make clear to her the reasons why he needed a break from all this, he had to keep up this frustrating remarshalling of his arguments practically day after day. The work that he did to feed himself and look after her he did in a room apart. When he did so, again she would be after him with another display of her cage mentality.

"I can't think why you have to always want to escape from me like that. All day you've only come to this room three times. Still, what's there to understand. That's just the sort of person you are."

"What are you trying to tell me you want me to do? In order to make you better, I have to buy food and medicine. If I'm just going to sit about here doing nothing, where's the money to come from? Are you asking me to do conjuring tricks or something?"

"But I don't see why you couldn't do your work here," she said.

"Well, I couldn't. If I can't forget about you at least for a while, I can't get anything done."

"That's right. You're the sort of person who thinks about work twenty-four hours a day, and you couldn't care less about me."

"Yes, your rival is my work. But that rival of yours is, in fact, always on your side."

"I feel so lonely."

"Everybody feels lonely. That's the way it is."

"It's all right for you. You've got your work. I've got nothing."

"Why don't you try to find something, then?"

"But I don't want anything, except you. And I just lie here, that's all, looking at the ceiling."

"Look, stop it, will you. We both feel lonely, right? And I've got a deadline. If I don't get the thing written today it'll be making a lot of trouble for somebody else."

"That's it. That's you. Your precious deadline is more to

you than I am."

"No, it's not. A deadline is a sign telling me I must not trespass upon the affairs of others. As long as I see and accept the validity of that sign, it is not permitted that I think about my own affairs."

"There you are, so rational, always so rational. God, I loathe rational people."

"As long as you remain a member of my household, your responsibility with regard to these contractual signs is the same as my own."

"You'd be better off not accepting things like that, wouldn't you?"

"Right. Then how do we live?"

"If you're going to be so unfeeling I'd rather be dead."

Whereupon he gave up and went straight out into the garden, where he took a few deep breaths. Then he took his shopping bag again and without saying a word went off to the town to buy the innards.

But there was his mind going round and round in circles tied up to the bars of her cage, and there was her mind inside its mental cage, and this cage mentality of hers with all her physical irritability kept on at him all the time, hardly allowing him a moment to breathe. Because of this, and because of the acuteness of this neurotic set of ideas she had created for herself within her cage, she was destroying the constitution of her own lungs every day at an ever-increasing pace. When he tapped her chest it made a light, papier-mâché sound. And then she lost all interest even in her favourite chicken innards.

In order to give her some appetite, he brought back various fresh fish from the sea, laid them out on the veranda of her room, and gave a little lecture on them.

"This is the frogfish, the pierrot of the sea who has tired himself with dancing. This is the large shrimp, and this is the small—they are the knights of the sea, fallen with their armour on. This is the saurel, or horse mackerel, the leaf of a tree blown off in a storm."

"I'd much rather you read the Bible to me," she said.

From that day onward he was obliged to take out the dirty, stained Bible and read it to her.

"Hear my prayer, O Lord, and let my cry come unto thee.
Hide not thy face from me in the day when I am in trouble; incline thine ear unto me; in the day when I call, answer me speedily.
For my days are consumed like smoke, and my bones are burned as a hearth.
My heart is smitten, and withered like grass; so that I forget to eat my bread."

Then another ill portent followed. One day, after a night of storm, they woke to find that the sluggish tortoise had gone away from the pond in the garden.

As her condition became worse, it grew increasingly impossible for him to leave her bedside. She started to cough up phlegm every minute. Since she couldn't wipe her mouth for herself, he was obliged to do it. Then she started to complain about severe pains in her side. Every twenty-four hours she had about five really prolonged and violent attacks of coughing. Each time she would fumble and claw at her chest with the pain. He felt that when she was like this he should try to remain as calm as possible. But this quiet detachment of his only seemed to provoke her into abuse of him, gasped out while these terrible bouts of coughing went on.

"I like the way you just sit there thinking about other things when someone's in pain like this."

"Look, calm down. If you shout like that now. . . ."

"So very calm and collected. You make me sick."

"Suppose I got excited now, what. . . ."

"Shut your damned mouth."

She snatched at the piece of paper he was holding, rubbed it angrily across her mouth to wipe off the phlegm, then threw it back at him.

Like it or not, he had to go on wiping away with one hand the sweat that poured out of her body, and with the other he had to unceasingly wipe away from her mouth the phlegm that she coughed up. His hips went numb with squatting by her side. The unbearable pain caused her to start flailing her fists about, hitting at his chest, as she lay there staring angrily at the ceiling. The towel he wiped her sweat away with got caught up in her nightdress. She kicked

off the bedclothes and tried to get up, panting and heaving.
"No. Stop it. You're not to move."
"But it hurts. It hurts me."
"Calm down."
"I can't stand it."
"You'll injure yourself."
"Shut up, can't you."
Her fists beat against him like stones rattling against a shield as he went on stroking and soothing the now coarse skin of her breast.
Yet even this extremity of suffering he found in fact several degrees less than what he had gone through when she was well and caused him to feel such jealousy. He became aware that her sick body with its corrupted lungs bestowed more happiness upon him than her healthy one had.
—There's an original thought for you. I must hold fast to this novel interpretation.
When he thought about this interpretation as he looked out to sea, he would burst into peals of laughter.
That would provoke her into another display of her cage mentality, and she would look at him with an expression of pain on her face, and say: "All right, I know exactly what you're laughing about."
"I doubt it. In fact, I was thinking how I am probably much better off as I am now than if you got better and could play about trying on lots of new clothes. For a start, that pale face of yours gives you a sort of dignity. So you stay in bed like that as long as you feel like it."
"That's just like you."
"It's because I'm like me that I can enjoy nursing you."
"You're always on about nursing, nursing. You bring it out every other word."
"Because it's something for me to be proud of."
"Well, if that's what your nursing is, I don't want any."
"However, if I were to go out of this room for three minutes, wouldn't you go on as if I'd abandoned you for three days? Come on, answer."
"What I ask is to be nursed without all this talk, all this complaining about it. I don't feel grateful for being nursed when it's done with that sour look on your face, as if it's all

such a lot of bother to you."

"Nursing *is* a lot of bother. Essentially it always has been and always will be."

"I know that. I just want to be nursed without all this moaning."

"Do you really? Then we'd better got the whole family and dependents over here, collect a million, and hire ten physicians and a hundred nurses."

"I'm not asking for anything like that. I just want you to do it yourself."

"Which means that you are telling me to give an impersonation of ten physicians and a hundred nurses and a man with a million?"

"I didn't say anything at all like that. It's only that I want you to stay here with me all the time, and then I'd feel safe."

"Exactly. In that case, then, the odd twitch of the lip on my part or the occasional moan will not be beyond the limits of your endurance."

"If I should die it will be through hatred of you. I shall hate and hate and hate, and then I shall die."

"No doubt I shall be able to live with it."

She said nothing in reply. But he could feel how feverishly her mind went on turning over in silence, sharpening itself to inflict the wound it was so desperate to give.

Despite her condition's growing worse like this, he still had to think about his work and his living, but all the looking after her and the lack of sleep gradually wore him down. He knew that the more exhausted he became, the less he would be able to work. As he became incapable of working he would also become incapable of earning a living. And then obviously the expense of her illness would rise, and it would rise in proportion to his increasing inability to meet it. Yet this was the one thing that was certain: he was becoming more and more exhausted.

—What am I going to do?

—I'd like to get ill myself. Then I'd show her how to die without one complaint.

He sometimes felt like that. And yet again there was always the hope that somehow they might be able to pull through this crisis in their lives. Then there was the desire to prove himself to himself. At night, woken by his wife, he would massage her stomach where it hurt her, and would mutter to himself as a form of habit: "Let more misfortunes fall. Let more misfortunes fall."

As he was saying so, one lone ball seemed to be struck across an enormous felt table, and rolled and drifted before his eyes.

—That's my ball. But who's been knocking it about at random like that?

"Rub harder, can't you? Why can't you do things as if it all wasn't such a nuisance to you? You never used to be like this. You used to be gentler to me when you rubbed me there. And now you. . . . Oh, that hurts there, that hurts."

"I am so tired, growing more and more tired. I don't think I can take it much longer. Then we can both lie down together and not bother about anything any more."

She suddenly became quiet, and then spoke softly in a pitiful voice like that of an insect crying from somewhere beneath her bed: "I'm sorry I've been so foul to you, always thinking about myself. You're not to be upset. I don't mind dying now. Everything's all right. So you sleep now. I can put up with it all right now."

Hearing that, he wept despite himself, and his hand went on rubbing her stomach because he did not feel like letting it rest.

The wintry sea wind withered the grass on the lawn. All day the glass windows shook and rattled like the door of a horse-drawn cab. For a long time he had been unaware of the enormous sea waiting there at his door.

One day he went to the doctor's to pick up his wife's medicine.

"Oh, by the way. I have been meaning to tell you for some time. However . . . ," the doctor said. "There's no hope for your wife."

"Yes."

He was very clearly aware of his face going pale.

"There is no left lung, and the right one is too far gone."

Along the seashore, swayed in a carriage like a piece of luggage, he went home. The bright, glittering sea lay loosely before him, a monotonous curtain concealing death. He felt that he didn't want to see his wife after this. If he never saw her again, it would be possible to think of her always as still being alive.

When he got home he went straightaway to his own room. He thought about ways of managing things so that he wouldn't have to look at her face. After that he went into the garden and lay down on the grass. His body was heavy, dead tired. His tears came feebly; he picked up blades of grass with great care from the dead lawn.

—What is death?

He thought it must be just a matter of vanishing from sight. He got his confused mind under control and entered his wife's room.

She said nothing, only looked fixedly at his face.

"Would you like some winter flowers?"

"You've been crying, haven't you?"

"No."

"You have."

"I have nothing to cry about, have I?"

"I know what it is. The doctor said something."

Having made up her own mind about this, she looked silently up at the ceiling with no particular signs of sadness in her face. He lowered himself into the cane chair by her bedside and looked unwaveringly at her face, as if to memorize it all over again for the last time.

—After a while the door will close between us.

—But both she and I have given each other what there was to give. Now nothing remains.

From that day onward he acted in response to everything she said, like a machine. This was to be his final farewell gift to her.

One day, after a particularly bad bout of pain, she said: "Would you mind, the next time you're out, buying me some morphine?"

"What would that be for?"

"I shall drink it. People say you drink it and then you go to sleep like that and never wake up again."

"You mean you die?"

"That's it. I'm not afraid at all of death. How good it must be to be dead."

"So even you have become brave, and I never knew. But when you reach that point it doesn't matter when you die. Any time will do, so not to worry about it."

"Only I feel so bad about you, causing you nothing but pain. I am sorry, truly. Forgive me "

"Yes."

"I've always understood what was in your heart. And all those selfish things I said, it wasn't me who said them. It was the sickness."

"I know. The sickness."

"I've written it down, all I have to say. But I'm not going to show you now. It's under the bed, so look at it when I die."

He made no reply. All this demanded the bitterest sorrow. But now he did not wish to hear her speak of things that demanded bitterness or sorrow.

Next to the stones of the flower bed, dahlia bulbs, being killed by the frosts, lay where someone had dug them up. Instead of the tortoise, there was now a stray cat that had come from somewhere and that nonchalantly walked into his empty study. His wife hardly spoke at all now, keeping silent with the never-ending pain. Unceasingly she looked at the horizon, at the far-off glittering headland which thrust out onto the surface of the sea.

He sat by her side, sometimes reading the Bible as she demanded.

"Oh Lord, rebuke me not in thine anger, neither chasten
me in thy hot displeasure.
Have mercy upon me, O Lord, for I wither away: O
Lord, heal me; for my bones are vexed.
My soul is also sore vexed: but then, O Lord, how long?
For in death there is no remembrance of Thee."

He heard that she was sobbing. He stopped reading the Bible and looked at her.

"What were you thinking about then?"

"Where will my bones be laid? I can't help thinking about it."

—She had reached the point where she was concerned

about her remains. —He was unable to reply to her.

—There's no chance now.

He felt his heart sink as if his head were sinking too. She was weeping much more now.

"What's wrong?" he asked.

"There's no place to lay my bones. What am I going to do?"

Instead of replying, he hurriedly started reading the Bible again.

"Save me, O God, for the waters are come into my soul.
I sink in deep mire, where there is no standing: I am come into deep waters, where the floods overflow me.
I am weary of my crying: my throat is dried: mine eyes fail while I wait for my God."

So they waited together, two linked stems of a flower that is dying, every day in silence. But they had made total preparation for death. Whatever happened now could be no cause of fear. The pure water carried from the hill brimmed over in its water jug like the heart now finally at peace in his dark and quiet house.

Each morning while she still slept, he walked barefoot the shore that had newly raised its head from the sea. Seaweed cast ashore at high tide the previous night wrapped itself coldly about his feet. Sometimes children who wandered the beach as if driven by the wind would clamber up the pointed rocks, slithering on the brilliant green seaweed.

More and more white sails appeared on the surface of the sea. Each day the white road at the sea's border became more thronged with life. One day the unexpected arrived, a bunch of sweet peas—sent by someone he knew—which rounded the headland to reach them.

At their house, so long made desolate by the cold wind, this was the first scent of spring to reach them.

With his hands covered in pollen, he entered her room holding the flowers as an offering.

"Spring has finally come."

"They are so beautiful. Aren't they beautiful?" she said, smiling and stretching out her thin and wasted hands toward the flowers.

"Really beautiful, aren't they?" he said.

"Where did they come from?"

"They came riding here in a carriage, along the shore of the sea, scattering the first seeds of spring as they came."

She took the flowers and hugged them full to her breast. Then she buried her pallid face among the bright flowers, and closed her eyes entranced.

Ideas of a Flower Garden

I

The clear windows of the sun room glittered among the flowers on the top of the hill. The steps leading up to the balcony stuck out like a white backbone.

He was returning from the seashore up the road that led to the sanatorium. Sometimes he would leave his wife's bedside and go out walking, then to return and see her face anew. Each time the face had advanced closer to death's border, a maintained and definite pace, each time a stage nearer. Suddenly from the brick building farther up a group of nurses swarmed out.

"Goodbye."

"Goodbye."

A patient was leaving, and they followed him, running and glittering in the sun like a white mantle on the road. They circled the bed of roses in the front courtyard, forming a ring, a single flower.

"Goodbye."

"Goodbye."

New, white patients lay sunbathing on the sloping lawn like heaps of fruit. He threaded gently through their fantasies toward the corridor. From the windows of the rooms along the corridor a column of eyes shining with despair pursued him.

He opened the door of his wife's room. Her face was still, a heartbreaking serenity in it, like the air filled and confused with flower petals.

She was probably going to die.

He watched her from the side of the bed. He recalled the virgin beauty given to him on their marriage night, and the face of that time floated before him, a pale blue outline fitting perfectly on this present profile.

II

The period of unhappiness between them was over. He could no longer recall how many times he had heard doctors condemn her to death. Each time he had found a different doctor. He had fought with her death with all the power that he had. Yet no matter how much he fought, nor how many times he changed her doctor, each proclamation of death only had more of truth in it than the last. It had broken him down, exhausted him. Now he had given up, and simply sat unmoving in this huge, vacant warehouse of nothing. Now all they could do was look with desolate eyes at this aspect of death that was pulling them asunder. It was as if death had appeared between them, and at mealtimes he scooped the soup up with the spoon and fed it into her mouth without speaking. It was as if death lay sunken in her stomach and he was feeding it.

One day he asked her in a quiet voice: "You're not even a little afraid of dying?"

"No."

"And you don't feel even a little desire to live?"

"I want to die."

He nodded his head. He felt their thoughts were open to each other, two faces looking through glass.

III

Now she was some alien animal stretched out in the space between life and death. What had happened to the woman who had loved him so deeply that she should so suddenly have vanished away? And what of himself? He who had loved so well was now no more than a machine, worn out by emotion, unusable. The result of so much suffering was that they were no more man and wife, no longer human. The alienating space between their eyes was now just empty, transparent air, docile and flexible. In this space between them, before death appeared and closed her eyes, the sun would rise and shine, the sun would sink and darken. That alone was certain. The time between them would not be lengthened or shortened by love; all that would appear between them would be the changes in natural light, the obvious rays of the sun giving light or taking it away. This was nothingness, a quiet absence of being. His wife's face in repose there was simply a part of that still life it made with the medicine tray and the table at her side. He was beginning to see her as a pure object.

To fill up the space between them, to restore its former living emotion and give it beauty, he went and took white marguerites and poppies from the flower beds. In the midst of this nothing, the white marguerites gave the shadow of a smile to his wife's unmoving face. He set the pliant poppies in a vase, and as they moved redly in the breeze she looked at them and gave a small sigh of pleasure. The vase, the medicine tray, the walls, her profile, the flowers, were a still-life painting in the frame of the square room, from which silence one small sigh of pleasure came, one line joining all together. In order to listen to the beauty that was hidden in that voice, he gathered together all the flowers he could lay his hands on and set them in the room. The roses swayed each morning under the water he gave. Hydrangeas, bronze leaf, wild roses, peonies, chrysanthemums, and canna lilies flowered by the three walls. The room was like a marvellous flower shop. Each night when he lit the candle, he would gaze at her sleeping face and wonder if that night death might not come as a customer to this green florist's. One night she suddenly opened her eyes, and said: "When I die you'll be happy, won't you?"

He said nothing and looked at her. Then he returned to his own bed and mournfully blew out the candle.

IV

To soothe his own weariness he began to try to make himself see all objects that entered the space before his eyes as purely beautiful. This was the only form of being left to him now, all that could be created in the empty space from which his feelings had vanished.

He liked his bed. It was similar to his wife's but was set on the veranda, a place suited to the only slightly ill. The veranda looked over the flower garden. When he woke up during the night he found the moon more troublesome than his wife. It dangled endlessly above his nose; he could never escape from its brightness. The moonlit night was like a portion of the sea, in whose depths the flowers made continual white circles, like pale moths fluttering together. The moon looked down on the heads of the flowers, on the flock of woolly pliant folds, and passed away over and out to sea.

On these nights he would leave his veranda and walk among the flowers like some truant night gardener. In the pond amid the damp lawns a fountain played and scattered the moonlight over the surrounding stones and flowers. It had the expensive grace of a household pet raised in some quiet home. Far off the two headlands that held the bay were bent like dark arms enfolding the flower garden. The horizon was a thread of glistening hair that hovered above the garden and swelled toward the moon.

Then he would walk back toward the always unlit wards. Then he would imagine innumerable lungs like fungae, rotting and black, spilled out and confused among the flowers. These decaying lungs were the products of attics of back streets untouched by the sun, or heaps of filth, and they were gathered and minced in machines, or sliced over and over, and then brought up to this garden on the hill. The doctor who stopped up the holes in these rotting lungs on their road to wretched death, who gave them new life and sent them back to the world, had himself had lungs like those he saved, had had the sentence of death read over him. In the joy of his own recovery he had decided to devote the remainder of his second life to curing other injured lungs. He had created the special treatment the breathing lungs received in this flower garden.

V

In this flower garden the most valued things were fresh air and sunlight and love and wholesome food and rest. While it was not night or cloudy, the only object that cast a shadow was the roof. The food was a skilful blend of mountain and sea produce, whose brilliant colours changed with the seasons and stimulated the appetite. The air was borne out of the various blues of the clear sky and sea and mountains. The only sounds were those of a silence that hurt the ear, or a light minuet from the music room, or a patient's cough, or the sound of the elegant fountain falling on the flower petals. And love? That flowed in the pure white uniforms of the nurses, chosen from the best hospitals in town, like a light breeze in May.

Yet love is never to be trusted. If one spends one's days gazing here at the sky and the sea and the flowers, and if what approaches is the gentleness of a light breeze in May, then a gentle desire awakens like a physical law. But sexual love is a poison fruit in this flower garden. If such love flowers it will fade also like a flower, and fall, since love's function here is different from that of the town, being to give peace to the sick. If love should flower among them, the brightness of the surrounding sky and flowers would cloud over before that strangeness. Yet in all this beauty of sky and flowers only a stone would not feel desire if assailed by the gay rustlings of the beautiful girls. Thus the nurses, while taking a patient's pulse, needed not only dextrous fingers but also a control over their faces and eyes worthy of an accomplished actress. Despite all their control, however, the girls had unmistakably real breasts. When the light went out in the wards and it was time for them to sleep, they would remove their severe uniforms, take off their makeup, bend their sashes round their hips, and the elegant soft lines of young girls would show through their undress. Yet these young girls would not chatter among themselves, but all remain in the weariness of fatigue, heavy with sleep. It was as if love had ruined them, and they endured this suffering, avoiding human eyes. One would be on her knees praying, another would be writing a letter, another would be sunk in thought, another would dress herself up and stand unmoving in the unlit corridor. Presumably she had no other time in which she could wear what she wanted.

Once one of them was discovered at night secretly entering the sickroom of her lover. She was dismissed the next day. When she left she strode boldly down the corridor, surrounded by the other nurses who were seeing her off, with only a token expression of shame, a slight blush, on her face. That she should have ignored what convention required in this way was her rejection of a life of ill-treatment and poor food, her revenge upon the suffering imposed on her by the hospital and its patients, and the pleasure of this showed in the deliberate poise of her shoulders.

VI

As the rainy season approached, the inhabitants of this garden had something to think about other than the internal affairs of the hospital. The village at the foot of the hill faced on a large fishing ground which supported the whole life of the village. Now that the fishing village had been capped with a sanatorium, it was inevitable that the market for its fish could not increase but only become smaller. Should one restrain the lively heart of the village, or should one simply ignore the needs of the dying lungs on the hill. The village, now beaten by these rival tides, divided into two factions. This had been bound to happen, since although permission for the sanatorium had been given, this did not mean that any of the hearts beating below had lost their sense of horror at what was above.

The heart which feared the rotting lungs began to torment the flower garden. Those points nearest to the garden were chosen as dumping grounds for rotting fish, mountains of manure made of that fish which could not be sold because of the rotting lungs. Flies swarmed, then flew among the flower beds and wards. In a hospital ward a fly is as great an object of fear as a pistol. The spaces that were windows were covered over with wire screens. Hammers disturbed the patients' rest for three days. One day of upset will cancel out half a month of convalescence. The temperature charts ran wild.

The war between the heart and the lungs continued. The heart learned of the defensive action of the wire screens, so fires of straw were lit to windward and smoke driven in at the lungs. Smoke obeys the wind rather than any concept of right and wrong. The flowers were covered all day by dense clouds. The smoke drove the flies energetically from the flower beds, but with ten times that power and effect it attacked the rotting lungs. The patients began to cough. One cough deprived them of one day of convalescence. The wards were closed in with glass doors. A stench of gas accumulated in the rooms. The temperature charts started to run wild again. The patients' appetites went down. People just sat and looked at the sky through the glass doors.

Thus his wife before her death was cared for by the people of the flower garden above, and made to suffer by those of the fishing ground below. Yet in the fight to keep hold of its superior position, the flower garden had simply to endure in silence. Every day his wife's cough got worse.

VII

One of those days he was quietly summoned to the room of the assistant director.

"I'm sorry about this, but it looks as if your wife. . . ."

"I see."

"Sometime toward the end of the month, I should think. . . ."

"Yes."

"We've done all we can. If there's anything. . . ."

"I should like to thank you for all you've done."

"That's nothing, I'm afraid. . . . Oh, by the way, if you are going to call in relatives, we'd be obliged if they didn't all come in one great rush."

"I'll see they don't."

"You must be pretty well worn-out yourself."

"I'm all right."

He was aware that he was standing alone in the corridor outside. All the forgotten misery struck in at him again, like a sudden violent odour.

He walked toward her room.

But perhaps it wasn't true. He stopped. He could hear the sound of a cello playing a lively gavotte coming from the music room.

Yet supposing reality was dragging his wife toward death, did that reality always have to be real?

No, it did not.

Suppose all one's sense impressions were false ones, and thus all the phenomena we apprehended were untrue?

Why do we have to experience misfortune as misfortune? Why can't we experience a funeral as if it were a wedding?

He had had too much of suffering, of bad luck. He had had too much of misery. So much so that all that suffering and misery had come to seen untrue. He could see it only as a false reality.

"She will become well quite soon."

"We will become happy quite soon."

He would use the power of his will in a new way. He decided that now. His will would be directed toward experiencing all the darkness of the heart as a form of light and joy. The long nothingness he had known was blown away like a momentary dream.

He breathed in the air deeply and walked back to her room. He sat at the bedside and said: "I suppose you're thinking about dying?"

She looked at him and nodded.

"But people don't die. Dying, death, there's no such thing, is there?"

Of course he had no idea what he was talking about. His wife said nothing but looked at him indifferently.

"You must understand this better than I do. Death is nothing, meaningless: ridiculous, in fact."

"I just don't want to go on in pain like this."

"Quite right. Pain is stupid too. You know there's no need to worry about me, just because I go on living. There's no need."

"I know. And I'm glad I'm going to die first, before you."

He smiled.

"You've worked that out nicely."

"You're the one I'm sorry for."

"Quite right too. A damn fool I look. I don't want to go on messing about in a place like this. You've done all right for yourself."

She smiled at him a little.

"I wouldn't mind living, if it didn't hurt quite so much."

"Don't be silly. What on earth for? I mean, what would you do? We've done all we had to do, the two of us. Think about it and you'll see."

"I suppose that's so."

"It is so. You can die easy. You've no regrets."

She looked up at his face but didn't answer, as if she were searching for whatever had caused him to change like this.

"You look as if you need cheering up. Shall I send for your mother?"

"Don't bother. As long as you're here I don't need anybody else."

He immediately wrote to her mother telling her to come.

VIII

On the next day his wife's face suddenly took on a soft, peachlike bloom. She looked out at the lilies on the mountain slope that filled her window. He set fresh flowers round the walls of her room. He said it was in place of her mother. Cyclamen and lilies. Heliotrope and bronze leaf. Roses, marguerites, and poppies.

"I wonder why your face has become so beautiful again. You look like a sixteen-year-old girl. You hardly touch a spoonful of soup, and yet you look as if you'd knocked back god knows how much meat. I can't figure you out. You must do it when I'm not looking."

"Please get rid of those lilies. They kill the smell of the other flowers."

"It is very strong."

He picked up the lilies and took them outside. He meant to throw them away, but the scent was so living and the colours so vivid that he could think of nowhere appropriate to put them. He wandered about the corridors, the lilies dangling from his hand like a kitten, until he came to the empty nurses' room. He looked in. It was hemmed in by its walls like a coffin, and scattered here and there in the fetid atmosphere were cast-off sashes and tufts of false hair. They would return soon and lay their weary bodies down here, and as if he were bestowing pure dreams of the natural world upon them, he set down the lilies like a sachet of sweet perfumes, and went away.

IX

One day someone kept on burning straw up on the hill. When he had time, he left the sickroom and made his way toward the fields from which the smoke was coming. From amid the grass a young man looked up at him, a sickle in his hand.

"How long are you going to keep that fire burning?" he asked.

"There's just that bit left," the young man said, pointing to the burning straw with his sickle.

"Do you have to burn it?"

The young man said nothing and cut another swath of grass.

"My wife's dying because of your smoke. If you don't have to burn it, then stop."

He didn't wait for an answer but went down from the hill toward the fishing ground. On that level space was a forest of bare, bronze, powerful thighs. They were drawing the fish from the nets, and then they would dash back with the nets into the sea, scattering foam above their heads. The children on the shore picked up trembling jellyfish and hurled them at one another. Barrels and thighs, then tunny, sea bream, and bonito, glittering with the colour of the sea, poured out of the boats. Suddenly the fishery was brilliant as if in the light of an unnatural dawn. The hairy thighs twisted and turned here and there among the waves of fish. Bestridden by those powerful thighs, the bream resigned themselves like rose-coloured girls; the tunny were quietly lined up, like shells stored up in readiness. Sometimes the erect forest of thighs would waver and the evening sun pierce through, scattering phosphorescence on the billowing crests of the fish like the slash of a knife.

From among the fish he looked up at the hill. The flower beds on the hill rose up magically among the waves of fish. Roses, tunny, peonies, bream, marguerites; and above those successive layers the always many-angled face of the sun room glittering in the evening, flashing off rays of light like eyes.

"The sanatorium is a çastle besieged by these waves after waves of fish. And the first to die in that siege will be my wife."

The fish were really an innumerable and intrepid host who hastened her death amid their smoke. They were also healing physicians who shortened the period of her suffering. Then the dull ranks of the tunny lined up like shells took on a different, disturbing meaning; became a black, black silence, and only that.

X

From that day onward he was no longer certain whether the cause of his wife's sufferings was the real cause, the fish in their fishing ground, or the flowers in their flower garden. While she remained in this flower garden, it would seem to be not so much the smoke that blew up from down there that gave suffering to her days, but the very length of days themselves.

That evening when the doctor came she looked at her legs and asked: "Doctor, why have my legs swollen up like that?"

"You don't want to worry about that. That's nothing, nothing at all."

The fluid has come round to her legs.

That's the end, then.

After the doctor had gone he switched off the light and lit the candle.

What shall we talk about?

He watched his wife's shadow, thinly cast by the candle, trembling above the heliotropes. Then he remembered when he had first met her and she had smiled at him with a light smile that seemed only for him. The tears began to flow. He bent gently over her and kissed her face amid the scent of the flowers.

"Do you remember how you used to come to see me silently at night, in that filthy upstairs room, and me always sitting in a heap of torn-up paper?"

She nodded in silence.

"That was the best time of my life. You would come up those stairs with your lovely braided hair into that dark hole I lived in. It was like . . . as if somehow a whole load of flowers had popped up into the place. Then all the depression and misery would go and we would romp around like children. It didn't matter, the poverty. I was happy then. We've been through a lot since then. Still, it's all right. We've both of us always wanted to have our own way. But I never did anything really bad to you, and you've got nothing to say sorry to me about. We've been lucky, and we should be thankful for each other. This is funny, I suppose, but at least it's thanks to your illness that I'm just about qualified to be a nurse, and I've stopped knowing what misfortune is or isn't, and that's a piece of luck you don't come across every day. You'd better go to sleep now. When you're a little better I'll take you on my back and carry you outside among the flowers."

"All right."

He was in danger of weeping again, so he stepped down among the flowers, his eyes brimming with tears. He buried his face in the crowds of night flowers. Then the tears poured over. As he wept he passed his face from one cold flower to another, drinking in their perfume like an insect. As he smelled the perfume he began to start praying violently.

"Please, God, save her. Please, God, save her."

He picked up a handful of primroses and wiped his face with them. The sea was pale and secret before the rise of the moon. A night crow drew an uncanny curve in the air, then flew over the flower beds like a sharp shadow. Like grief itself he walked countless times around the quiet fountain, until his own heart quieted too.

XI

Early the next morning his wife's mother arrived. She looked at her daughter's face and burst out crying.

"What's happened to you, love, you're so thin. I wanted to come earlier but I've had so many things to do."

His wife had the same indifferent expression as always, and gazed at the fuss that the other was making.

"Does it hurt you? Your mother has never stopped thinking about you all this time. I've wanted to come so much, ages ago, but then everyone in our house is sick, aren't they?"

He no longer felt like filling out the details of what he had written in the letter about his wife's illness. He left her with her mother and went to the sun room. The morning patients were all lined up, reclining in long wicker chairs. The sea was graceful and clear in the arms of its two headlands. Two nurses appeared laughing together, and received the sun full on their faces as they stepped down among the glittering beds of flowers. They bent down in their white uniforms among the red poppies. Then a red smile appeared and rippled among the flowers. They were laughing.

A young girl patient reclining there smiled also.

"It must be wonderful to be happy like that."

An emaciated lady by her side replied: "It must be, mustn't it? Still, you'll soon be able to walk about like them, my dear."

"I wish I could be sure of that. I don't. . . ."

"But of course you will. The doctor said so only yesterday."

"How lovely it would be to walk on those lawns in the mist."

"Of course it would. And you will. You'll be able to laugh again quite soon."

The nurses appeared again from among the flowers, each with a flowering branch in her hand. They walked between the purple bed of bronze leaf and the bed of roses laughing cheerfully, entangled in morning sunlight. Above the bed of peonies toward which they walked the fountain threw up a steady morning rainbow.

XII

The number of injections made in his wife's arm increased every day. All she now had for nourishment was water.

One day at dusk he climbed up to the balcony to look down on the deepening twilit sea below. He was thinking. "All I am doing is waiting on her death. What do I expect to get out of moments like these?"

He knew nothing. All he felt was that the unmoving balcony on which he was riding was perpetually voyaging above time.

He watched the pace of the sun's half-circle as it sank beneath the sea's horizon.

"That is the pace at which her life is worn away."

One could see the process. The sun swayed and trembled, then was swallowed by the horizon. The surface of the sea was a chopping board over which the blood ran. The sun stifled a cry, and sank. On the sea's surface, boats lay unmoving like fallen birds.

Then in the air he felt a sense of omen like a dark sound. He descended hastily from the balcony. His wife's mother was hurrying along the other side of the corridor. They passed each other without a word. Then the mother called after him to stop.

He turned round and looked at her.

"She may go tonight, mightn't she?"

"She might."

They both stood for a while in silence in the middle of that long, tubelike corridor. Then the walked off toward his wife's room. The duty nurse approached and stopped him.

"I suppose I'll probably be needed tonight?"

He nodded.

He opened the door and went and sat at her bedside. Her eyes were wide open, and stared at him like deep pools of water.

"You'll soon start to get better," he said.

There was no answering response in her face.

"You look tired. Why don't you try to get some sleep?"

"I called you a little while ago," she said.

"Then it was you just now. I was on the balcony and I felt something strange inside me."

"Would you lift me up a bit. I feel I'm falling down, right down into a pit or something."

He raised her up with both hands.

"I haven't put my arms around you for a long time. Is that all right now?"

He had raised up the pillows and laid her gently against them.

"You don't weigh much, do you? It's like holding a bunch of flowers."

A little happy smile trembled on her face.

"You put your arms around me. Now I feel safe."

"I feel safe too. But you must sleep. You haven't slept at all since last evening, have you?"

"I just don't feel like sleeping. When it's not hurting too much, all I've wanted to do all day is talk."

"That's no good for you. It's better not to talk. I'll stay here, so at least try to close your eyes and get a little rest."

"All right. I'll try to sleep. But you stay here, please."

"I will."

She closed her eyes, and he switched off the light and opened the window. The swaying sound of the trees was like the sea. An elderly nurse walked lonely in the dark, moonless garden. His wife's mother stood on the veranda with her face resting against the glass, gazing out into the garden. All hope was now totally gone. Motionless shadows were cast on the curtains of the distant wards. The tops of the flowers stirred, like pale hands searching for something in the dark.

XIII

That night, at high tide, the agony started. The doctor came. Camphor, salt, and Ringer's solution, one after the other, kept the small spark of life in her body. But there was no going back to what she had been yesterday. Finally, as a last surge of activity, the oxygen equipment began to foam and bubble by the side of her head.

He put the mouth of the inhaler over her mouth, covering it. The mother was breathing in unison with the tortured breath of her daughter, her face contorted, determined not to let her go.

He took the inhaler away from her mouth. She was struggling for breath.

It can't be long now, he thought.

If the inhaler could stop the suffering, he would sit through eternity holding it to her mouth. Yet it was clear that the machine's only function was to prolong her torment. He began to feel that the people from the fishery below had been kinder to her in shortening her going, than the doctors with their medicine had been in trying to hold her back. The doctor believed in his medicine; he was talking about trying another injection.

"No, I don't want it." His wife cut the doctor short even before he did.

"All right, then. Calm down. We'll stop the injections."

"It's no good anymore, you see."

"Come on. You're going to be all right."

"Oh, it hurts."

"It'll be all right soon. Don't worry."

"Oh why, why won't you let me die!"

"You mustn't say things like that."

"It hurts so much. Do you want to hurt me more?"

He began to resent the way she wanted to die.

"Just hold out a bit longer. The pain will go away soon."

"Where are you? I can't see your face anymore."

His eyes were blinded by the storm. She was staring about the room, thrusting her hand out toward him. He concentrated all his love into his hands and set them on that one arm.

"Don't give up. I'm here."

"Yes," she answered. She grasped his hands with all the strength remaining to her.

"You know, I am going already," she said.

"Can't you wait a little for me?"

"It hurts so much. I shall die before you. I am sorry. Forgive me."

Instead of replying, he burst into loud sobs.

"I have caused you . . . such trouble . . . for so long. Forgive me . . . for that too."

"You've been so good to me. So much. So good."

She raised her head and nodded firmly.

"I have been so happy . . . nobody more than me. Now you'll be alone . . . all by yourself. When I die . . . nobody . . . to look after you."

Her mother started weeping loudly beside the withered marguerites.

"I'm sorry . . . about everything . . . mother. Forgive. . . . Remember me to my . . . brother . . . and everybody. . . ."

"You don't have to say that. They'll all be here soon."

"Must I wait for them? . . . It hurts so much."

"They're just coming. I telephoned. They're just coming."

"I'm sorry. . . . Excuse. . . . Want to die. . . . Hurts . . . so much. . . ."

"Don't worry about them. There's nothing to worry about anymore," he said.

She nodded and gazed all round the room with wide eyes. A crow took up the sounds of the husband and mother and cried above the flower garden. His wife gave a smile of loving recognition and murmured: "Clever crow, to be so quick. He has cried already."

He bowed his head before the greatness of her prepared spirit. He wept no longer.

After a while she said, "Goodbye."

"Yes. Goodbye," he replied.

Her mother called her name.

But there was no reply. Her breathing had changed into great, violent spurts of breath. As her head gradually declined, the grasp upon his hands stiffened like wood, then grew slack. Then death came suddenly over her face like a vivid dawn.

That is it.

He remained awhile absorbed in the beauty of this death before him, then stood up entranced, and drifted, a scrap of blown paper, down into the garden.

The Machine

At first I sometimes used to think that the boss must be a maniac or something. One observed that he would get annoyed with his child, who was hardly yet two years old, because he claimed that the child didn't like him, and what right did a child have not to like its father? Then the child would be toddling about and fall over slap on its face and he would suddenly start thumping his wife saying that she was supposed to be looking after the child and what did she think she was up to letting it fall over like that? It was a right comedy to look at, but the man was so dead in earnest that you started to wonder, on the contrary, whether he wasn't out of his mind, or what. There he was, a man of forty, and when the child stopped crying a bit he would have it up in his arms and caper about the room with it. If you thought he was like that just about the child, you'd have been wrong, since he showed the same kind of innocent simple-mindedness about almost everything, and so it was only natural that his wife should have been actually running things. Since the wife thus became the centre of what went on in the place, it was also not very surprising that the people who were in with her were the ones who were doing all right for themselves. In my case, and I suppose you'd have to say I was connected with the boss's lot if anything, the result was that I found myself getting landed with all the really rotten jobs in the place, the ones nobody else wanted to do. These rotten jobs, these really lousy jobs, since they were a part of the life of the workshop that had to be done by someone or else the whole place would come to a halt, and since that someone was me, meant that it was me and not the boss's wife who was the central figure in the set-up, although since the whole lot there thought that only someone who couldn't do anything else did the lousy jobs, then all I could do was shut up and get on with it. It's weird when you think about it that someone who couldn't do anything else at all should be doing things that nobody else could do, and since that was so and since this workshop made name-plates, which involved the use of various chemicals, my jobs were always those that were just about drowned in particular lethal ones, as if some niche had been craftily prepared for disposing of someone who couldn't be made use of in any other way. Once I'd been dropped into this particular hole, I found not only that my clothes and indeed my skin were ceasing to be of any real use to me through the effects of handling iron chlorides that were used in the corrosion of metals, and that the effects of bromine stimulation had been such that I could no longer get any sleep at night, but also that the very structure of my brain was altering in some way and my power of vision was beginning to fail. It wasn't at all likely that any serviceable person should have been dropped into so perilous a niche, and since the boss had learned the same jobs that people could not do when he was young, no doubt he must have been the same sort of useless and unemployable person as myself. However, I certainly was not going to hang about here like a fool forever in order to become a wreck. The fact is I'd just left a shipyard in Kyushu and I happened to meet a lady on the train up here and that's how all this started. The lady was somewhat over fifty and her husband had died and the house went with him, and since she didn't have any children she'd decided to impose herself upon some relations in Tokyo for a bit and then start a boardinghouse or something like that. I said as a sort of joke that in that case I wouldn't mind imposing myself upon her in her boardinghouse when I got myself some work, upon which she suggested why didn't I go with her to these relatives of hers and give a hand with the work there? I didn't have any work to go to as yet, and I felt I could trust her because of the nice way she spoke and dressed, and so I simply traipsed along after her to this place and drifted into this work. Well, it looked a cushy job at first sight, but I gradually realized that the chemicals were basically depriving me of my powers of labour. So while I kept thinking to myself that I'd leave today and I'd leave tomorrow, I found myself feeling that since I'd put up with it this far I might as well stay until I'd got the real hang of what the job meant, and so I decided to try to work up enough enthusiasm to volunteer for the most dangerous bits of work. However, the man working alongside me, one Karube, came to the conclusion that I was some spy who'd got into the place in order to steal trade secrets. He came from the house next door to the boss's wife's family and so he could pretty well do what he liked, and yet he had this big thing about the boss and the business coming first, as if his main pleasure in life came from giving this fine portrayal of the faithful old family retainer. I only had to take a bottle of poisons down from the shelf and there he would be, staring pointedly at me. I'd be hanging about in front of the darkroom when he'd start clattering about somewhere to let me know that I'd better look out because he was watching me from over there. I found the whole business ridiculous, and yet since he was serious enough about it, it all began to give me the creeps somewhat. For him the cinema was the supreme source of edification about life, and in particular he seemed to consider detective thrillers as exact replicas of reality, and undoubtedly someone like me who'd just wandered in like that would be very solid, indeed inevitable, material for his detecting concerns. Particularly as Karube wasn't thinking of spending all his life in this one shop. He'd get himself set up in a branch, which would mean setting up a nameplate workshop of his own, and obviously he'd no intention whatsoever of letting me get hold of that secret method of making red nameplates, a process worked out by the boss, before he'd got his hands on it. I myself simply wanted to learn the work as such and had no plans for making any living out of it, although there wouldn't have been much point in explaining that to Karube, since it would have been beyond his powers of understanding, and of course once I'd learned the work there was always the faint possibility that I might somehow start making some kind of livelihood out of it, and anyway, however all that might be, it struck me that it would be a good thing to put old Karube's back up a bit as a slight taste of liberal education for him, whatever he might be thinking about me, and in this way I stopped paying proper attention to him to discover that his feelings of animosity toward me had grown at a very remarkable rate, which made me first feel what a damn fool he must be, and then take to thinking that being such a fool, and because he was such a fool, perhaps he wouldn't so easily be made a fool of after all. When someone decides you're their enemy when in fact you're not, you can have yourself a good time laughing at them while it's all going on, and you don't realize that it's this that leaves you wide open to the other person; so when I quite casually tried moving a chair or working the margin cutter and a hammer fell down bang from above my head, or when a whole stack of brass sheeting crashed down just where I was walking, or when a bowl of a harmless mixture of varnish and ether had suddenly changed into one of a dangerous solution of dichromic acid, at first I thought it was some slip on my own part, and then when it struck me that it was all Karube's doing, it made my blood run cold as I thought about it and realized that if I was not very careful it could be a question of my life. Particularly because, although Karube was a fool all right, he had still been working there longer than I had and was well up in the preparation of strong poisons, and he knew that with a spot of ammonium dichromate in someone's tea, and if that someone drank it and died, it could well look like suicide. When I had my meals for some time after and saw something yellowish, it would come to me that it might well be a bit of dichromic acid, and my chopsticks would stop moving in that direction; but after a while all this vigilance on my part began to seem just comic, and if I was so easily to be killed off then let's just try it out, and so again quite naturally thoughts of Karube went out of my head.

One day I was working in the shop when in came the boss's wife and said that her husband was going off to buy some base metal and would I go with him and keep hold of the money all the time. The fact is that when he kept the money himself he almost invariably dropped it somewhere on the way, and so the thing that she was most concerned about was not letting him have any. The truth is that most of the misfortunes of the house came from this one particular piece of stupidity, although no one could work out why the boss was always losing money in this way. There's no way of getting lost money back no matter how much you blame and swear about it, although when it's money everyone's sweated their guts out to make and it simply evaporates because someone's been idle, you don't much feel like simply creeping into bed and choking back your silent tears; and also it wasn't only once or twice but all the time, if he had the money he dropped it, that was a fact they said, and so in this shop there had grown up quite naturally a very different way of running things, a different kind of work discipline. Obviously we couldn't even start to conceive how on earth a forty-year-old man could go about losing money as soon as he got hold of any. For example, his wife would tie his wallet on a bit of string around his neck and then slip it inside his breast pocket, and yet even in such a case the money within it would have smartly disappeared, which would imply that he must have dropped it when he was either taking the money out or putting it in, although given the fact that he'd lost the money before you would have thought that he'd now be watching himself as he did it, be a bit careful. There was a time when I convinced myself he must be being careful and that he wasn't losing the money at all and that it was all a cunning ploy on the part of his wife to put off paying money out to people, but the fact is that the boss was so odd that after a while, because his behaviour was so weird, I found myself all of a sudden having to believe that what she put out as the truth was in fact so. It's said to be one of the marks of the wealthy that they don't think of money as money, and yet our impecunious boss, despite the fact that he could only just about scrape enough coins together to take a bath, would still blandly give away to somebody who was short himself the money needed for buying the base metal for his own shop. In the past I suppose he would have been some kind of holy man, some wild hermit in a cave. However, people who live with a holy man find themselves in a continual state of suspense. It wasn't just that he couldn't be trusted to do anything, but what one person ought to have been able to go out and do now required two people, and just how much wasted effort his presence caused in the people around him I do not know; yet although all that was so, the fact of his being there was what determined the extent to which our shop attracted customers. It seems fairly certain that the reason why no one had a really bad word to say against our place was because of the boss, since although people criticized the way he was tied to his wife's apron strings, the fact that so decent a person as he was should be there like a kid, as it were, peeping out from behind her apron was naturally so comic that everyone felt pleased with him, and whenever he got a respite from her overseeing eye he'd be off like an escaped rabbit, scattering money in all directions like someone back from somewhere, and that sort of thing only increased his popularity that much more.

Thinking about it in these terms, I became obliged to consider that the central figure in the set-up was not his wife, or myself, or Karube, but the boss himself, which is the old employee's loyalty coming to the surface in my case no doubt, but then I liked him, everything about him, so there you are. You could get an idea of what my boss was like by imagining a kid of five years old who'd arrived at the age of forty without changing at all. Even though we found the idea of a man like that utterly absurd and wanted to look down on him because of it, when you looked at him you couldn't despise him and instead he made you think about yourself; he made the ugliness of your own grownupness, that coming of age which had sometime happened, almost painfully clear. This sort of response wasn't limited just to me; indeed, I could see that the same sort of process was going on inside Karube, and it struck me afterwards that Karube's antipathy toward me did in fact come from a virtuous impulse on his part to protect the boss. What made me feel that I couldn't leave the place was this supreme virtue of his, and it was no doubt this same virtue that caused Karube to drop hammers onto my head, which only goes to show how virtue can move in very mysterious ways.

Anyway, I went off with the boss to buy the base metal, and while we were out he told me that something had come up that day, which was that he should sell his process for making red nameplates for fifty thousand, and did I think that it was a good idea or not? A question to which I couldn't reply, so he went on that if the red plating process was never going to be worked out by anyone else, that would be that, but the fact was all the other people in the trade were working on it like mad, and if he was going to sell out, now was the time to do it. I could see what he meant but I didn't feel I had any right to make suggestions about what was the fruit of how many years of heartbreaking research on his part; and then I thought that that was all very well, but the truth was if I just left it to him no doubt at some point he would do what his wife told him to do, and since she was someone who couldn't see any further than her nose, I thought I must do something about it for him, and then very oddly that became the one thing that started to obsess me. When I was in the shop everything in there, everything going on there, started to look as if it were waiting until I got it sorted out, and even Karube began to seem to me like a sidekick I should order about, which was all right perhaps, but in spare moments I noticed that even his voice, that damn hectoring voice which he must have copied from the narrator at the silent movies, was starting to get on my nerves. Then I began to notice, on the contrary, that he had become again most horribly sensitive to what I was doing, so much so that while I was in the workshop his eyes almost never left me. The boss's wife must have told Karube about the kind of work that had been going on recently and also about the question of selling the patent for the red plating process, although I couldn't work out if the wife herself had told Karube to keep a watch on me or not. However, when I considered that I myself was now thinking that might not the boss's wife and Karube be secretly plotting together to steal the boss's secret and sell it and maybe oughtn't I to do a bit of watching, then I could hardly laugh off the idea that the wife and Karube might be having exactly the same suspicions about me. Well, when I observed myself as being the object of their suspicious glances, it's true it wasn't a very nice feeling, but even so I was a bit disturbed to find that this was all somehow very amusing to me, particularly if I boldly reversed the situation and went on supervising what they were up to. It was when things had reached this very point that the boss told me about the new researches he was engaged in: for a long time he'd been working on ways of getting the black out of the base metal without using the iron-chloride corrosive process, but things weren't going the way he'd thought they would, and he asked me if I would mind giving a hand whenever I had a spare moment. I had my doubts about whether he ought to let slip something important like that, no matter how nice a person he might be, but still I had to be grateful, and I was, that he should have trusted some a bsolutely like that. Of course, if you think about it, it's the person who's trusted who finally loses out and that's no doubt why the boss was always one up on everybody about him all the time, but since his infinite stupidity was not something that one could acquire, that was where his real greatness lay, and so I told him that I would do everything in my power to assist him, and thanked him from the bottom of my heart; upon which I felt that I'd like at least once to be able to make someone thank me from the bottom of their heart. Still, the boss didn't think in that petty way about who made whom do what, which only made me bow my head that much lower before him. Struck through by some vital force that came out from him, I felt like a disciple transfixed by a magical phrase from the Master. Miracles are not imposed upon us from outside; they are produced by our own poverty and ugliness of spirit. And so from then on I started to become like Karube, always putting the boss first, and I started to take exception to everything his wife did since she controlled everything that he did, not only questioning just how much a wife like that should be allowed to monopolize so splendid a husband, but also even considering from time to time ways of getting rid of her for him, and I felt I now had really grasped what it was that gave Karube such a down on me, and I knew that when I looked at him I was automatically also seeing myself, and the whole thing became more and more a source of fascination for me.

One day the boss called me into the darkroom; when I went in he had some aniline-coated brass over an alcohol burner and he explained that when changing the colour of a plate it was above all the changes under heat that you had to be most attentive about and that this bit of metal was purplish at the moment but it would turn blackish brown and eventually black, which meant that already it would have reached a state whereby in the next stage of the experiment it would be broken down by iron chloride and rendered useless; all of which meant, he informed me, that the knack in colouring was in the intermediary stage of the change from one colour to the next, and he wanted me to make as many tests with the burner of as many chemicals as I could. I found the organic relationships that existed between elementary substances and their compounds of growing fascination, and as this interest deepened I learned to understand what I had not been aware of before, that in inorganic substances there existed sensitive organic behaviour patterns whose logic I could grasp, and that in the minutest things there existed a mechanism, a machine like law, which could be broken down into its moduli and then grasped as a whole entity; all of which, when I understood it, became the first step in my awakening from my idealistic slumber. However, when Karube was aware that I had gained free access into the darkroom, into which up to now no one had been allowed, even the colour of his face changed when he looked at me. All that time spent putting the boss first, and now here was a newcomer like me permitted something that was not permitted to him; of course Karube would be thinking that all his vigilance over me had come to nothing, and also that if he didn't watch out, his own position within the place might come within my jurisdiction to dispose of as I pleased. Given this, I realized that I ought to be a bit more circumspect toward him, but after all who was Karube that I should have to keep on looking to see if Karube was upset about this or angry about that, and so I kept on treating him as I always had, since no matter what he might do it would only make life a bit more interesting, and I didn't have any sort of fellow feeling for him anyway, so I kept on as I always had, treating him with a complete and cool disdain. Well, I could see that made him pretty annoyed, and then one day I was thinking of using the punch for making holes that Karube had been using, when I couldn't find it, and I said weren't you using it up to just a moment ago? To which Karube replied that whether he'd been using it or not, it wasn't here now and since it wasn't hadn't I better set about looking for it myself until I did find it? He's right you know, I thought, so I started looking for the punch but I just couldn't find it anywhere, when where should it be but right there in Karube's pocket; so I didn't say anything but just slipped it out, when who the hell do you think you are taking things out of people's pockets, he said. People's pockets are people's pockets, I said, but in this workshop all pockets are the same; whereupon he said, it's people like you who think like that who've got the damn nerve to go around stealing the boss's work. When did I steal the boss's work, and if helping the boss means stealing his work, haven't you been stealing his work as well? I said, and that shut him up a bit but then his lips started trembling and he began ordering me to get out of the shop. All right, I'll get out, I said, but I don't want to let the boss down and I will if I don't stay until the present researches have got a bit more forward, and so he said, right, then I'll leave. I tried to explain to him that leaving now would only put the boss in a fix and if he was going to leave he should wait till I did, but even so he kept on and on about leaving. All right then, I said, since that's the way you feel, you'd better go and I'll do the work of both of us after you've gone, at which he ups and grabs the calcium powder by his side and heaves it into my face. I admit it was me who was in the wrong, and I knew it at the time all right, but the fact is that doing the wrong thing can be very interesting. The more he got worked up, the more clearly I could see the honest and righteous indignation that kept him trembling in front of me, and the cooler I became savouring it all. I knew this was no way to go on so I started thinking of ways of quieting him down a bit, but the fact is that from the start I'd never been able to take Karube seriously, which was wrong of me I'm bound to admit, and that being the case, to start now trembling with him and before him as he got angrier and angrier, well it would have taken a pretty special sort of person to have managed that, and I couldn't. It's always a worthless sort of person who puts himself out in order to get somebody else worked up, and as Karube got angrier and angrier I got the feeling that I was measuring my own worthlessness, until finally I didn't know what to do with myself or my own feelings, and what I could do about Karube I had no idea. I'd never before had such a strong feeling of not being able to manage myself. It was like my mind only existed to fill the space of my body, as if people were right in claiming that the mind and the body do fit absolutely and perfectly into each other. After a bit I went off as I was into the darkroom and I started heating some potassium chromate in a test tube in order to precipitate some bismuth for dye that was already in preparation there, which as far as Karube was concerned was again something I ought not to have done. It was my being able to go into the darkroom that had already caused Karube to have it in for me, and now having just made him go off his nut like that, this returning immediately to the darkroom was merely adding insult to injury, so it wasn't surprising that he should have got all excited. He opened the door, got hold of me by the scruff of the neck, dragged me out, and threw me onto the floor. I let myself be thrown; indeed I felt as if I were almost throwing myself down, since the only way of getting any response out of someone like me is by the use of violence. While I had a look to see whether the potassium chromate in the test tube I'd been using had been spilled or not, for some reason or other he had an excited scamper around the place and then came back to where I was, and since his little scamper hadn't turned up any results for him he just stood there and glared at me. However, I realized that if I so much as moved a muscle he'd most likely put the boot in for lack of knowing what else to do, so I just lay there as I was, and although I did start to wonder myself what I was up to and how long I was going to remain in this strained position, finally I just felt sort of vague and half-witted, deciding that I ought to let him have a good old rage and swear, let him do just as he wanted and get it all out of his system, which then made me feel calm and indifferent, fed up with the whole lot, so I started considering just what effects this Karube fellow's raging had had on the situation and discovered that my face had taken most of the damage, being all scrabbly with calcium from my lips right into my ears. Still, I wasn't yet sure when it would be safe for me to get up. There was a large pile of gleaming aluminium sections, which had fallen from the margin cutter, heaped up just in front of my nose, and I looked at them and felt really surprised that I'd been able to get through all that much work in three days. So I said to Karube, shouldn't we stop this stupid quarrelling and get on with the business of coating the aluminium, but it seemed he had no wish to do any work like that. What about polishing your face up a bit instead? he said, and took hold of my head just as I was laying down like that and thrust it right into the pile of aluminium fragments and shook it about as if giving me a good wash; and so I got a picture in my mind of my head being polished in a great heap of all the little doorplates with numbers on them of the houses in the streets, and thought to myself that of all the terrifying things in the world the most terrifying is violence. It wasn't just that as my head was swayed about each time the corners of the bits of aluminium jabbed into and scratched at and pierced the lines and contours of my face. The fact was that the lacquer, which had only just about dried, was sticking onto my face and wouldn't come off, and of course it would all start to swell up. Well, having taken that much from Karube without a word, it seemed to me I'd just about done what duty demanded of me by him, so I got up and made as if to go back into the darkroom. Upon which he took my arm again, twisted it behind my back, and pushed me up against the window, then started bashing my face against the pane, meaning no doubt to slash it open with the resultant splinters of broken glass. Here was I thinking all the time he'd soon stop it and there was he looking as if he was going to keep it up forever, and now I really did begin to wonder if this violent behaviour ever would come to an end. However, the expression on my face was beginning to change, not only because the apologetic feelings I had felt toward him had just about exhausted themselves, but alto because I was finding it more and more difficult to maintain that look of being eagerly desirous to make things up at the earliest possible opportunity, because my face was all swelling up like that and was now becoming no more than another pretext for exciting more violence on his part. But I was also aware that Karube was no longer actually in the mood to be angry but was just going on with it because his anger was somehow something he could do nothing about. When he started taking me away from the window to the side of a vat of potent corrosive acids, I suddenly turned to him and said that his wanting to take it out on me was his own affair, but that the experiments I'd been working on in the darkroom were ones that no one else had done, and that if they were successfully completed the boss would probably really start raking the money in. Not only would he not let me get on with them, I said, but now he'd gone and spilt that bismuth solution which I'd been all that time slaving over. Now you can damn well tidy it all up, I said, upon which Karube asked me why I wouldn't let him work with me. Let him work with me or not, someone who can't even read a chemical equation is only going to be a hindrance if he helps in an experiment, but I couldn't tell him that so probably out of a little bit of spite I took him into the darkroom and showed him my notebooks all crammed with chemical equations and told him that if he found it amusing to keep on mixing and mixing elements in different combinations as it was all written down there, then let him have a go at it and keep on with it every day instead of me, and for the first time I really had him, and continued to from then on.

Now that the fighting with Karube was not likely to occur again for the time being, I was just finding things had got easier for me when suddenly there was a monster great increase in the work that both Karube and I had to do. Some Town Hall wanted fifty thousand plates made for all its streets in ten days, which pleased the boss's wife all right although we both knew that for the next ten days we'd get almost no sleep. So the boss decided to take on loan a worker from another shop, run by a friend of his who didn't have anything much on at the time, and put him in to work with us two. At first we didn't give much thought to it since we were just about smothered by the sheer volume of work and simply got on with it, but gradually I began to find there was something in this newcomer, called Yashiki, which started to attract my attention. Well, he was clumsy enough and stared hard enough at people to suggest he was a worker, but I couldn't help thinking that in fact he might well be some sort of agent sent round here to get the shop's secrets. However, if I was to let any of this out to Karube, God only knew what he might do to him, so I decided to keep quiet about it for a time and simply watch what he was up to, and I discovered that Yashiki most concentrated his attention upon the way Karube had of shaking his vat about. Yashiki's job was to put the sheets of brass into a solution of caustic soda after Karube had finished with them, and wash off the varnish and glue that Karube used together with the iron chloride in the corrosion process, and since that part of Karube's work was one aspect of the number two speciality of our shop, and something which no other workshop knew how to duplicate, it was natural that Yashiki should be interested in it, although that natural interest in itself only made him appear all that more suspect if one was already thinking in terms of being suspicious of him. But since Yashiki was watching him, Karube became all full of himself and started to show off shaking his vat about with its iron chloride corrosives inside. Since he was always ready to be suspicious of me, you would have thought he would have shown some sort of suspiciousness toward Yashiki, but not on your life, and instead he started explaining the whole shaking process, saying that you always laid the inscribed surface face down just like he was doing then, like that, since all metals can be relied upon to work upon themselves by their own weight, and so the uninscribed portions alone got eaten into and worn away by the iron chloride very quickly, and explaining all this in such difficult terms that I wondered who he'd learnt it all from, and then inviting Yashiki to have a shake of the vat himself. At first I could feel myself going cold all over as I stood there listening to Karube chatting away, but finally I decided that as far as I was concerned if somebody wanted to know some trade secret you might just as well tell him, and I decided I'd stop watching over Yashiki, and one very important thing I did gather at that time was that the leakage of any secret resulted from the conceit of the people who worked with it. Still, it wasn't just Karube's getting carried away with his own conceit that had caused him to blab out his secrets so eloquently. Undoubtedly there was something in Yashiki's bearing that got Karube to give everything away like that. Yashiki might stare hard at people, but his eyes, despite this customary hardness, were also capable of a softness, a rare charm which could make people lose track of what they really ought to be keeping in mind. I could feel the pressure of this same charm from him each time he spoke to me, but I was so rushed off my feet, what with getting up early and heating the brass on the gas and then putting the lacquer on it and then dyeing it and then putting the metal sheets that had been coated with ammonium dichromate out in the sun to sensitize them, and then putting on aniline, and then dashing round from the Bunsen burner to the charcoal burner to the brass polish to the margin cutter and back again through the whole performance, that I didn't have much time for Yashiki's charm. And then about the fifth day I woke up in the night and saw Yashiki, who was supposed to be working away on night duty, come out from the darkroom and go off in the direction of the room of the boss's wife. I was just wondering what business he could have in that lady's room at this time of night when as luck would have it I fell off to sleep again because I was so worn-out. When I woke up the next morning the first thing I recalled was Yashiki's carryings-on of last night. Unfortunately, as I thought it over I found I had no idea whether I had dreamed it or it had really happened. On other occasions when I'd been tired I had had experiences of this kind, and in this case in particular it seemed more than likely that I'd dreamed the whole thing. Although it wasn't beyond the reach of imagination to work out why he should have gone into the darkroom, what possible reason could he have had for going into the boss's wife's room? It was unthinkable that there was some deep connection between the two of them, all unknown to us, that would have had to have been going on for some time prior to his coming here, and so I decided it was pretty clear that it must have all been a dream, when that midday the boss laughingly asked his wife if something unusual hadn't happened last night. Upon which the lady replied that no matter how heavily she might sleep, at least she knew it was he who had taken the money. When she added in a very proper voice that if he were going to steal money she would prefer him to steal it more intelligently, that only increased his enjoyment and he laughed even louder. Then I realized that the man I'd seen going into the wife's room last night hadn't been Yashiki but had been the boss, though I must say it seemed a bit funny that although undoubtedly he was never allowed any money, even so he should creep into his wife's room in the middle of the night to get at the purse by the side of her bed; so anyway, I asked the boss if it wasn't him I'd seen coming out of the darkroom but he replied that he'd no idea what I was talking about. So now I couldn't work out whether the person I'd seen coming out of the darkroom was indeed Yashiki, or again whether that bit was only something I'd dreamed. Still, since it was now quite clear that the man who had gone into the wife's room was the boss and not Yashiki and that was something that really had happened, it became pretty inconceivable that Yashiki's coming out of the darkroom alone was something I'd completely dreamed up, and so my suspicions about Yashiki, which had disappeared for a while, now came right back and grew deeper and deeper. But I also realized that having doubts of this kind all on my own was in effect just a form of having doubts about myself and served no useful purpose. I could have found out by asking Yashiki straight out, but if I had asked him and it was true, he obviously wouldn't have known how to answer but just have got all bothered. At this juncture there was nothing to be gained on my part by bothering Yashiki, but still the whole business was so absorbing to me now that I really didn't want to drop it just like that. And it was, after all, important, since the secret formulae for my compound of bismuth and zirconium silicate, which I'd really slaved and sweated over, and for the boss's special red colouring process using amorphous selenium were both hidden in that darkroom. If they became known, not only would this be a massive loss for the shop, but also my secret's no longer being a secret would deprive me of the one thing of interest in my life. If someone was trying to steal my secret, why shouldn't I try to hide it? Well, I decided all I could do was consider Yashiki a plain crook. This was the same way in which Karube had suspected me before and I felt that now it had become my turn to suspect somebody; and yet when I recalled the great time I'd had making mock of Karube, I thought how I was about to bestow the same unceasing delights upon Yashiki; but on reflection it seemed that at least once in my life I ought to be made mock of by someone and so I began to really observe him, gave him the full treatment. I don't know if he was aware of my glittering eye, but he did start making a point of always looking somewhere where his eyes wouldn't meet mine. If I pressed him too hard it might produce the undesired effect of making him push off somewhere, so I tried to introduce a gentle nonchalance into my gaze; but eyes are funny things, and when two people have been thinking at the same level of consciousness and their wandering gazes meet, they pierce right through to the back of each other's mind. I'd be working away polishing up a bit of brass and while we were chatting about this and the other my eyes would ask him if he'd stolen the formulae yet, and his eyes seemed to flash in response that he hadn't yet got round to it. Hadn't you better hurry up about it, I'd seem to say, and then his eyes would reply that now that I knew about it these things were bound to take time. But you know, I'd go on, those formulae of mine are still lousy with mistakes so they wouldn't help you much, to which he'd reply that once he'd looked them over he'd fix them for me. So for a while Yashiki and I worked like that with these unspoken conversations going on in the middle of my head, so that gradually I started to feel close to Yashiki, much closer than I felt toward anyone else in the place. Yashiki's charm, the charm that had seduced Karube and made him blurt out his secrets, was now beginning to take possession of me. I would share my newspaper with Yashiki and we found our opinions always matched when we talked about something we'd both read. When we talked about chemistry, too, things went very smoothly, despite variations in the pace at which our understandings worked. Our political views and social aims were the same as well. The only point on which our opinions varied was the question of stealing someone else's invention, which I considered an immoral act. His interpretation of the matter was that the theft of an invented process could hardly be considered an immoral act if one thought in terms of the progress of civilization. In truth, the person who stole such a process was probably acting in a superior way to the person who did not. In that case one would have to conclude that if one compared my attempts to conceal the boss's invention in the darkroom with Yashiki's attempts to steal it therefrom, then only Yashiki was making a contribution to society. Thinking about that and thinking about Yashiki trying to make me think like that, I began to feel even closer to him, yet even so I wanted him at least to remain ignorant of the boss's original creation, of the method of colouration using amorphous selenium; that I did not want him to know. So although I was always the person who got on best with him, inevitably it was me who went on being the biggest stumbling block to him.

I talked to him once about the way when I had first arrived here Karube suspected me of being a spy and about the dangerous incident that led to. Yashiki replied that he'd been trying to work out why Karube hadn't given him the same treatment, and added with a laugh that it must be because he had had his fill of it with me. Anyway, he said, having a little go at me, I suppose that's why you were so quick yourself to get in a little bit of suspecting practice with me? All right, I said, but if you were so quick to realize that, you must have been pretty well prepared for those suspicions when you arrived here, to which he replied that he had been. That was as good as saying straight out that his object in coming to our shop was to steal our methods, yet the thing that most surprised me was that he had the nerve to say so. Perhaps he'd decided that since I'd seen through him, if he said it right out like that I'd be taken aback and maybe even respect him for it; so I just stared at him awhile thinking what a crafty bastard he was, but Yashiki being Yashiki he'd already switched to his next act, which was a complete changeabout, saying that having come into a workshop like ours the way he had, of course we'd all assumed that he must have something on his mind, although as we should have known there's nothing that people like him and me can do anyway; but since he still had no intention of explaining and apologizing for himself, which would only have made things more unpleasant, he'd just got on with the work and let people think what they would think, although at this point he had a go at me in a direct way saying that the thing that had most upset him was having someone like me around looking at him as if discovering things he was doing that in fact he wasn't doing at all, touching him on sore points that weren't in the least sore. That remark touched me on a sore point that really was sore, since I realized that I had kept on probing and prodding at him in the same way as had happened to me and I felt real sympathy for him, and I said he couldn't be liking things very much if he always had to talk like that about working here, whereupon Yashiki suddenly perked his head up, looked fixedly at me for a moment, then gave a quick laugh and let it go at that. So I decided not to bother any more about what he might be plotting to do. Most likely a man like Yashiki would have seen everything of importance that he needed to see in one visit to someone else's darkroom, and since he'd have seen everything one couldn't do anything about the evil consequences that would come from that, as long as murdering him was out of the question. As far as I was concerned, the opportunity to have met so accomplished a man in this quite accidental way was no doubt one for which I ought to offer up thanks. Indeed I felt more than that, since I began to feel that I should profit from his example, and making use of the trust and affection the boss placed in me, I should try as far as possible to steal those secrets for myself, now. So one day I said that I myself had no intention of staying in this place for very long, and I asked him if he knew of any good jobs. He replied that he'd been meaning to ask me the same question, and since on that point we both seemed to be very much alike he couldn't see what I'd got to be talking to him in that superior way about. I said I appreciated why he said that and tried to explain that I hadn't been doing a sort of crafty digging into the recesses of his mind or anything, because the truth was I had a great respect for him and I wanted to ask him to let me work under him; upon which he said "under me?" and gave a little bitter and I thought scornful smile, but then he suddenly looked serious again and told me to just go and have a look once at an iron chloride factory, where the whole surroundings for a hundred yards are just blighted trees and dead grass, and then everything would work itself out after that. I couldn't quite understand what he meant by "after that," but I did at least get some inkling of the reason why ever since he'd first laid eyes on me he always seemed to be making a fool out of me, although how far he would go in this I was growing less and less sure about, which was not a very nice feeling to have about him, although as I felt more and more like this about him I thought there might be something to be said for looking down on him too; but having once admired him this attempt to despise him didn't come off, and in fact it all seemed merely comic to even attempt doing so, although I must say it was a matter of some considerable regret to me that it seemed that now I had come face to face with this great man I was to be put through a slow and painful process of indoctrination. However, just as we were finally getting on top of the order from the Town Hall, one day Karube suddenly got Yashiki down under the margin cutter on his face with his arms twisted, and started ordering him to confess, you bastard, confess. He must have caught Yashiki in the act of creeping into the darkroom, and when I entered the workshop there he was sitting astraddle him and pummelling the back of his head. He's caught it at last, I thought, but I didn't feel the least inclination to help him out of it. In fact I felt more an upsurge of curiosity, exactly like that of Judas I imagine, to see how the man I'd always looked up to would behave in the face of violence, and I just coolly and calmly gazed at his contorted face. Yashiki had one side of his face all sticky in some varnish that had been spilled on the floor and was straining and trembling with the effort to get up, but each time Karube simply pushed him flat back on his face again with his knees, and he lay there with his clothes all riding up showing his fat legs floundering about in an ungainly way on the floor. This by no means token resistance on Yashiki's part really seemed to me quite absurd and I was disconcerted to find how repulsive the sight of the man I looked up to suffering like that was, because his expression was so ugly that it seemed to indicate some corresponding spiritual deformity as well. What then started to annoy me about Karube's use of violence was the ethical breach of manners whereby he deliberately imposed that ugliness upon another's face, and not the strong-arm methods themselves. But Karube couldn't have cared less whether his opponent looked ugly or not, since he went on throttling and banging him with increasing vigour. I began to have doubts about whether it really was right for me to just stand there watching someone else's sufferings and doing nothing about it, but if I were to move one degree from this static position of mine and take the part of either one of them I would be putting myself quite definitely in the wrong. However, the more I looked at that horrible face of Yashiki's, in spite of which he still wouldn't confess to anything, it began to strike me that surely he must have stolen something from the darkroom, and so I began to strive to read off his secret from the lines created by the contortions of his face. Stretched out like that he still looked up at me from time to time, and whenever he did so, in order to spur him on to greater efforts I would sneer contemptuously at him, which seemed to really get him since he suddenly put all of himself into it and tried to roll Karube off him, but Karube was much too strong and the only result was that whenever Yashiki tried anything like that Karube really flailed away at him. What upset me most was that as I grinned at him and as he responded to this grinning of mine by these frantic efforts of his, I got the feeling that at last he was really giving himself away, as if the upshot of all this was that as soon as people start to do anything they are obliged to give themselves away like that, and so while I went on grinning at him I found that I really had come truly to despise him and I stopped grinning; and the reason was that he insisted on doing something, insisted on moving his body about, when doing so could serve no function whatsoever. I knew now that Yashiki was no different from us but just an ordinary man, so I tried telling Karube to stop hitting him, since surely talking would be sufficient, wouldn't it? Upon which Karube started smothering his head with brass shavings rather as he had once buried mine in something similar, put the boot in a few more times, and then told him to get up. Yashiki got up and edged slowly and nervously back up against the wall as if still expecting Karube to do something, and keeping a wary eye on Karube he said hastily that he'd gone into the darkroom to look for some ammonia because he couldn't get the glue off the base metal with caustic soda. Then if he needed ammonia, why hadn't he asked someone, since anyone knew that the most important place in any nameplate workshop was the darkroom, Karube replied, and again started thumping him. I knew all right that Yashiki's explanation was a lot of rubbish, but Karube's fists were making such a hell of a sound that I told him that at least he might stop hitting him, upon which

Karube suddenly turned on me and said that we must be in it together. I was going to reply that just a bit of reflection would show whether we could both possibly be in it together or not, but then I started to reflect myself and realized that we could well be considered as both being in it, and not only that but that even if we were not we'd certainly been behaving as if we were. I mean I'd let Yashiki go into the darkroom like he had and get away with it, and I'd been considering that my not stealing the boss's secret was actually the wrong thing to do, and so I had been behaving exactly as if I were in a conspiracy with him; upon which I began to feel a certain amount of pricking of my conscience, which only made me take on a rather cocky air and say that whether we were in it together or not, that was just about enough thumping for one person, upon which Karube started on me, clipping me smartly on the jaw a few times and saying that I must be the one who had let Yashiki into the darkroom. By this time I wasn't bothered by being hit by Karube but instead I found it all very cheering since now in front of the man so soundly thumped up to this moment, in front of Yashiki, I could show myself taking his sins upon my shoulders, and this I wanted him to see. However, while I was being punched by Karube I became strangely apprehensive that Yashiki might end up thinking, even though I was being knocked about like this, that it was Karube and myself who were in fact in league together, and that we had previously arranged that it should just appear that he was hitting me, the whole thing being simply an act that we had got up together; and so I had a glance in the direction of Yashiki, who seemed to have gathered some sort of satisfaction from the fact that now there were the two of us who were receiving the treatment, since he suddenly became all very lively, and calling out "Go on, bash him one," he started clouting Karube from behind. I wasn't particularly worked up about any of this, but I found that the exercise of hitting back toned me up a bit and relieved some of the pain I had from being punched, for which reason I was giving Karube a few pokes in the face. Now that he was being attacked from behind and before, Karube turned his principal energies toward Yashiki and tried to bang him one, but

I was pulling at Karube from the rear and spoiling his aim, and Yashiki took the opportunity to push Karube over, sit on him, and carry on thumping again. I was astounded at this great show of vitality on Yashiki's part, and I assumed it was because he imagined that I'd lost my temper at being so unreasonably struck and would thus be with him in the struggle against Karube. But I didn't see any reason to carry my revenge any further so I just stood there doing nothing and watching Karube get hit, so that Karube immediately had no trouble in throwing Yashiki off him, getting on top of him again, and banging him even more mercilessly than before. So Yashiki was in just as hopeless a position as he had been at the very beginning. Karube went on hitting him for a while but then it must have crossed his mind that I might attack him from the rear, since he suddenly got up and rushed at me. It was a foregone conclusion that I would lose to Karube in any man-to-man punch-up so while waiting for Yashiki to rise again I just let Karube hit me, offering no resistance; but when Yashiki did get up he unexpectedly started punching not Karube but me. If one was too much then there wasn't a thing I could do against two, so I just lay where I had fallen and let them do what they liked, although I was wondering just what exactly I had done that was so wrong, and as I lay curled up with my head protected by my arms I considered what kind of badness it must be in me which required that I should be beaten up by the two of them. Of course ever since this whole business started I suppose that as far as they were concerned my behaviour must have been very hard to interpret. Still, as far as I was concerned, hadn't they been behaving in a peculiar way as well? For a start, there was no reason why Yashiki should have hit me. Even if he were to claim that I hadn't joined him in the attack on Karube, my answer would be that Yashiki himself had been a fool to try to get me to join in with him at such a time. While I was thinking about it I realized that the only one who hadn't been set upon by the other two was Yashiki himself, and considering that he was the one who most deserved a thrashing, he'd done all right for himself, and I began to think it might not be such a bad idea to pay him a few back, but the fact is we were all of us absolutely worn-out. The real truth of the matter was that although one could say that the cause of this ridiculous set-to had been Yashiki's going into the darkroom, in fact a much more considerable cause had been the fatigue created in us by making fifty thousand nameplates in so short a period of time. In particular with the corrosion of brass, the bromine from the iron chloride, especially when its effects are in large quantities, produces a kind of nervous exhaustion and starts to confuse a person's sense of rationality. On top of that, instinctive reactions become more acute, revealing what a person's character essentially is, and so there wasn't much point in getting worked up about an incident of this sort in a workshop of this kind, although I wasn't going to forget that I had been hit by Yashiki, particularly by him. I was wondering what attitude Yashiki would take toward me now that he'd hit me, and I was thinking I'd like to make him feel really ashamed of himself if he'd give me half a chance, when after the business was over, although how it actually ended I could not say, Yashiki said to me that he'd felt genuinely sorry while having to hit me like that, but if he hadn't done so Karube might have gone on hitting him forever, so he'd taken the liberty of letting me have one just to bring it all to an end; and he really did apologize, he said. The fact is that although I hadn't realized it at the time, I did recognize now that if the two of them had not hit the person who least deserved to be hit, namely myself, the whole business might still be going on. Even so, I perceived that even during this affair I had again been safeguarding Yashiki's theft, and all I could do was smile bitterly to myself, and as for the pleasure I had thought I would receive from making him blush with shame, well that had quite gone, and I simply had to take my hat off to the remarkable ingenuity of the man, a state of affairs which I found very provoking so I said to him that since he'd been so clever in making use of me he must no doubt have also made good use of his time spent in the darkroom, to which the clever lad replied that if I said things like that it was no wonder that Karube should have hit him, and anyway wasn't I the one who first put the whole idea into Karube's head? And he laughed and avoided my question that way. Of course if he maintained that I had started Karube off, there was nothing I could say in reply to that, and I began to think that maybe he really had hit me because he thought Karube and I were in collusion with each other, and no matter how I tried to work out what either of them truly thought about me, I found it becoming harder and harder to arrive at any answer. But amid all this uncertainty, one thing certain was that both Yashiki and Karube were suspicious of me; and yet were the things that seemed certain to me in fact real? And in what way and to what extent could I calculate the reality of these apparent certainties? But even if I could not calculate these things, there was somewhere within our midst something that could, something that seemed to understand all in absolute clarity, some mechanism that we could not see, a machine which was unceasingly making calculations about us and which then directed our actions according to the light of these calculations. However, although we remained mutually suspicious of each other, we were dreaming about the following day when the job would be over and things would be easy again, and we were enjoying the thought of the wages we would get for our work, and so we forgot our fatigue and our quarrels and we got through that day, and the next day came and with it a new and unescapable happening not one of us had dreamed about: after he'd received the complete payment for all the work we had done, the boss had gone and dropped the whole lot, all the money, on the way home. We hadn't had one decent damn night's sleep in ten days and all that effort had been for nothing. And yet when the boss had gone to get the money, his elder sister, who was the same lady who introduced me to this place, went with him because she had foreseen he might well drop the money somewhere, which was indeed the only part of the whole business that did come out as expected, but it was some time since the boss had made so much money and he was so happy about it that surely it would be all right to have the money he'd earned in his hands just for a moment, and that was her undoing, since she sympathized with his request and she allowed him to hold the money for a while. It was during that period of time that the fatal flaw worked itself out with the total precision of a machine. Obviously nobody thought the lost money would turn up again, so after the police had been informed the whole household were all horribly pale and nobody had a word to say, and as for us workers, we wouldn't be getting any wages and suddenly we felt absolutely worn-out and we just lay down in the workshop for a while and didn't say a word. Then Karube started smashing all the wooden signboards that were within reach and flinging the broken pieces about, and then turned on me and asked me what the hell I was grinning about. I didn't think I was grinning particularly, but if that's how it looked to Karube I suppose I must have been smiling somewhat. I suppose it was because the boss really was such a total nut case. If you thought about it, that was probably the result of all those years of being affected by iron chloride, and surely there's nothing so horrifying as the idea of mental deficiency. And yet what a weird turnup of the system it was that those very deficiencies in the boss were what drew us to him and prevented us from getting annoyed with him. But I couldn't talk about things like that to Karube so I said nothing, and then suddenly the Karube who'd been glaring at me like that clapped his hands, suggested we go and drink, and then stood up. Even if Karube hadn't suggested it, one of us would have soon done so, and thus that it should have been him was pure accident, for there was nothing unnatural in that our thoughts should have glided in the direction of drink. The truth is that the only thing young men can do at such times is drink, and there's no doubt that not even Yashiki could have had any idea that it was the drink that was to cost him his life.

That evening the three of us stayed on in the workshop drinking together until past midnight. When I woke up later, Yashiki was dead; he had mistaken some leftover ammonium dichromate for water and drunk it direct from the earthen bottle. The people from the workshop that had sent him here said that Karube murdered him, but even now I still don't think so. Of course although it had been me who had been working as usual that day on the gluing process, a part of which required the use of the ammonium dichromate that Yashiki drank, I hadn't been the one who suggested to him that we start drinking and it was quite natural that suspicion should fall at first upon Karube rather than upon me; yet even so, the idea that Karube had deliberately got Yashiki drunk as part of a deep plot to murder him would imply that we had all decided we wanted to drink much earlier than we in fact did. Since I had made up the ammonium dichromate long before we thought about drinking, suspicion should more properly have rested on me, and I suppose the reason why Karube was suspected was that tough look about him, which at first glance seemed to indicate a love of violence. But I cannot say outright that Karube absolutely did not kill Yashiki. All I can say is that as far as I can know about these things, it is possible to say that he did not, and that's all. Ever since he'd caught Yashiki going into the darkroom, he must have realized, as I already had, that there was no way of keeping him ignorant of our secrets now other than by murdering him. Then if you considered that I myself had decided that if one were to kill Yashiki the one way to do it would be to get him drunk and then get him to drink ammonium dichromate, then he must also have thought in those terms. Even so, it wasn't just me and Yashiki who were drunk but Karube as well, so he could hardly have given that poison to Yashiki to drink. Right then, so let us suppose that what had been on his mind for days was transformed into action in his drunken state through the workings of his subconscious mind, and thus he caused Yashiki to drink that ammonium dichromate; but by the same process of reasoning, the same thing could be said about me. I mean there is no way by which I can say with absolute certainty that I did not kill Yashiki. Wasn't I the one who had always been afraid of Yashiki, more than Karube, more than anyone else? Wasn't I the one who whenever he was present was always watching him, always on the lookout to make sure he didn't go into the darkroom? And more than that, wasn't I the one who hated him most because I thought he was going to steal my formula, my discovery of that compound of bismuth and zirconium silicate that I was still working on? Yes, I was. It might well be that the person who did murder Yashiki was me. I was the one best acquainted with where the ammonium dichromate was kept. Right up to the time I became drunk I'd been worrying myself sick over the fact that Yashiki would be free to go tomorrow, and then where would he go and what would he do? And if he had been allowed to go on living, wouldn't I have lost more by it than Karube? And hadn't my head at some time or other been taken over already by the iron chloride, reduced to the same state as that of the boss? I have reached the point where I no longer understand myself. All I feel is that there is the sharp point of some machine coming slowly toward me, getting closer and closer to me. Let somebody take my place and judge me. For if you are to ask me what I have done, how can I be expected to know?

The Carriage

It was Taki who arranged for Yura to go to a hot spring that was said to be particularly beneficial for mental ailments; the hot spring was in Taki's home village. The doctor had claimed that the cause of Yura's particular illness, his mental affliction, was exhaustion from overwork, and truly it did seem to him as if all the water had been used up in the cells of his brain, leaving his head squeezed dry, and he had a constant and splitting pain there. When he tried to read, the columns of print seemed to float over the page and collide with each other; even just when thinking about things the words would form in his mind, begin to move forward, and then they would break formation, becoming disorderly and confused, the verbs jumbling about all over the place, the nouns alone coming to a halt in perfect order in one particular spot; and the concern of his brain, its very existence in fact, became a quest for order, all of which seemed to make his already chronic sense of anxiety only the more acute. He thought he had better see a doctor and have himself looked at, so he went to one who was an acquaintance of his. The doctor had examined him and then said: "Look, you're walking along the street, for example, and you start thinking at some point of which direction you ought to go in, and that's what your head can't take. Make up your mind for once and for all that you're going to avoid any kind of thought process, any kind at all, and keep it up for a year."

So one mustn't think, meaning one must live for a year on feelings only, reverting to the state of a three-year-old child; obviously this impossible proposal was just the same as telling him to become a lunatic. Anyway, Yura didn't possess the kind of money that would have allowed him to idle about for a year; the whole thing was out of the question. Not only that but there was a younger brother and also his mother in the background, two people who depended upon him for support, and thus for Yura the doctor's proporal had been felt as a piece of arbitrary and irrelevant callousness. From that day onward he had tried to avoid any work, amusement, or other form of activity that would make him use his eyes, and so he had employed various devices to create a world about him of sound only, his eyes firmly closed. Sound had never stimulated his mind much before, and he imagined that it would afford rest to his brain in a way that the stimulations of the visual world never would. One day Taki had come over to see him and they talked about these things, and Taki mentioned that there was a hot spring near his parents' house which almost no one knew about, and that Yura should go there until he got better. The expenses could all be paid whenever he liked direct to Taki instead of to his people, so Yura had made up his mind to take this opportunity offered to him and go off immediately to the house of Taki's parents. He felt that if he didn't do so, it would mean that the sick portions of his mind would go on debating if they were really sick or not just as they did now, his condition would only get worse, and as long as he went on sitting in that tiny room of his there was no chance of his head ever getting better.

The hot spring was in the mountains, so far in as to seem virtually buried in ferns, the hills covered all over with green leaves firmly pointed like the teeth of a saw. When you walked over the moss, moisture would ooze up between your toes; the sort of quiet place that enjoyed all the amenities of nature. The hot spring water came out perpetually from crevices in the rocks at the bottom of a small decline and accumulated there, and this being an out-of-the-way place only the locals made use of it, and consequently it was peaceful and relaxed in a way the normal hot spring tends not to be. Yura was marvellously pleased with things as soon as he arrived there; the people at Taki's house gave him a place all to himself somewhat detached from the main house, but particularly he was taken with the wonderfully unspoiled natural setting he was in, and delighted at the thought that with this setup his head would certainly get better in only a short space of time. He worked out a routine of bathing three times a day in the hot spring, once after getting up, once again during the afternoon, and finally at night just before going to bed; and if he got bored in between times, he could go for walks in the surrounding mountains and countryside.

On the afternoon of his second day he was out taking a walk as he had done on the previous day, along a mountain path between tall bushes that came right up above his head, when before him in the direction he was going he saw a man standing alone and stock-still by the trunk of a tree, a person quite unknown to him who nevertheless on seeing Yura's face immediately made a most impressive and polite bow, all the while maintaining complete silence. Yura returned the compliment since although he did not know the man such courtesy obliged him into some gesture on his own part, noticing as he did so that the man did not raise himself from his original bow but only descended lower and lower. Yura was horribly taken aback by this courtesy now totally transformed into a controlled and classic gymnastic posture, but since it crossed his mind that this was probably a lunatic or at least someone somewhat wrong in the head like himself, he thought he'd better not get involved in anything and walked right on by. Then, after he'd gone a little farther on, this time it was a man squatting down with his head in his hands, looking silently into the grass with an occasional muttering to himself, and thus too absorbed to notice Yura's approach. He had now met two apparently insane people within a distance of only a few hundred yards, and he hadn't met anybody normal at all, and thus it seemed most likely that the whole area around that part must be swarming with people who were wrong in the head and who had assembled, like Yura himself, at the hot spring to take its beneficial waters. Which was all perfectly natural and certainly nothing to be astounded about, since what else would you expect in the vicinity of a hot spring that was efficacious in mental complaints than that it should be crawling with people who were wrong somewhere in the head?

After three or four days of taking the waters it was clear that all who came there to do so had something weird going on inside their heads just like Yura. At first glance there wasn't anything particularly odd about them, but if he got into conversation with any one of them, any number of obscure points of no contact would make their presence felt, not only statements that were disconnected or totally self-centered and thus with no chance of getting through to any listener, but obsessions that went on whether anyone was listening or not, such as a man perpetually chattering away about the dates of the festivals in the region as if he were reciting them from a calendar, or another who when he was in the water would loll out his tongue like a cow or some other breed of domestic animal and slop it all around his face, or another who at the least opportunity would go on and on about pillows, that pillows performed the function for one-third of each day, thus for one-third of all lived time, of accumulating blood in the neck and thus preventing it from reaching the brain, and that consequently the degree of softness or hardness of the pillow was something essential to be taken into consideration if complaints of the brain were ever to be cured, all this delivered with great opinionatedness indicating he was most likely a follower of the Tenri sect,* and there was a woman who never once looked sideways out of her eyes, and there was someone suffering from saint Vitus's dance who would occasionally let forth a weird howl while in the water and suddenly break out in uncontrollable twitching; all of which made Yura feel that the whole place was like a farm and these mountain fields covered in ferns were pastures where lunatics had been let out to graze. At first he would keep himself quite still in the water with his head just above the surface, but this silent and furtive catching of other people's eyes he found oddly and unpleasantly awkward. There was something funny hidden somewhere in all of them, and even when they were peaceful like this there was no knowing when and where some paroxysm might break forth, although on reflection that itself wasn't all that terrifying. Still, if one forgot about all that, there was the flow of the clouds across the sky and the movements of the wind among the trees, a wind that one soon felt cold on the skin. The heat of the water became too hot and one would climb out onto a rock until one felt the cold, upon which one went back into the water again, and a whole day could be got through in this way without doing anything or talking to anyone, and there was no necessity to be bothered about anybody. So Yura decided that this was how things

*A recent Shinto sect appealing to lower-class people which lays emphasis upon the mental cure of physical ailments in a way fairly reminiscent of Christian Science.

were and there was nothing to worry about and that the thing was to relax as much as one could, so that when he took the waters he endeavoured to amuse himself with the deer of the village that grazed in common here and that would come very close, or else he would play about collecting the sulphur sediment that deposited around the places where the hot water came out and stopping up the holes with it, or he would gaze down at various weeds and flowers growing on the bottom of the pool, or he would swim about. However, he gradually came to feel how deadly boring all this was, this deliberate abstention from thought, this willed attempt to have an easygoing, relaxed holiday.

Then one day Yura went to bathe as usual, and there was a man, a distinguished gentlemanly figure in his fifties with a closely shaven head, sitting on a rock with a set of small bamboo divining rods in his hands. The gentlemanly figure noticed Yura, deliberately looked him up and down, and then said all of a sudden: "I shall read you your fortune."

Indifferent to the fact that Yura still made no reply, he raised the fifty divining rods in both hands above his forehead, closed his eyes, then, with a slight grunt, broke his hands apart and thus the set of rods into two portions, and then counted out the rods that were in his left hand. Yura submerged himself in the water, reflecting that here was another one queer in the head, and quietly watched what the other was up to; which was that he performed the same operation again twice, then wrote something in the earth with a piece of stone.

"I say, the signs are quite hopeless for you today. 'In Heaven and Earth stagnation' has turned up. 'When the ten thousand things are blocked, the ways thereto impassable, patient withdrawal is required.' "

Yura looked at the good, clean, smiling face of the gentleman, and saw this as a way out of his boredom.

"That is all very unfortunate. I suppose you wouldn't feel like doing it again? It must come out better next time."

The gentleman made an expression of outrage.

"Absurd. Impossible. The first cut proclaims. The second or third defiles—defiling, there is no truth therein. I suppose you don't feel like trying your hand at this divination thing yourself, do you? You could learn how to do it. Help you to pass the time at any rate."

As he was saying this he had plopped into the water and approached Yura, and on Yura's admitting his interest and a desire to learn, he crawled out onto the rock again, took up his divining rods, and intoned away rather as if he were reciting Chinese.

"Since remote ages there have been numerous theories relating to the Law of Changes and how that may be ascertained by the rods of divination, among all which the true forms have only been three in number, namely those referred to as Original Divination, Middle Divination, and Concise Divination, and of the other forms it would be no exaggeration to say that they are mere arbitrary perversities and falsifications. Original Divination is that set forth in the earliest Chinese Classic on this subject, and is the Law of the Eighteen Variations. Middle Divination is then a reduced form of this, being the Law of the Six Variations, and Concise Divination is a form further reduced to the Law of the Three Variations. For general purposes it is perfectly in order to make use only of this last Concise Divination with its Law of the Three Variations, since the Art of Foretelling declines complexity of method but aims instead at a wholeness of heart and mind, a oneness of the soul which finds access to the god and thus receives the divine indications of what is to come. Therefore one can say with confidence that there is no objection to the Concise Divination of the Three Variations being used."

No doubt this gentleman had instructed numerous and various others in exactly the same way. His words poured from his tongue as if they had been memorized as he explained to Yura that the bases of the Great Law of the Art of Foretelling was in the control of the breath. That is, that what determines the act of Foretelling is that primary instant when one breaks the divining rods apart in one's hands, that fraction of a moment when one finally can no longer bear to retain one's breath, when at the extreme of endurance unthinkingly in an act that is beyond mind or intellect one draws up all one's strength behind the solar plexus and breaks the rods apart, for it is in that moment that the will of the god is naturally revealed. The gentleman put great energy into this explanation so that the very colour of his eyes changed in almost a weird manner.

"Considering that aspect of Divination, or the study of the Law of Changes, that is concerned with the root causes of creation, of life and growth in all things in heaven and in earth, it may be thought of as a form of speculative philosophy. Again, considered in that aspect by which it demonstrates the creation in relative terms, in terms of change and connection, in terms of the mechanism of such movements, it is a natural science. And as it clarifies human fatality, not merely in terms of where success or failure lies in wait, in terms of what is fortunate or what is unlucky, but in that it also instructs in what courses of action should be taken in the face of each individual circumstance, it is a form of life philosophy, a doctrine of the art of living. And furthermore, being a precise science that calculates that which pertains to the fortunes of a particular country as a whole, its fortunes both good and evil, and since it provides models for conduct in such matters, it is a form of political science. And from its elucidation of disasters in heaven and earth, of orders and disorders in the weather of the world, with planting and reaping, with sowing and harvest, for which it provides models of conduct to be used in due season, it is a form of applied science, a science of practicality, a form of 'pragmatism' which has no superior in the West. And yet this 'pragmatism,' though a method of instruction is not instruction, though a form of scholarship is not scholarship, being boundless, without limit, a study of Fate, of the mysterious that eludes, the depth too far to grasp, and in the words of Yü Shih Nan it is the very 'regent' or learning. And yet even with this Law of Changes, this precious study of a hundred and one uses, the speediest way to arrive at the heart of this Art of Divination is, beyond all else, to entrust all to one's last movement of breath, since in that last moment when the breath gives way, the spirit motions of all things in the created order, of everything in heaven and earth, in that emptiness of the soul created in that moment, then appear in their totality within the self, and thus a complete integrity, a oneness of the spirit, is essential in that moment when finally one lets go of the breath."

Yura had got out of the water and was now sitting next to the gentleman on the rock and, as he listened absorbed to this almost sung form of language, he began to feel that this man was no ordinary maniac but unquestionably someone of culture and learning far above that of the ordinary person. It appeared that the gentleman now felt that Yura had begun to show the kind of quiet respect toward him that one expects in a pupil, and thus after a while he began to speak of himself, that he had been the headmaster of a Higher School where he also taught physics and chemistry, but since he had gone mad he had been obliged to come to a place like this, although now he had calmed down enough to make the study of the Science of Fate possible without undue worry, and, in particular, as he had the habit of shutting himself up inside a closet when the fit of madness came upon him, while he was outside like this he was perfectly all right. Yura asked in response to this if he was aware himself of the fact that he was about to go insane at those times when he did, and he replied that he was always perfectly well aware of when it was going to happen. He explained that up to the point when he had his attack of madness, it was as if there were a lever swinging inside him like a pendulum, right in the centre of his body, and that the arc of its stroke grew gradually smaller and smaller until it finally stopped absolutely still pointing straight downward, and then it was as if his body were being torn apart into small fragments and a terrible feeling of profound unrest overtook him. Yura decided that a person with such a tendency to run mad must be more reliable in his forecasting than the ordinary person, and on asking him whether his study of the Changes did not tend in fact to be more precise than that of normal people, the gentleman with unconcealed delight took up his account of the Law of Divination again with even more vigour than before. He said that the very success of his own divinations had unfortunately led him into being negligent of his own proper subject, which was natural science, although in fact the only real difference between natural science and divination studies was in the one point of whether one was to consider the Unknown as that which was merely not known and thus discount it as an object of study, or whether one was to consider the Unknown as the Unknown and treat it as such, and since there was no other aspect of variance there could be no point of contention between divination studies and natural science, once one had set aside the question of the Unknown.

"For example, if you consider the water of this hot spring and analyse it according to its chemical components, you would get sulphur, calcium sulphate, sodium sulphate, potassium sulphate, hydrochloric acid, aluminium sulphate, sulphur silicates, something like that, which is all a matter of total indifference to the human body, which is concerned with the question of what matters to itself, namely, does this hot spring cure people or does it not? Now in medical terminology this hot spring is primarily beneficial for skin diseases, in particular leprosy, or Hansen's disease, and then for mental complaints, then for diabetes, in that order, and yet the question of whether it will really work in a particular case, the question which is the vital one insofar as the sick body is concerned, this question is beyond being solved except by the methods of the science of divination. Thus those former natural scientists who have wished to cast out this doctrine that gives play to those distant features of existence to which natural science cannot reach, to reject this phenomenon which of all natural phenomena inevitably and undeniably exists, those scientists must, I say, be considered as ignorant dwellers in utter darkness, unacquainted with the Great Law that governs Nature as She is in all things, being mere perfect believers in the omnipotence of the Material, lowly keepers of swine and lesser cattle.

"Now, the three hundred and eighty-four variations that are the basis of all the various forms of the Changes are in effect as countless as there are numberless atoms, this being in accordance with the laws of increase and change, of creativity, and they comply with the innumerable particles of the whole Creation. And if you thus follow the complex aspects of the variations as they appear according to the laws of time, then you may observe the ascendance or the descendance of the opposing principles of Yin and Yang, the harmony or discord of the male and female principles, thus knowing the mechanism of progress and repulsion, of life and death. And not only is all this knowledge vouchsafed to you but also the ability to avoid disasters before they occur, the method of rendering harmless those calamities that befall men in the events of their lives by reading the signs for ill and good fortune before they happen, and thus divination studies are a spiritology, a necromancy, as well as being a philosophy."

His language became more and more forceful and Yura began to wonder when this sermon would come to an end, so he immersed himself in the water again and said that he certainly found all this extremely interesting but he also assumed that since it appeared that the gentleman had also come here to take the waters, he presumably believed that by so doing he would be cured. The gentleman said that he was quite right in his assumption and that he had been here about a year, and having thus recovered this much probably none of his predictions would ever turn out right again, upon which he gave a tremendous and loud maniac's laugh, lifted his bundle of divining rods, and pointed with them at a small village far away at the foot of the mountain.

"That village you see over there is a leper colony, and I have told the fortunes of most of the people in that unfortunate place. But they invariably come out bad. When I saw what was foretold for any one of them and realized always how unlucky the signs were, I regret to say that I felt obliged to tell them untruths concerning it, out of pure commiseration, you see, which is the principal reason why my control of this ancient and unchanging art tended to be set off balance; although as I saw it the Way of Divination was a sovereign art that aimed to demonstrate to the unfortunate how they might attain to good fortune, and thus to show the clear face of misfortune to the unfortunate would be only to thrust them one stage lower into that misfortune, and would thus be in opposition to the Way, which is one of salvation for the people and alleviation of their troubles. So I finally decided to tell them lies, with the result that I might perhaps justly be despised as a mere mountebank, a dealer in superstitions, a raving fortune-teller of the cheapjack sort, particularly as I came to see that indeed there was no necessity of telling them lies, since all of them are people in the last depths of misfortune, and as far as any further misfortune for them is concerned, since they are no longer truly existent in this world, that which men most deeply fear, the fact of death, has no terrors for them, since it would be preferable to life as they now know it, and thus my fortune-telling had become that much more an impotent and useless thing for them. No matter how black my predictions, for them all is good fortune, and thus one could even refer to that place as a true paradise. A paradox, you may say, but then that village is the Mysterious which is the heart of our study, the true form of the Unknown."

Yura had been listening to all this for some time with no misgivings of any kind, but then, instead of the words, he suddenly noticed the weird smile that played over the other's face, and he began to have doubts whether the man really was completely cured, whether he was still not in fact a lunatic. Despite these doubts, Yura raised himself out of the water and looked in the direction in which he pointed toward the melancholy lone village, and his doubts about what the man said on this point vanished away, since he had heard about a leper colony in these parts and presumably that could well be it, and thinking so he felt a coldness that seemed to seep up from the very depths of the rocks. He remained standing in silence imagining to himself what kind of life those wretched people might live, when the gentleman asked him if he wouldn't drop in at his place for a bit, for if he did he would lend him some detailed studies on the subject of Fatalism which he had there, and he urged him so repeatedly and insistently that Yura himself began to feel that since he had nothing to do he might just as well spend the time studying divination, so he agreed and got up out of the water. As they were both putting on their clothes there was a group of villagers who always came to bathe at this time coming up from below, among them a young woman of a composure rare for her age and with a poise and refinement about her that seemed to have some shadow of melancholy, of darkness, within it, who looked in the direction of the gentleman and smiled affectionately at him. However, the gentleman gave not a flicker of a smile back and as soon as the girl got near enough he asked her brusquely what she wanted, and then hurried off down the slope without waiting for a reply. But the girl went on saying something softly at his side and walked along with him, and Yura, since he did not know how far the two meant to go together, hung back, not wanting to intrude, whereupon the gentleman turned toward him and hurriedly introduced the girl as his own daughter. Yura was completely taken by surprise by this, and the girl seemed as flustered as he was since she blushed, and after greeting him with great reserve, she said no more but politely allowed the talk to be between Yura and her father, following behind the two of them. Yura had noticed the remarkable beauty that appeared in her when she greeted him, and he was ceaselessly aware of her presence, which seemed almost to beat into his back, so it was as if his legs had suddenly gone weak and were trembling and floating over the ground, and as this uneasiness increased he began to feel that he might make a fool, or maniac, of himself in some way, and therefore it would be better to leave before he disgraced himself, so he decided to go home. When he suggested this to the gentleman, he behaved in exactly the opposite way to his earlier persistence, another odd about-face on his part, since he merely said he would see him tomorrow and they parted.

Yura had hoped that from now on whenever he felt bored he would be able to see and talk to him, but the gentleman didn't come at all after that parting, so he was obliged to spend his days getting in and out of the water in company with the tedious chatter about pillows, the silent woman who never looked sideways, the idiot who slopped his long tongue about his face, et cetera. And yet ever since he had met the gentleman he found he could not avoid thoughts of the leper colony that had been pointed out to him as he stood up there in the water, and now it was an obsession for him, something that continually and forcibly intruded into his field of vision. He would take every precaution so that he need not see the village, but none of them worked since there would the village suddenly be, and he had seen it.

Now all his everyday habits were altered by this new habit

that had overtaken him. The things he had most enjoyed, such as lazing about and gazing up at the sky through the tangles of moss and rampant wild flowers, through the drifting roots of the wild orchids in the clefts of the rocks, or looking toward the face of the mountain and the movements of the freckled patterns of the deer and the fern leaves fluttering like wind across it, or looking up to the mountain peak and the perfect balanced flight of the kites circling above it; all this was changed, since should he but once recall the mountain foot and its unlucky village, then the stench of sulphur would rise up from the hot water about him and overcome him in waves. He told himself that the village was no concern of his, but all the objects of nature had taken on that same dark melancholy and become unbearable to him. He decided he must find out once and for all that the village he could see before him with his eyes really was the village of misfortune, so he had better ask somebody to make sure; and when he made this resolve he happened to be sitting near the Tenri man, who was plopping and bubbling his face in and out of the water, so he asked him. The Tenri man confirmed for him that the village was indeed the unfortunate place in question, and he implied surprise that Yura should have been ignorant of that fact until now, and he went on to give a precise, detailed account of life in the village called Yumedono,* and also of its contacts with the outside world. According to him, in this unhappy village of Yumedono there were shops, inns, workers; there was even a brass band, and the village had been created from people who all had the same illness, in particular from those who had come to this hot spring to find a cure, and they married among themselves and one could see fresh young children running about there who were, in his phrase, bursting out all over like bright shoots of new green among the old withered leaves. Communication with the outside world was carried on by those who were only slightly affected by the disease

**Yumedono* means "dream hall" or "vision chapel." It is also the name given to an octagonal shrine within the precincts of the Horyuji temple near Nara, and it is where Prince Shotoku Taishi, the father of Japanese civilization, used to retire to meditate and enter into communion with Buddha and his saints, and where he had his visions or dreams.

or by those who had been cured, and thus everything went very smoothly.

"So somebody is always coming and going between the village and here?"

He replied to Yura's question that of course that was so, but that the one person who came on various errands from there to this village was in fact not a patient of any kind. She was a most beautiful lady who did so out of charity from the fullness of her heart, the Tenri man said, and then suddenly changed the conversation, asking him if he knew of the existence of a man who carried divining rods and often came to this spring. Yura said that as it so happened he did at least know about him, whereupon the man explained that he was indeed the father of the lady in question, and he had come here from Tokyo and was apparently a most remarkable scholar. Then this benevolent lady must be the daughter introduced to him by the gentleman, and Yura began to think about the woman he had met some days earlier, about her beauty that had hidden within it a melancholy that could not remain in hiding, and his thoughts about her were many and various. Really, why were they here? To come all this way from Tokyo to a rural village like this, of course you could call it pure goodness of heart, but there was something between the woman and her father, something that suggested there was a definite reason why they had been forced to take this extreme step; and his interest in the beautiful girl became so strong that he suddenly and deliberately went and sat right next to the Tenri man.

"So that learned man is a kind of permanent resident here, is he? He did introduce me to his daughter the other day, and given the situation I can see why he should be here so much. I had this place recommended to me as soon as I became. . . . But in his case, I mean, what made him come all this way from Tokyo in the first place?"

The Tenri man didn't reply for a while but just looked at Yura's face, and then gradually began to edge away from him as if trying to escape, crossing over to the rocks on the other side of the pool. Observing this remarkably sudden and motiveless change of attitude, Yura perceived that he must have been questioning him too persistently, reminding the Tenri man that he was after all dealing with somebody, Yura, who was a lunatic. Certainly up to now there had been a number of occasions when Yura had been questioned by people, or looked at in a secretive way when nobody else was about, so as to suggest that he also was being considered a lunatic, and in a place like this with so many queer-looking patients all collected together, in the same way that he suspected others of being mad it was perfectly natural that those others should suspect him also of being so. He started to recall those occasions, remembering the comic, bewildered postures those people had taken, and the mirth that had started to rise somewhere within him then now bubbled up again, and no matter how much he tried to restrain himself, it bubbled over onto his lips and set them trembling with laughter; so he decided he must get hold of the Tenri man and put an end to his doubts once and for all, and he then swam in pursuit of him across the water. But having swum up next to him, he found that he did not know what he should say, and quite naturally he began talking about the learned gentleman again, asking where on earth he was hiding himself away all this time, and realizing that he'd said the wrong thing again, the laughter started up within him again and appeared in grins and smirks which he had no way of suppressing. The Tenri man told him that the gentleman stayed in a house just over the bridge called the Omiya, then got out of the water straightaway and hurriedly started to put on his clothes. Yura decided not to pursue him any more, since the effort to persuade him now that he was not a maniac would be, the more he thought about it, a task of some magnitude. Whatever he tried to say, the same meaningless smirk would rise to his lips, so obviously whatever he said the man would not believe him; and after all he could explain as much as he liked that he was not crazy, but once having made the other man believe that he was so, well even the most distinguished physician cannot function without the appropriate instruments; indeed the more distinguished he is, the less he can function. Thinking along these lines it struck him that he did have an appropriate instrument, just one, and that was the question of pillows. He'd trust him if he talked about pillows. Once he got onto that subject, especially since the Tenri man himself was slightly unbalanced about that particular question, he'd be able to show him the rightness of his way of thinking, and thus of the condition of his brain, in that matter at least. So he once again went insistently after him, saying that he'd done as the Tenri man had said and used a slightly harder pillow than usual, but today his head felt a bit bad somehow and ought he to go on using the same pillow tonight?

"Ah, well, in that case the pillow must be slightly too hard," the Tenri man replied, soon smiling amiably, innocently ensnared; and he advised him to give the pillow a good pummelling tonight and not to rest his neck on the pillow but only the back of his skull when he slept. If that didn't work out, he should try a wooden headrest instead of a pillow, since that applied no pressure to the flow of the blood and was thus the best possible thing for the head. He seemed to have completely forgotten his suspicions about whether Yura was a madman or not. The two of them decided to go for a stroll together, went down from the hot spring, and continued their conversation about pillows until such time as Yura decided it was a suitable opportunity to take up again the only subject he wanted to talk about, that of the learned gentleman and his beautiful daughter.

"Um, as I was saying a little while back about that scholar fellow, er, I made a promise a few days ago with him to learn how to do fortune-telling, and left it at that, which is how it stands now, so since I'll be going to see him to learn about it sometime or other it seems to me I ought to know a bit about what he's like or there's no saying I won't do something to offend him, so I suppose you couldn't sort of tell me anything that you might happen to know?"

Immediately the Tenri man shut up tight as he had done before, and walked a little way away from Yura as if to reproach, even to warn him. Yura realized that he'd been wrong in thinking that the Tenri man suspected him of being mad. In that case, then, it was even more puzzling why the man should behave in this childish fashion whenever the subject of the learned gentleman came up, becoming cold and distant like that, and for a while he walked beside him lost in thought about these things. The Tenri man seemed eventually to find this silence of the two of them rather preposterous, and after a while he said in a half-muffled voice that he himself had been persuaded into studying divination and had gone to the gentleman's lodgings a few times, but since the daughter kept coming there direct from Yumedono village he thought he'd better be careful, so . . . and as he looked at Yura his face started to grow more and more red. His previous inexplicable actions were now quite clear; he had been jealous of him, Yura reflected with amusement, because he had taken over his former position, and it struck Yura that if the fact of someone else doing divination was so unpleasant to him, unquestionably there must have been something between the Tenri man and the learned gentleman's daughter. However, if he was going to take over the Tenri man's place and learn the art of divination, and if on top of that he was going to meet with the sort of experience that had put that unmistakable and mournful look in his eyes, which was obviously not something to be slighted, then as the learned man's perhaps umpteenth disciple it was essential that he should ponder whatever remained of the Tenri man's experience. In particular there was the daughter, that strange beauty which lay deep down within that immediately felt melancholy of hers, and which from the first had caused motions and disturbances within his heart.

Now that the cause of the former unpleasantness between them was clear, and seeing what a small-minded person the other was and it was not surprising that he should suffer from disorders of the brain with a mind of those dimensions, Yura decided he must be cunning in ways of putting the Tenri man's mind at ease, so he said that since according to what the Tenri man said this business of visiting the learned gentleman seemed to be fraught with various dangers, he himself was thinking of dropping the whole thing, to which the other replied that he would indeed be advised to give up the idea, upon which he looked highly pleased and burst out laughing quite meaninglessly with a shrill giggle like that of a woman. Also while giggling he began to come closer to Yura, and since there was now nothing else in sight except the thick although now withered high autumn grasses, he started almost to snuggle up against him, twisting and wriggling his body as if in some sort of physical pain, and he said, "Oh, I'm so glad to be walking with you like this!"

Yura could feel his skin starting to creep and the hair of his body standing on end, and he made a movement to withdraw slightly, but seeing that the Tenri man was now sufficiently at ease to edge close in this way, obviously one could not suddenly withdraw and spoil everything, so he had to endure things as they were and walk along without saying anything.

"I've been so much wanting to be alone with you like this for the past few days, really I've not known what to do with myself. You've no idea how happy it makes me, just being with you like this for a bit. You won't ever desert me, will you? It would make me so happy if you didn't," he said, even letting forth a sigh as he did so, muttering away almost as if he were talking to himself. Yura could think of no appropriate answer to this, and occupied himself with suppressing his rage and looking in the opposite direction, when it suddenly occurred to him that perhaps that girl had met with a similar experience with this man in almost this identical spot, and he looked at the surrounding grasses and tried to imagine how she must have felt. Not that such reflections were relevant, since what had caused this man to behave in that stupid way just now was not any form of dislike for him but rather the opposite, and clearly what had caused the Tenri man to be annoyed with him before was not a feeling of protective jealousy toward the girl but a jealous feeling against her, assuming his feelings in these matters were as abnormal as they seemed to be, and thus a jealous fear that Yura's affections might be stolen by the girl. Admittedly, what had seemed clear up to now turned out to be suspect again so there was no certainty about this; however, Yura's thoughts about what he might shortly have to undergo at the hands of this person became more unpleasantly ominous; and yet of course he had to admit that the original approaches had been made by himself, and even if it did result in a slight amount of unpleasantness he imagined he could probably put up with it, at least for a certain amount of time, and so he walked with him through the tall bushes, then along the side of a stream, the bottom of which was coated with sediments of sulphur and where he could feel warm upon his sleeve the steam that came off from the great bubbles of hot water that rose up through the cold stream water, and then the two of them went up a path on a small hill. Having walked some distance, they had in fact come round in front of the village of Yumedono, and suddenly there it appeared before them through the leaves of the ferns, and Yura was aware that he had stopped still.

"Here, isn't that the village of Yumedono?"

"Yes, that's right. We've taken a shortcut here—the quickest way there is, actually."

Yura felt himself grow absolutely cold, but since the Tenri man seemed quite unmoved at his side, he was not able to give full vent to his feeling of shocked surprise, and so walked after the man, who himself suddenly gave a little startled cry and pointed back in the direction of the leper village. Yura was now almost shaking with fear, as if he had been shown a certain portent of the immediate appearance of some ghostly apparition, although he braced himself despite the fright he'd received; when looking at the other's face he noticed it was all wreathed in smiles, and wondering what on earth he was on about, he himself looked toward the village and understood that it was none other than the strains, admittedly faint, of the village band playing a nautical march, whose harmonies could be heard straying down the slope from the high ground above.

"The patients are getting ready for a festival, you see. That's them practising now."

The Tenri man seemed delighted by this practical demonstration of the truth of what he had told Yura and started off walking again, and Yura himself sensed that the fear which had always so unnamably and unreasonably seized him at the thought of the village of Yumedono was now over and done with. Late autumn in the meadows: the tree of winter, the holly, let fall its white powder like flowers, one then another, drop after drop flowing down, and the whole surrounding scene entered into his mind, took hold there, for certainly she would have walked here, every day this path from the village back to where her father was, and how many times she must have let fall tears, he thought, at the coldness in the world which enclosed her and in which she was obliged to live.

"The daughter of that learned gentleman, I suppose she must have to come this way every day. What it's all for or why it is, I don't understand, but I can't help feeling what a waste it is, what a terrible thing for her."

"You're so right, of course. It is an awful thing to have happened to her. But if one's to talk about the whys and wherefores of it, then it's the father who's to blame. He's the one who's responsible for it."

The Tenri man seemed to have released the taboo from this particular subject, and he started to enlarge upon the life story of the scholar and his daughter. According to him, the girl's name was Kona Hanae, the eldest daughter of Professor Kona, who was also a man of considerable independent means. One day a swelling appeared on the girl's leg which gradually changed to a deep purple colour, because of which the professor took her to be examined by a doctor acquaintance of his, who diagnosed it as a form of leprosy. The effect this had upon the professor can be imagined, although he tried to consider what should be done despite the great confusion of mind this had thrown him in to. He felt he could not discuss the matter with others, not even with relatives, and he made up his mind that it was better that the daughter herself should remain ignorant of the truth, so under the pretence that he was merely taking her on a trip to some pleasant spot in the country, one night he had her brought all this way in a car, and then shut her up here in a state of virtual imprisonment. One year passed, then another, and Hanae still had no abnormal symptoms, so she was examined by a different doctor, who said that physically there was absolutely nothing wrong with her. Yet Hanae had lived so long in a state of misery that her heart had lost the aptitude for joy, and she seemed to feel nothing joyful in the news, choosing instead to remain in Yumedono and reject the world of everyday life, devoting herself to nursing the sick in the village and performing whatever errands were required between it and the outside world; thus she had remained till this day.

Yura felt the pain of this with such intensity that he was

shaken into silence, into a numbness of mind that cancelled out all the world about him. Then a sudden rage rose up within him.

"All because of the father," he murmured to himself.

"Yes, he *was* in the wrong, and it was all because he became flustered and excited, you see. But that's what drove him mad as well. So that shows he really felt he had been in the wrong. He really felt the responsibility very deeply, that he'd done wrong."

The Tenri man had noticed how seriously Yura was moved by this, and he now assumed an expression he'd never shown up to now, of a real grown-up person thoughtfully scrutinizing and judging these weighty matters, and he even gave a little cock of the head to one side as indication of the profundity of this process; all of which made Yura feel slightly sick, and he felt like shoving him aside and asking him who the hell he thought he was, being so big and cocky about things he couldn't understand half of, but when he looked at the foolish calm face of the man who perceived none of the torment that was going on inside Yura, he calmed himself by thinking that this too was a part of the man's sickness, so he returned home with him all along the level road through the hills as if nothing untoward had happened.

After hearing the tale of Hanae from the Tenri man, Yura found that he had been so painfully disturbed by it as to require deliberate efforts on the part of his mind to forget it. Sometimes he would be lying relaxed in the sun, and would remain too long, and then he would remember, and all the pity of it and the wonder that such things should be would take hold of him, and he could not get the remembrance of her face out of his mind. He no longer cared what the Tenri man might think, but only wanted somehow to open his heart a little to Hanae and show his sympathy for her, although he knew that no matter how many such opportunities he might have, he would never be able to speak, and the possibility of showing what he felt in some act or other was even more remote. If he did nothing like this, behaving as if he knew nothing and felt nothing, could there indeed be any exchange of understanding between a man and a woman?

This coldness in the speech, this giving nothing of oneself away, it was certainly the custom in the East to behave like that out of a feeling that restraint should always be shown in such matters, but Yura began to feel that rather than showing restraint it was more like a form of obscenity. And then again, he thought about Hanae so much there was something odd about it all, and it seemed she must have bewitched him in some way for this to be so. He must fight against it, cast her out somehow; for what was so terrible about her situation that it required such consolation? It was absurd in him to think so. Rather save one's concern for the people who were really in agony, now, in that leper village. And could it be that there was a coldness in her also, a lack of feeling, a lack that had prevented her from feeling joy when she learned that she herself was not ill, a lack that prevented her from leaving the village? But could he look at her as she was and not feel anything himself?

One day he went to the Omiya house next to the bridge and asked if Dr. Kona was at home, and on hearing that the professor had caught a cold a few days ago and had been in bed but it seemed he could get up today, he explained that he had received a standing invitation to call some few days ago, and he would like to see him now if that were possible, and he was then shown after only a very brief time to Professor Kona's room. The scholar's room was a reasonably spacious one of eight mats in size, and next to his fortune-telling tools, divining rods and square calculating blocks, on the desk a number of ancient volumes also relating to that art were scattered about as well; and nothing else. The scholar crawled out of bed, greeted Yura plainly, sat down formally with the rods in his hands, and immediately began talking as if giving his usual practised lecture.

"Now where did we get to the other day? Well, the starting point is that these rods are made of a special kind of bamboo, and the fifty or so stems are all taken from the same plant, all from the same root, and are of a length of four or five inches. Now some six thousand years ago an extremely notable Chinese by the name of Fu Hsi proclaimed that all created things were a combination of eight separate elements, which he named as Air, Water, Fire, Thunder, Wind,

Lakes, Mountains, and Earth, and he discerned that whatever alterations occurred in things were a rearrangement of these elements and of no others. Well, if you consider that chemistry has only in modern times got round to seeing air as a material substance, you can realize what really astounding insight that was on his part. Since the creation of the Way of Changes, Shen Nang, Huang Ti, Yao Shun, and other holy men have used divination as the law whereby the basic truths of the divine gifts and the ruler's way of true order might be understood. Moreover, since the time of the Duke of Chou for one thousand five hundred years up until now those true forecasts only have been collected and set in order and their findings understood, with the result that the extreme complexity of human affairs in society has meant that in dealing with the basic principles that govern all change and the changes that result from the combining together of those principles, the eight elements of Fu Hsi have been increased eightfold, and then again sixfold, to their present number of 384 variations. Now you can see, therefore, as you have seen, that the one true difference between natural science and the Science of Fate is that our Science of Fate considers the human spirit as the same as any other object in the natural world, as a material substance, whereas natural science does not do so, saying that the human spirit is no substance, being in fact a fictional construct without scientific authentification and having no place in the natural order of things. Very well, now since the Meiji era of enlightenment and civilization so-called, only this form of knowledge, natural science, has been accepted as such, and yet by this one fact alone you may well perceive what an uncivilized form of knowledge it is. No matter how complex and detailed its analyses of its 92 elements in nature, from hydrogen through to uranium, the question is what does all this analysis have to do with human destiny, with the fate of men?"

"But look, sir, surely presentday psychology does in fact give sufficient attention to the treatment of the human spirit as a material substance."

Yura hadn't really wanted to say that, but the words just slipped out, upon which the scholar struck his thigh vigorously with his divination rods and said: "That's it. You've put your finger right on it. All right then, now suppose this psychology does treat the human spirit as a material substance. Yes, but what is it actually dealing with? It's dealing with a falsehood, with a lie, it's something totally nonexistent that it deals with as a substance, and it certainly does not concern itself with the positives given by direct intuition of the world. As proof of that, isn't this psychology no more than a variant of physics that has been separated off from its parent discipline? What sort of 'science' do you call such foolishness? As far as the thing that most concerns human beings, those insights into the future and into what fate awaits them, this science has nothing whatsoever to offer, not one experiment in which you could place any confidence."

As Yura listened to his words, he could hear mingled in with all this his anger and resentment against the science that, in the form of a doctor's mistaken diagnosis, had condemned his daughter to this living death, and he lowered his head out of sorrow for him and said no more. He went on with his diatribe against science for some while longer, stressing the superiority of the Science of Fate on a number of points, and at last when the tone of his voice had softened he began to instruct Yura in the methods of divination. This instruction was remarkably simple compared with the complex preamble that had gone before it, being the same as in all mainstream divination in that one merely broke the rods apart, placed them with the calculating blocks, and interpreted the portents that appeared; and that, it seemed, was enough. However, if one didn't follow the methods of interpretation as laid down in the manual based on the Book of Changes, one got oneself into a complete muddle. Since one had to do things by the book like this, Yura could not see what all this training in holding the breath until one's headached was really for, so he decided he'd have to learn that part gradually in his spare time, and said: "I wonder, sir, if you feel like taking the waters today? I'm sure it would be perfectly all right, particularly as I should be with you."

The scholar was delighted with this suggestion, which he agreed to there and then, and the two went out together.

When outside, he still went on with his talk about divination, saying that since it was a direct apprehension of what kind of fortune lay in store by a method dependent upon complete wholeness of mind, the first thing for a beginner in the art was to purify himself in body and soul, then sit in a precise posture in a quiet room, and after that finally take up the rods. However, Yura was clearly a man of considerable mental accomplishment so the place or the environment would not affect him in any adverse way, and therefore he could perform divination whenever and wherever he liked. This was high praise, and he went on to say that providing one had the knack of achieving perfect uniformity of the spirit within oneself, the rest did not really matter. He went on to offer as examples of this truth the spiritual progress of the three thousand of Confucius's disciples in this art, and talked of the methods of study of Arai Hakuseki, all with a scholastic passion of that intensity which Yura always found in him when he got onto the subject of divination, and which made him begin to feel again that surely the man was a lunatic.

"I was wondering, sir, if before your illness there had ever been anything physically at fault in you?"

"No, physically there has never been anything particularly wrong with me, at least not so that you could say I had bad health or anything. The only thing was that just before my mind gave way I had the habit of reckless spending, both on things for the school and also for my own use, and only on those things that were very expensive. How about yourself?"

Yura found the fact that the scholar looked upon him as a lunatic like himself so funny that he could not immediately answer. However, although he himself did not have the habit of reckless spending, he would sometimes find himself getting worked up into a rage for no good reason, and in his dreams he had a vivid sense of smell and of colour; also he sometimes had extraordinarily distinct remembrances of the distant past, all of which might conceivably mean that he was himself now in a period preliminary to going mad, and the whole thing suddenly stopped being a joke.

"My head seems to be all right so far, but I have this feeling that suddenly my mind might give way, and it's that anxiety that I find most worrying."

"Quite right. That sort of anxiety will do you no good at all. You must be very careful about that. Now when I'm about to go mad I leap inside a closet, and that's because when I'm inside, my mind becomes at peace because it feels it knows that my body is not going to be scattered in little pieces all over the place. The great point is to gain this sense of peace and certainty toward things. As you make progress in divination you will find yourself gradually attaining to a state of peace of mind, and your anxiety will go away, and your physical condition will improve as well. Since I started divination the confusion I used to feel about things doesn't occur anymore. Before that I was engaged in some studies on ballistics, practical questions relating to gunnery, in particular the problems concerning the boring inside the barrel of a gun and what sort gives the greater degree of velocity. I really slaved over the question, worried day and night about it until I reached the point where I could not see how I or anybody else could go further in the matter than I had done, no matter who he was, and that thus there was nothing left in this field of research. And then we tested the gun and it was all wrong. I don't blame myself, I blame the science itself. So I dropped ballistics and took up fortune-telling, and I understood that the limits of scientific practicality when compared with the extent of the uses of divination were very narrow indeed, as feeble in its usefulness as the abilities of a small child. If that's all the hairy foreigners have got to boast about, then sometime during my life I'd like to show those hairies something about the real extent of the powers of divination. That's what I'd like to do."

They crossed the bridge and started to ascend the rise, the scholar still talking away and Yura still at his side waiting to see if he would ever let anything slip relating to his daughter's tragedy, but instead he only became more and more abstruse until Yura felt that all it was giving him was a headache.

"Do you think, sir, we might leave the subject of science

for today? I'm finding it rather a strain to listen and I'm beginning to get this pain in my head."

"Pain in your head? That won't do. When you find your head's causing you trouble, the great thing is to stop all that activity inside it for a while."

"What do you mean by 'stop'?"

"Just leave it alone. Let it do what it wants for a while, exactly what it wants in its own way. Let it run wild."

That was interesting. For the scholar, of course, the act of going mad was a kind of holiday that was given to the mind.

"So it is possible to let the mind run crazy? You do it at your own free will?"

"It's all a question of practice."

Of course madness was a question of consciousness, of the consciousness losing control, and since the consciousness went mad it went on being mad, and the very act of trying to affect that consciousness with the consciousness itself, to cure the crazy consciousness by the consciousness, would only mean a spiralling process of more and more madness. That was obviously so, thought Yura, and he warned himself that the learned man's statements thus could hardly be treated as trustworthy. Then it struck him that the man was no doubt having him on, amusing himself at the expense of his nervous and gullible opponent. So in order to turn the tables, as it were, and confound his own enemy, Yura suddenly burst out into loud peals of laughter.

"I was wondering, sir, what is the limit of sanity? Where is the boundary point where one can say one goes mad?"

Yura felt he had got in a good telling thrust at the scholar, who'd been having it all his own way so far at his expense, but the other continued his way up the rise, his towel dangling from his hand, and leaving Yura behind as he moved toward the spring, he replied: "The borders of madness are said to be there where the spirit forgets its own body. At least that is how natural science will see the matter."

This give-and-take of question and answer was much like the *mondo* catechism of Zen master and disciple, and Yura felt quite cheerful as he thought that, the first time he had felt so for some time, and he too went up toward the hot spring, when suddenly the Tenri man, who would seem to have been in hiding listening to what the two of them were saying, appeared from out of the bushes, looked toward the two of them with a most fierce expression, although what was on his mind Yura had no idea, and then came down toward them. He came right up to Yura, glaring at him all the time with a threatening glint of obvious fury in his eyes as if he were going to really show him what was what this time, and then cut him dead and walked by. Yura had completely forgotten that he previously promised that he would not go to the scholar's home, and so for a time he could not work out what had got into the man; but then he remembered and realized that must indeed be it, and again the absurdity of it all overcame him, and, looking at the retreating back of the Tenri man, he opened his mouth wide and burst out into howls of laughter. On hearing this the man turned round and glared back at him, then covered his face with towel, and as if in deep mortification he dashed off down the slope. Then just about at that point where he should have disappeared among the bushes, he seemed to catch his foot hard in something and crashed forward upon his face. Yura stopped laughing immediately, but whether he was still fallen over or not he could not say, since the form of the man was hidden in the long grass, so he remained standing where he was, holding his breath in expectation of the man rising again. No matter how long he waited, however, he saw no sign of the risen man, so he went back in that direction to find that he was, in fact, nowhere to be seen.

"Toba," he called out, "Mr. Toba," wandering all around the area, but there was no reply. So he went off back to the spring, got in the water, and a little later while he was pouring water over the scholar's back he mentioned Mr. Toba to him, since he had heard, he said, that he had taught him the foretelling art, and he wondered if Toba had had any success; upon which the scholar replied none whatsoever. The Tenri man's method of divination had been mere guesswork, superstitious indulgence, and he denounced it out of hand. Yura could imagine how remarkably badly they must have got on with each other, and thinking how infuriating it must be if the Tenri man were to see this next disciple pour water over teacher's back, he desisted from it, slipped himself back into the water as deep as he could, leaning his head back as he always did and looking up into the sky, when suddenly while admiring the brightness of the fallen leaves, of which there were so many now all over the face of the mountain, what should he notice but the face of the Tenri man staring this way. He had his body motionless and concealed within the shadow of a rock that jutted out of the ferns in this direction. Now this really was going too far; the man's persistent pestering made him want to puke, since after all what did it matter if he had made a silly promise with him about going or not going to the scholar's place. It was his own business what he did with himself, wasn't it? So Yura decided that from then on he was going to ignore the fool entirely.

So from then on whenever he had time to spare he would go to the scholar's place, and as long as his head didn't start to hurt he practised the methods of divination under him, at first merely messing about with the interpretation of the signs that appeared, and then rather horrifyingly finding that as one started to get the hang of it all it gradually became more and more fascinating, like pursuing a deer and thus becoming aware of the true depths of the wood, not knowing how far one should go, losing the sense of where one's studies should end or lead to, losing the sense that knowing how far one should go mattered, until finally one had lost all restraint or sense of proportion, merely wanting to divine what was in store for people, to judge, to do it all the time. For Yura this was most disturbing. The scholar had once said to him that if the signs for someone were bad, one had to remember that even one bad sign was something really in that person's life that he would suffer from, and thus one could not foretell in an indifferent or casual way; and for Yura, since this was something that was totally dependent upon sincerity of heart, it was hardly something that could be done as a profession either. His teacher said that fortune-tellers would speak of most of the many people who came to consult them by saying that "a dead person has come," this being because when everything is considered seriously and things are seen as they undoubtedly are, those fortune-tellers, out of the full confidence that the fate of all things is shown to them as in a bright and perfect mirror, become unable to see the ignorant people wandering in this transitory world as truly existing but only as the dead; all of which seemed to Yura quite reasonable on their part. Fortunately only those portents which appeared if one's own hand were seriously involved in its task directly with someone could be considered as the true judgements on a person's fate, and thus often, for the sake of practice only, the two of them would work upon incidents that appeared in the newspaper, or happenings in the village that their divinations could not affect in any way, or they would work out their own fortunes, competing to see which of them would turn up the nearest answer; this playing about was, in fact, what they usually did.

Although Yura was enjoying himself on his visits like this, and although he was growing to feel a deep respect and affection for him, indeed because of this, he had only to look a little deeper to know that the tragedy of the man's daughter was always somewhere within his mind, a deep source of anxiety to him. The daughter certainly seemed to visit her father on occasions from the village of Yumedono, but perhaps because he was never there late in the day, in the afternoons or evenings, he had not met her again since the time he was first introduced to her. Finally, one afternoon just as Yura was getting ready to leave for his bath, Hanae came to visit her father. When Yura saw her he felt again as he had that time before, and he felt he must go or otherwise it would be too painful for them, and he was about to take his leave when the scholar said a few reassuring words and persuaded him to stay. Yura remained sitting as if he were just on the point of departing very shortly anyway, when he recalled the portent he had turned up for himself that morning. It was "Water, Thunder, Initial Difficulty," which according to the Chinese manual meant, "Man Woman First Meeting Problem Arise: Action Perhaps? In Danger," which meant that when the ten thousand things were in dire straits, patient withdrawal was required. Yura found this so comically apt he felt he had to laugh, but he could hardly start chuckling in an unintelligible way in front of Hanae, so in order to find some different and more acceptable outlet for his mirth he mentioned to Hanae that today her father had produced the portent "Heaven Fire Companionship" for himself, which was very good for cooperative actions, in particular for marriage connections, even for unlawful passions. Her father retorted that his hand had been completely put out today by Yura's baneful presence. This amused Hanae, who said that she'd come today because there was something she wanted to talk to him about, so he at least hadn't been totally out in his prediction, and presumably she could also expect her father now to be very cooperative.

"However," her father put in, "the primary and most relevant meaning of 'Heaven Fire Companionship' is a political one, abjuring inferiors not to acquiesce in the mandates of their masters. How about it, then?"

This retort made both Hanae and Yura almost collapse with laughter, which had the effect of dispersing the shyness and caution that surrounds the first being together in a room with another person; and after only a short time they were talking with great interest and pleasure to each other. Yet this very attempt to be interesting and amusing finally produced the contrary effect in Yura of setting in motion all his past anxieties, among them a host of unpleasant ones that he did not want to remember, and this in turn caused him to think of the unhappiness between the father and his daughter and that they would also be thinking of all their misfortunes, which might even cause them suddenly to burst into tears; and his mind revolved in this complex and detailed manner so that he began to feel a powerful sense of irritation against himself and things in general, and merely waited for a break in the conversation to say: "I'm afraid, sir, I really think I must be going, if you'll excuse me. I've still got to take my evening bath."

It was already dark when he left but the moon was bright and he could see where he was going well enough, so instead of going back home first he took the direct route to the hot spring with his towel over his shoulder. Walking up the slope he recalled all the light in her face when she happily laughed, and then he contrasted that with those times when the smile faded away for a moment and the melancholy dark came back, and his heart went cold as ice. No doubt the learned gentleman did see things with the eyes of a father, no matter how much one might call him a lunatic; he saw his daughter, and he must be thinking unceasingly about what sort of person would be right for her husband. Thus while he was teaching a young man like Yura the art of divination every day, surely it was inconceivable that he had never put the thought of Yura and that of his daughter together in his mind. Yes, it was inconceivable, Yura thought; yet supposing the father accepted the idea of his marriage to his daughter, what would he himself have to say? While still pondering that question and still unable to answer it, he arrived at the pool, and there he could see, low under the bright moonlight and stretched out across a rock, a man flat out and all black like a snake. The first thought that crossed his mind was that this must be the Tenri man, who'd been on the lookout for him, seen him leave the house, and then taken another way round and got here before him; so he stood for a while looking down motionless at the water, but just by the moonlight he could not see clearly who it was, and even if it was the Tenri man he could hardly allow himself to be so cowardly about this that he should simply go back home after coming all this way, so he stripped naked and got into the water. The only thing was that as he watched the man on the rock, he realized that he never once altered his position at all, remaining absolutely motionless, so that he began to think that it was probably no person at all, but a shadow cast by a rock or a bush, and as he started to think like that a sense of the unpleasantly weird, then of the uncanny, began to occupy the water with him, and so he immersed himself right up to his chin. All around was total silence, not a single sound, with only the radiance of the moonlight falling, and he found that unconsciously he was avoiding making any splashing sounds and assuring himself that if the man moved he would be holding himself in readiness, his fists clenched under the water. But there never was movement of any kind from across the pool, and he finally decided that it truly was not a man, feeling a sense of letdown in a foolish awareness of the ridiculousness of it all.

And then again he began to feel that if it were not one of the lunatics, since such a person would hardly bother himself about Yura and thus certainly move sometimes, then it might be, indeed almost certainly was, somebody from the leper colony at Yumedono who crept down here to take a bath when nobody was about. On thinking about it, that seemed the most likely answer, and then he remembered the "Water" portent he had turned up today could also mean "Danger by Water," and if he went on sitting here like this anything might happen, so he crawled swiftly out of the pool. He put on his clothes, pulling the belt tight and firm about him and reflecting that his foretellings were gradually becoming more accurate, and as he was about to descend the path he noticed with some trepidation that the person seemed to have slipped off his clothes, leaving them in the same spot as before, and got into the water; when from among those discarded clothes, suddenly, like the tail of something, a face snaked smoothly out. He felt his whole body run cold from the soles of his feet upward; and if he were to respond like that to an experience as trivial as this, then what it would be like if for some reason he were condemned like Hanae to spend the rest of his life in the village of Yumedono, he could not even attempt to imagine. So as he went down the slope he kept thinking about Hanae, one thing after the other, and he wondered why it was only when he was going up and down this slope that ideas of Hanae and remembrances of her should come so clearly into his head like this, and if this was going to turn into a habit, then quite seriously what would be the meaning of his head getting better if it was merely going to be smashed to pieces again in this way with obsessions about her?

On the evening of the next day he again went to study divination with Professor Kona, who told him that a new problem had just turned up which he thought would serve very well as an exercise in the art. A railway was soon to be opened through the neighbouring town to Yumedono village, but it had been decided that neither the inhabitants of the village nor any visitors to it should be allowed to use the trains, so the leper colony had sent representatives on a number of occasions to argue and negotiate with the Town

Council, which had so far brought no results of any kind, and consequently the village negotiators had worked themselves up into quite a state and at last come to the professor for his advice. Yura assumed that it had been over this business that Hanae had come the evening before; and it was no surprise to him that in view of the extent to which the village aroused a sense of fear in him, the people of the town should share a similar fear, nor could it be considered all that unreasonable, given the traditional attitude toward the disease, which was one of horror only. However, in this area the one feature of any prominence was the certainly remarkable one that it was able to accommodate so many lepers in the village of Yumedono, a feature which none of the other regions round about shared, and thus to create a railway which would be of no benefit to the only distinguished natural feature of the place, i.e., the lepers, could be thought of (and Yura thought so) as actual and deliberate opposition to the will of nature.

"Then I suppose, sir, you've already looked at the signs for this?"

Yes, his teacher had looked at them that previous night, but he wanted to see in what way his would differ from those that Yura produced. Upon which, considering what the problem was, Yura left that he would not be able to treat this as half a joke as he normally did when performing divination; this time he would have to put as much of himself as he could into the act of breaking apart the rods, but it was as if he were surrounded by the sick bodies of the lepers, smothered with them like soft foam, and the sad face of Hanae rose and sank somewhere within him, and he was unable to achieve that composure of mind that he required. But his indrawn breath was now almost gone, and the pain severe now and severer, waiting for the face of Hanae to fade in the distance, and now it had, and he gasped and broke the rods apart. He looked at the signs, read them from the manual, and they were "Water, Heaven, Waiting": "Great Haste would lead to Great Misfortune." It principally meant that if one proceeded cautiously, good fortune would certainly follow, and that would seem relevant to the village of Yumedono; he turned to his teacher and asked his opinion, and he replied that his own had things in common with that and also points of difference, and changing the pointers of the calculating blocks, he laid out "Wind, Fire, Dispersal." That meant that misfortunes would melt away, and that the signs for celebration were good, which certainly had something in common with what Yura himself had produced.

"Then that shows, sir, that I'm able to act in your place. I think that some form of certificate is called for as soon as possible," Yura said, laughing.

"A certificate, is it? All right, I'll provide you with some form of certificate shortly," he answered, and Yura left with that.

As he went outside, the Tenri man was standing by the doorway by himself, and he glared at Yura's face. Yura walked past ignoring him, but the Tenri man followed after him and would not go away. They reached a point where there were no more houses to be seen, only bushes, and since Yura could not be sure what the man at his back might do, he stopped, turned round, and said: "Look, are you after something? Because you're starting to get on my nerves a bit. Come on. Get it over. What is it?"

Upon which the Tenri man appeared to grin foolishly with all his teeth showing. But on looking a little harder, he realized that this was no grin, but convulsions of rage which set his two lips moving alternately away from and toward each other, and then he thrust his face without restraint toward the unretreating Yura, and said: "Read the signs?"

"Signs? What signs?"

"Your signs, friend, yours."

Yura turned away from him without replying and walked off. He understood that the man must most likely be continually reading his fortune in secret, and the thought of this creature following on and on after him was beginning to give him the creeps. Suppose the man said that Yura was going to die soon? Of course that would be a piece of nonsense he would have made up, but Yura's head in its present state could well make that the hint for running absolutely wild, and he wanted to get far away from him, as quickly as possible; yet the fact that he had read his signs and was still, despite his anger, coming on pigheadedly after him like this probably meant that there was some essential connection established in the signs that the man had read, and he began to feel overwhelmed with doubts and uncertainties about where he himself was going. By now he had arrived at the place he was staying, and ignoring the Tenri man he hurried inside and dashed into his own room, although once inside he began to feel certain that the man would have gone round and be standing there outside; so he opened the window and sure enough there he was, standing quite motionless and looking in this direction.

"Look, you must be after something. Well, aren't you?"

"I want to have a word with you."

"All right, come in."

However, the upshot of their conversation was that the Tenri man could not discuss things except in the open, so would he come outside, which Yura reluctantly agreed to, slipped on some sandals and went out to the garden; then the other suggested that they walk some more. Well, a long skinny streak like that couldn't do much anyway, so he followed along behind him, keeping his hands free, out through the back gate and up into the high field. From that point on, the Tenri man crept close to Yura as he had done on the occasion before. Yura could not work out whether this was an expression of the same intimate emotions he had given vent to before, or if it was a plot to lull Yura's suspicions since he was planning to do him some damage in this spot. Whichever it was, he had certainly come today after reading the signs, thus presumably with the intention that some profoundly felt wish of his might be fulfilled that night, and having come to that conclusion Yura suddenly realized that the long skinny streak now looked quite different from his daytime self, was even beginning to appear quite strong and forceful.

After a while the Tenri man said out of the silence, "I've been wondering whether you're not thinking of marrying Professor Kona's daughter," then went silent again and looked him in the face. Yura said he was thinking of no such thing, and the other wondered if that were true. True or false, he'd met his daughter only twice, hadn't he? At which the other grinned and said that the reason the professor taught the art of divination to any young man who happened to be around was an attempt to get such young men tied up with his daughter, and he ought not let himself get caught in that way, and then he started complaining about why Yura didn't spend more time with him, going on with a lengthy account of the loneliness he felt when they couldn't be together. So this was what he'd been threatening him with, was it? This was becoming more and more ridiculous, Yura felt, and said that unlike the Tenri man, he had never thought in terms of who was or who was not spending time with anyone else, since he didn't have the time or inclination for these childish obsessions about who was playing or not playing with whom, and if he wanted to visit at any time he'd always be perfectly glad to see him. Also, why was he always running away and hiding and then creeping up like this? To which the Tenri man replied that it was because the signs he had read stated that Yura was going to marry the daughter of Professor Kona.

"Then that just shows how hopeless you are at reading the signs."

Yura said that merely to get rid of the other man's anxieties, but having said it, that particular worry rebounded upon himself. Supposing he did get into the awkward position, as the Tenri man's signs foretold, of having to marry Hanae, what was he going to do about it? He realized that he had made no kind of effort within himself even to start to grasp what such a situation might mean, and inevitably he now felt the full and confusing force of his inner unpreparedness. For the truth was that in any normal situation if he'd been asked to marry Hanae, he would have almost jumped for joy. But to marry Hanae as she now was—one had to recognize that, since she had been working in Yumedono village, the fact that at some time or other she would be visited by the same disease as that of its inmates was a real possibility that could not be ignored. In that case—and then for the first time he understood the terrible fear that must have overcome Hanae when after two years in the place she understood that she was not ill with the place's disease, and his heart seemed to stop beating. Two years believing one was ill, those two years passing and discovering one was not, the joy in that and then the new fear swiftly falling, and how great the long swing from one feeling back to the other, and back again, and back. If one went back to the normal world there would always be the ignorance as to when that illness with which one must now be contaminated might appear, always the threat beneath only the one layer of skin, and he understood that he himself would have lost the desire to move from a place to which he had become accustomed. And yet if he understood the enormousness of that fear, as truly he did, how was it that he could be thinking of marrying the girl? As he walked along he understood that he must now think positively about the fate in store for him, of which he still knew nothing. In particular he must think about how horribly friendly Hanae's father had become toward him, and didn't that mean he was secretly judging the fortunes of himself and Hanae? And wasn't that why he had become that much more friendly? Yura began to feel that it was so, that something was after him and was finally tracking him down, and his whole body became tense at this thought.

Being thus obsessed with his own fate, he had completely forgotten about the Tenri man at his side until he broke in upon his thoughts, suggesting that they take the waters since they hadn't done so together for some time. When Yura looked up to see where they were, he saw they were indeed on the path up to the hot spring, which they shortly arrived at, so Yura followed suit with the other and stripped off his clothes and got in. When in, he noticed that despite the fact that it was quite dark now, the man with Saint Vitus's dance and the woman who never looked sideways were also there, the Saint Vitus's dancer twitching and trembling in the water beside the woman and making the water ripple as he occasionally let out those weird cries which made him look as if he were suddenly swallowing something. What could that woman with her unmoving eyes be thinking about? She looked perpetually at the same spot two or three yards ahead of her, always directly ahead, saying nothing to anybody, her arms always folded above her breasts, with only her thumbs moving as she twiddled them round and round each other. Then the Tenri man started his usual antic, thrusting his head into the water, dashing it out, thrusting it in again, like a cormorant diving for fish, when suddenly he was at an entirely new game as he grasped Yura's leg in the water and started licking it. Now at last he was truly revealing himself, thought Yura, but since he could hardly give him a good kick, there seemed nothing else to be done than let him have his own way for a time while showing no response on his own part; which only led to the Tenri man's lifting Yura's leg higher and higher until Yura pushed the man's head forcefully away and climbed out onto a rock. But the Tenri man raised his head from the water and came up to Yura again, and asked him in a low voice if he wouldn't please put up with it for a little longer and keep still, please help him by thinking of it as Yura's own illness which might get better in this way, upon which Yura said that he had not the faintest idea what the other was up to but he had had enough of it and was going home, whereupon the Tenri man became suddenly hectic, seizing hold of Yura's leg, begging him to please stay a little longer since he was almost finished, or something to that effect, and then again sealed his tongue against Yura's leg and started licking again, all the time gazing up into his face. As the man's lukewarm tongue moved over his skin, he had a quite nauseous feeling, and yet if this sort of thing was necessary to cure the man's illness it must be a pretty wretched sort of illness to have, and so he decided that he could put up with it for a while, and when he felt the other had had enough he withdrew his leg, dressed, and left without waiting for him. On the way home, thinking about the behaviour of the Tenri man toward him that night, he began to feel that everything the man had told him about the professor, about Hanae, about everything concerning them in fact, was all merely things he had made up for himself; and so completely did he come to doubt these things that he felt like going back and trying to get the truth out of him, although he did not.

The following morning Yura decided not to go to the scholar's place that day and instead stay in his room and think over things. But the thought of the Tenri man's jealousy produced the thought of going there, and then he began to feel that this caution toward people who had come so close to him was ridiculous, and then perhaps today and perhaps at this very time Hanae would be there, with the result that he could no longer bear to remain shut up like this and he left for the professor's house.

When Yura arrived there, the professor was in the act of putting some white cocaine powder on the tip of a piece of bamboo and thrusting it right up inside his nostrils to clean them out, and while doing so he told Yura that his portents had come out dead right, referring to the question of the railway and Yumedono village. What happened was that the Town Council had been so obstinate in their refusals that at last the inmates of the village decided to invade the town, breaking into the house of one particular town councillor, and neither the councillor nor the police could actually prevent them from doing so by handling them, so things went very smoothly and everything was settled happily there and then. Yura imagined the town full of lepers, and among all those cloudlike faces the figure of Hanae leading the struggle came into his mind, and he thought also of how at this moment she would be in the village surrounded by them, drinking healths to their victory. Rather than feeling any sort of sense of achievement at his own forecast having come out so well, he was thinking about himself and Hanae, and they were married, and so he had to kidnap her away from that village, and the inmates rose up with that same force and suddenly all thrust in upon him, and why when nobody had ever made the least hint of a request that he marry Hanae, why was this alone always inside his head? Did it mean that he would simply drift meaninglessly into marriage with her? And yet how could he leave her as she was now? It was too cruel, and he knew that he could not now erase her from his mind.

That evening when he got home he took out the divining rods and thought he would try the portents for their marriage without letting anyone else know. But the only person who had ever mentioned the idea of such a marriage was the Tenri man, since which time his head was always racing with thoughts of her, and thus if he did turn up signs that pointed to their marriage, would it not be inevitable, horribly inevitable, that his own fortune-telling would then gradually incline all his feelings in the directions to which it itself pointed? Particularly, given his success with the portents over the village, he was beginning to feel confidence in his own powers. Now that he had this confidence in himself, he would have more successes, and more. Then he began to feel within the depths of himself a uniquely unamable terror, so he shut his divining rods away in the cupboard and went straight to bed, but the face of Hanae that had appeared to him before he slept troubled him unceasingly in his dreams. Not only that, but unlike his waking dreams of Hanae, the dreams of her while he slept had the same characteristics as those that had first troubled his mind into illness, in that they presented her to him with all the brilliant colours and live odours of the real. Thus waking life again became pleasant to him in contrast to this, since sometimes in his dream Hanae would be walking among the bushes and some garment with damp flesh clinging to it would wind around her legs and he would attempt to kick it away and then it would cling to him and he could not get free, and he woke sweating. There was faint light in the sky and the night would seem to be over, and thinking that the night would soon be over, back into his dream world came the figure of Hanae, and he was all of a sudden so close to her and the night would soon end and it must not end so quickly, so close was he unto her when he slept.

When he woke the next morning and looked round at all things under the morning sun, it was as if he had been living together with Hanae for many years, although he knew that if he were to meet her now all the vividness and life of this long closeness would go and he would be reduced to the awkwardness of the time when he first met her. And yet to think like this was only to tie himself closer to her, to make their marriage more and more of a certainty, and he suddenly understood that if he once faltered, there would be no escape this time, and that what he must do was take the fatality in himself that carried him toward Hanae and alter it; he must do everything he conceivably could to derange his own fate. If he had to marry her, then she, and finally he as well, would have to live in that village, that hall of dreams, for they would be lepers, a burden which he would have to, and of course could not, impose upon his family, upon his relatives, for the rest of his and their lives. Thus now not merely was he thinking of refraining from going to see the learned gentleman, but also, since his head truly did seem to be recovering, he decided he should be thinking of making preparations to go back to Tokyo. And then as various devices for keeping Hanae out of his mind were just beginning to take effect, one evening he ran right into her. It was already dark outside, and Yura was wandering in the direction of the hot spring when he met her in the middle of the road going from her father's to the leper colony. Their eyes met and they stopped at the same time, both feeling they had nothing to say to each other, bowing to each other and passing by. And yet as Yura saw her waist bend as she greeted him, saw her with her lantern as she slowly shuffled by away from him, he felt almost a sense of wonder at the thought that this was the girl who might have been his wife; or might be going to be his wife, for suddenly his breast seemed to be full with her again, cramped with her, and despite all his resolutions not to go with her he felt himself weaken and be drawn in toward her, and he had to go after her, strolling only, but after her.

"Hanae. Hanae," he called out, and as he did so he knew that he was drifting and there was no way back. "It's dangerous in the dark like this. I'll see you back some of the way."

"No, please, it really is all right. I know the road very well. But thank you."

Despite this, Yura still walked along with Hanae, and as he did so he imagined that this degree of solicitude was no doubt shown to her by the Tenri man before, and probably any number of times by other disciples of her father before that, and if he were to care for her more than all of those, he would have to show such love by going as far as she was to go, by entering with her into that most dreadful of villages. But he could not believe that he was capable of that, capable of entering the village of visions and dreams now, with her, like this.

"Well then, thank you very much. This will be just right, just here. The carriage will soon be here."

Yura wouldn't reply to those words, standing slightly distant from her as if angered at what she said; but then he understood that she talked like that because of not wanting to show him the direction in which she was to go, and so he thought it would be all right to leave things as they were and say goodnight. Yet having reached this point, he thought that more than knowing himself where he was with regard to Hanae, it was necessary to find some way of letting her know what he was to her, and there must be a way, and he was unable to go away but just stood there with her, when far off in the late autumn wind he could hear the light clattering of a carriage coming toward them. Now Hanae went on telling him to please go home, please go, and Yura himself felt that if he stayed there any longer he would seem to be spelling out the fact that he was sure of her feelings for him, and so he said: "Then I think I'll say goodbye now. If there's anything I can do for you in Tokyo, please let me know."

She said there was nothing at that moment, and she behaved so restlessly as if to say that all she wanted was that he go away from there now, and he understood why she should feel like that and he had no quarrel with it so he went away from her. But when he had reached a point where he imagined that Hanae would no longer be able to see him, he stood among the long grass and looked back in her direction. The small shabby carriage in which no one was riding came swaying toward her and stopped. She got in, then blew out the light of her lantern. The carriage started up again, rattling over the stony road across the fields, and he watched her and the carriage go, she leaning against the post of the carriage as if she had given a long sigh of relief, swaying with the carriage's motion; and he stood there with the late autumn wind beating against his face, and realized fully at last that he might struggle as hard as he pleased but it seemed unlikely that he would ever be able to part from her now.

Smile

"We'll go into the country next Sunday. The trees will be looking their loveliest now."

Kaji heard that from among the various voices that passed him by. It was so: late spring, and the new leaves at their best. He hadn't been in the habit of forgetting things like the changes in the seasons for some time now. Then he heard that programme on the radio last night, an outside broadcast from a mental hospital, someone interviewing the patients. At the end a psychologist said to the interviewer: "You know this kind of patient isn't all that rare nowadays. In fact you could well say that, get a group of ten people together and you'll find one lunatic among them."

"If that's the case there's nothing to stop you saying—if you mean people who are just a bit weird—that in Japan at this moment there must be five million of them, ah, ha, ha, ha, haaa."

A weird and ugly laugh had drifted under the light. A crowd of five million lunatics and they would all be laughing together like that, probably at that same moment. It had been no normal voice.

"Ah,ha,ha,ha,haaa."

A long, extended laugh: Kaji imagined it within himself and gradually the laugh changed into a chuckle, a gurgle that had nothing of the human left in it. It was the voice of something that had somehow entered into the human race.

It is hard for a man to think that he himself is mad; even harder than imagining that he is not. Even so, there was still something that Kaji was not clear about. There was a saying that every man possessed something of the madman within himself, and there was one particular and peculiar memory which among all the recollections that had been effaced remained clear, and gained in clarity.

That time had also been late spring with the new leaves all suddenly out.

"There's this young man who'd like you to write something for him. Just a few lines with the brush on that coloured paper you have. If you wouldn't mind."

Takada was an acquaintance of his, and made what was a common request of Kaji. It wasn't at all a rare event for him, but just this time he felt a special interest quite different from before as he took up the brush. What Takada had said about this as yet unknown young man was enough to raise this exceptional interest in Kaji. The young man went by the name of Seiho, which was not his real name but the one he used as an amateur of haiku. He was a pupil of Takada (who was a haiku poet), twenty-one years old, and a student at the Imperial University. He was reading mathematics, for which it seemed he had a quite extraordinary genius, but at present he was at the naval base at Yokosuka, having been taken by the navy as a research student and consequently shut up there.

"Surrounded by military men and M.P.s it seems he feels suffocated by it all. So when he does manage to slip out, he uses his haiku name and nobody knows what his real name is. Well, he has dropped the name of Saito but that's an assumed name too, for the same reason no doubt."

Takada went on to say that Seiho had already invented three special weapons, and was now employed on a final one which if perfected would bring the war to a definite and successful conclusion. Kaji was aware that Takada was of a peculiarly volatile sensibility, and Takada himself made no claims for the truth of any of this, simply presenting it as rumour. Yet the war was clearly being lost on every front, the air raids would soon be starting . . . and it was late spring, fresh green in the air. Even if it was untrue, everyone was hungering for some cheerful untruth. Then the concealed joy he sensed in so warm and human a person as Takada, that affected Kaji inevitably as well.

"What kind of weapon?"

"Something pretty terrific, apparently. Anyway, I'll bring him over here in a few days' time and you can ask him yourself."

"I suppose it wouldn't be this atomic bomb thing that people talk about?"

"No, I don't think it's that. From what I've heard it seems to be some kind of very powerful light ray. I don't really know about these things, though. . . ."

The great incline, the long descent to defeat; who would not wish for some as yet unseen strength that would permit a reemergence, a powerful upsurge against all that? And what could be more right, Kaji thought, than that it should appear from beyond a horizon on which no sign of such strength was, flash out as light, a single ray of light. The illusion of a dream perhaps; but better than the image of defeat and suffering, this joyful fantasy had the power to sway Kaji. Kaji imagined the young man, imagined him as another Archimedes with his Grecian homeland facing defeat, on the walls at Syracuse besieged by the Roman fleet, Archimedes absorbed in inventions, cranes that raised boats by their anchors and smashed them down, a mirror whose light would set enemy ships on fire.

"So we seem to have a remarkable young man among us again," Kaji said excitedly.

"But he has a lighter side, you know, a sort of charm about him. He does his experimenting at night, and since it makes pretty much of a noise he's always getting kicked out of his lodgings. The present landlady, however, has a young daughter, so it'll be all right this time, he says, that sort of thing. They say he's had his doctorate accepted."

"A doctor at the age of twenty-one, as young as that? It must be the first time ever."

"That's what people are saying. The thesis points out a number of errors in Einstein's Theory of Relativity, apparently."

Kaji saw in Takada's face that he was striving to be modest about his brilliant pupil, deliberately avoiding exaggeration of any kind; and putting his faith in that, he found the day becoming cheerful and pleasant.

"One needs to hear something like this sometimes. Everything else is so dark. One wants something to clear the mind, fine weather there if only for a day."

Kaji's fantasy entered into him quite clearly from so simple a feeling as that, and began to spread within and occupy him. After all, if this colossus who could conceivably save the country had now appeared in Kaji's vicinity and was wandering about there, this could be one of the biggest moments in his life. And it was all thinkable; it was just a question of believing what Takada had said, and then hope and fantasy were the same thing.

"Yet it's a bit queer that he wants my autograph on coloured paper. It's hardly the time or place for that," said Kaji, and then thought about what he had said.

"Well, you know he's only a lad. The reason he wants your autograph is that one of his friends who's also reading math apparently stole the doorplate with your name on it from your house one day, and he's still got it. So Seiho says that made him decide: Right, I'll get hold of an autograph."

Kaji remembered a time some ten years ago when he kept having his doorplate removed, no matter how many times he had it replaced. The longest a doorplate would last was three days, and sometimes he even lost two or three in the same day. The postman had started grumbling about it. Then he had had the plate firmly banged in with nails instead of just hanging by the front gate, but it kept on being removed. This trifle had got on the whole household's nerves. And now instead of a doorplate it was his autograph, the half-serious whim of a young man, and yet Kaji felt an involvement, a direct concern that meant this was not a matter that could be of indifference to him. Seeds of a former irritation had fallen on unexpected ground, and now suddenly there was a tree putting forth its leaves. He wanted to meet Seiho as quickly as possible. One looked at a group of annoying young men, a lump, meaningless—one looked through that to their sufferings, their anxieties—then it was something else, his doorplate being like a leaf to be nibbled at and discarded, something necessary for a young scientist or rather the chrysalis of one for the spreading forth of its wings; and then he wanted to see the suffering in the face of that chrysalis struggling into birth. If he were then to compare the melancholy of his own face to that, there would be a meaning in his lost doorplates, in the wave of coincidence which now broke back upon his shore.

One afternoon he heard the sound of footsteps coming up over the stone path leading to his front door. Kaji had got into the habit of calculating the nature of a visit from the quality of the sounds that the visitor's shoes made on the stones. "Sermons in stones"; this lifetime habit of listening to the reverberations these stones could make had led him into making that sort of joke about it, and yet recently he had come to see this as an almost frightening and mystical power that the stones possessed. It was probably some electromagnetic process that produced the varying sounds they made, yet that day they brought forth a strikingly odd one. It was a tremendously regular and precise resonance. It was the sound of four feet that were in total unison, quite different from the footsteps he normally heard, which would have the confusion of hesitancy, the heaviness of scepticism, or the low, lost sound of solitude. But this was a rhythmical, clear resonance, the full expression of a body overflowing with energy.

Kaji stood up, but immediately recomposed himself in a sitting position. He was listening for the quality of the sound of the door being slid open. If the sound of the door opening did not match the sound of the footsteps leading up to it, he made a point of not going himself to the hallway to welcome the guest.

The door opened.

"Hallo. Is there anyone at home?"

Everything about this guest from the first sounds up to this voice carried an identical rhythm. Kaji went out to the hallway, and standing there was Takada with behind him a young man wearing an Imperial University cap and smiling the same smile as Takada.

"Please come in."

The doorplate had at last returned. When he sat facing his guests in the living room, he felt himself full of a cheerfulness that he had lost for so long now, although where it had been in hiding he could not guess. Takada formally introduced Kaji and Seiho to each other.

Even with his university cap off, Seiho looked young. Scampering along back streets, doing mischief and never getting scolded for it, smudges all over his face; Seiho was that kind of youth, looking like the typical naughty boy. The young ticket collector at the small suburban station who leaves the passengers to their own devices as he chases after his pals, clipping his clippers like a pair of scissors, careering around after them; that kind of young man.

"From what I hear, you must be having quite a time of it every day."

Kaji started with that and Seiho simply smiled in reply. It was a smile like a flower bursting open, literally bursting with a real sound, early in the morning. It quickly vanished, like the dimple a baby makes when it first learns to smile. Kaji found it absolutely impossible to conceive that this youth had received his doctorate, but the smile, the guileless and innocent smile, in that second when it appeared and disappeared from his face, made all such doubts seem beside the point. Kaji did not feel like asking him about his scholastic labours or about the tribulations of his researches. Also he hardly imagined that he could understand anything even if he did ask.

"Which part of the country do you come from?"

"From A prefecture."

"My wife comes from there."

"Which part?"

On hearing that it was T city, Seiho said that perhaps they knew the Matsuya hotel in the hot spring of Y, which was nearby. Kaji not only knew it, but the family, who were in the habit of going to that hot spring often, had in fact stayed at the hotel a number of times.

"That's my uncle's place," Seiho replied, flashing out his smile.

Kaji's wife came in with the tea, and on hearing about Seiho's uncle began chatting away quite unreservedly with him, and as the two of them talked about matters limited to their own part of the world in extreme and exhaustive detail, Takada and Kaji were rather left out of things. As Seiho became more and more carried away he began to drop back into a distinctive regional accent, using it without any sort of restraint before Kaji's wife.

"Everyone says the air raids are going to start soon. It frightens me just thinking about it," Kaji's wife said.

"Not one plane will get through," Seiho replied. The smile flashed on again.

From the small talk of this day and from what he had learned before from Takada, Kaji was able to piece some of his life story together, and very involved it turned out to be for a youth only twenty-one years of age. Top of the class at school, grade one in judo, he had been accepted into the preparatory course at the university on the strength of the marks he had received for mathematics while only in the fourth form. It was during his second year there that a series of disputes with his teachers over mathematical problems had got him thrown out, and then drafted to the naval base at Rabaul. On his return he entered the university proper, it appearing that someone of influence there did not want to lose him and had pulled a few strings. During this period there were problems at home to trouble him as well. The mother's family had been Loyalists for generations, and since the father had been jailed for left-wing activities, they decided, both formally through the family register and also in practice, to take the mother and the son back. The separation of mother and father was a constant source of private grief for Seiho, but a personal problem of that kind was not one that Kaji wished to touch upon. The conflict between old Imperial loyalties and the Left was a central problem in the country; if one touched it, one would be drawn immediately into that whirlpool. Seiho had grown up struggling for life in those swift currents, so it was not difficult to imagine the strivings of his young spirit to decide which side he should be on, beaten by the two opposed systems of thought. For him the one problem would have two different truths, two opposed solutions; if he chose one, the other would collapse, and if he chose both, both truths would necessarily become untrue. The Law of the Excluded Middle, the mathematical law that would allow no mediatory intermediary truth, would be no abstract problem for him but a real one of the relationship between father, mother, and son.

This was not something confined only to this particular question of Loyalists and the Left, and the whole question of probability involved in the Law of the Excluded Middle was not something to trouble merely the mind of a mathematician like Seiho. Those questions of contradictory possibilities, of probabilities that had to exclude each other and yet seemed mutually to exist, were problems at the centre of human psychology, ones that must trouble the mind of anyone involved in the struggle now going on in the world. To turn one's face away from all that, to ignore it, would be the same as maintaining that the substance of all that existed was mere falsehood. And yet to take this most problematic of all problems, a problem that with austere beauty took everything and let it collapse into nothing and then as austerely departed—no, he had not wanted to show that now to Seiho to assault and beat down his young mind. It would be splitting open his own mind as well. And yet the world was still . . . indeed there still was a world: and that world was at war. Although truth must be thought to exist somewhere, all that offered itself as truth was the aspect of war, and at the centre of that insoluble riddle only a disciplined violence, violence for the sake of its own discipline, glowed white hot, casting off rays of brilliant light.

Does it mean that all that exists is unreal? That all things that visit the eye are ghosts? How can we prove that even the sensation in the hand is other than that ghostly existence? . . .

Sometimes he was visited by the image of a human head, the images of human heads severed from their bodies, but still convulsed, still moving as human beings unconsciously move: such phantoms would rise up in his mind. This problem that had troubled the old Masters of Logic in the past had never left him over the past ten years. The war would end in victory or defeat but the problem would remain unaltered, the problems that the Law of the Excluded Middle gave rise to, the stern law that a truth drove out other truths that would not conform to it. These problems remained unchanged, unchangeably unsolved.

"About how powerful is this light ray of yours?" Kaji was thinking of asking Seiho that, but something about the question troubled him and he decided not to. Instead he said: "This V-1 that the Germans have just started to use, they say that a mere boy first came across the idea. And, well this is something I just heard, but anyhow, what is really being done in the world of mathematics is apparently done by people between the ages of twenty and twenty-three or -four, and the centre of creative energy, as it were, moves from a man to his successor in about six months. At least so a mathematician I know told me. I suppose it's about the same in this country, if the truth were known. What do you think?"

Aware that the question made direct implications about himself, Seiho replied to it only with his sudden smile. Kaji felt the temptation again to ask him something about the secret weapon, but he might thus draw him into divulging secrets of national importance and get him into deep trouble, so that was something to be avoided at all costs. As if he were groping down a very narrow path, Kaji searched for something to say.

"Have you been writing haiku for long?"

That was harmless. A safe road suddenly opened out before both of them.

"No. I've only recently taken it up."

"What was the attraction?"

"I've got to let my head have a bit of peace and quiet sometimes since I can't seem to stop it working, and I saw some of Mr. Takada's poems in a magazine so I got in touch with him straightaway and asked him to take me on. The only thing that keeps me sane is the poems. Everything else is just a source of anxiety and trouble. But with haiku, that releases me, makes me feel at rest."

Seiho sat smiling and looking out at the sunlight upon the leaves. Kaji realized that he could ask him nothing of importance. His head would be full of whether crowds of people should be indiscriminately allowed to live or die. Was it a reality that he could already see, or was it still only a dream? For Kaji the whole question was too large; even if he tried to grasp it with his mind, he was quite unable to feel it.

"But you can get out and about quite freely like this, so they can't be watching over you all that strictly," Kaji said.

"Don't you believe it. I can only get permission if I say I'm going to a haiku meeting. All the other rooms in my lodgings are occupied by military police, all of them, all surrounding my one room. The only bit of freedom and privacy I get is with poems. I can't stand much more of it.

Why, even today the M.P.s followed me, nearly all the way here, but I told them I had a meeting and managed to get rid of them at Shinagawa station."

Now he realized the importance of his autograph as evidence to show to the military police. Of course helping out Seiho with a piece of paper might bring trouble on his own head, but there was the business of the doorplate and the sense of connectedness created by that, so he wrote what Seiho wanted.

"I don't know much about science, but unfortunately there's all this scrambling for secrets going on and whatnot, so you'll need to look out for yourself. You've got to be careful, you know."

"You're right. Only the other day a gifted mechanic was shot with a revolver. He was a very gifted man. You should come over to Yokosuka sometime. I'll show you round our workshop."

"There wouldn't be much point in my seeing a place like that, since I wouldn't understand a thing. Better off remaining ignorant. There was a lot I wanted to ask you but I've decided I won't. Still, those mistakes of Einstein's, what were they?"

"The basic hypotheses were wrong. Einstein's argument leads from one hypothesis into the next and so on. Just knock over the original hypotheses and the whole lot comes down."

So even Einstein had just been dreaming, creating castles in the air, and Seiho had applied his scrutiny to them, like a magnet throwing the whole pattern out of order. That was really something, and Kaji was immediately out of his depth. Even if you were to claim that Seiho must be crazy, not one of his answers rang untrue in any way that would support that idea.

"You know, your mathematics seems to be something peculiarly your own, of your own making. I was wondering just what part the concept of zero, of nothing, plays in your system. I have always thought that it should be completely central, but I don't know that. . . ."

"That's it! Absolutely!" Seiho became tremendously excited and started smiling and talking away at great speed.

"For me, myself, everything starts from that. And nobody, not one person, understands what I'm getting at. I've been just recently struggling with people over that very point. You see, the Japanese warships, they're all wrong. There's a miscalculation in the hull and I'm trying to get it worked out, and if they'd only do what I say the speed would go up by six knots. Yet it doesn't matter what I say, since no one pays a blind bit of notice. It's the curvature of the hull: they've got the zero placement wrong."

On a point about which no one else could offer judgement Seiho continued his lone, solitary struggle. That he should want to revolutionize the placement of the zero point and thus throw aside all the fixed basic ideas on the subject: obviously nobody else at this juncture would respond to such brashness. Yet it was precisely in that aspect of the way Seiho attacked an intellectual problem that one saw the marks of his genius. That a youth of twenty-one should have set his mind upon the question of zero showed how complete his questioning of basic concepts must be. Clearly there would be nobody who would recognize him.

"Do people accept your ideas?" Kaji asked.

"Not really, although I did finally succeed with my point about the ships. All the scientists were trying to put me down, but I said, 'Produce your evidence,' so there wasn't much they could do about it. From now on ships will start to go faster."

When he thought of the world and all the indifference and incompetence in it, and then thought of this brilliant mind that could pierce through all that in its progress, Kaji felt even stronger all the stupid and useless struggle of the adult world, and that uselessness loomed like a mountain.

"Just come and have a look at my workshop. I'll show you round. It's an interesting place. If I said my haiku teacher was coming, they'd soon give you permission to look round."

Kaji understood that Seiho was slightly put out because he did not ask him about his new secret weapon, for he looked pointedly at Kaji's unresponsive face as he made the invitation.

"That's precisely what I would rather not see." Kaji had wanted to avoid that kind of direct answer.

Seiho said nothing but looked even more displeased. During the whole period of their relationship this was the only time Kaji remembered him looking annoyed.

"It wouldn't do me any good going to see a place like that. I wouldn't understand anything."

Kaji felt that he was being slightly cruel to him, but then the world that Seiho represented, the world of Science which kept changing the foundations of things, aroused painful emotions in him that he found difficult to name. He had a momentary sensation of joy, anger, misery, and happiness all confused together, and then a hatred for his own constipated idleness, his own powerlessness, and also a real enmity toward Seiho's world, even to the point of wanting to fight against it; finally a lost, solitary despair at the thought of watching a murder machine take shape and of the tiredness caused by the excitement of imagining victory. No, it was best not to go and see it. Then he felt isolated in himself by the envy in him that would not let him do what Seiho most wanted of him, and miserable that he should take this position of refusal, of denial of everything for which Seiho stood.

"I'd like to hear your opinion of the Law of the Excluded Middle. It's something that's troubled me in my work more than anything up to now."

Kaji had not thought he would ask that or any other question like it, but one could not avoid saying something, and he looked up at Seiho, who gave a little gasp of pleasure, pointed his finger at the fan revolving on the shelf in front of him, and said: "It's nought point five."

Seiho's answer came like a flash of light, and naturally at that moment Kaji could make nothing of it. Still, he had no desire to repeat his question. In the way Seiho had behaved in that moment he felt something almost horrifying, and he most wanted to keep him quiet and peaceful.

"Let us say the centre of the fan is zero. You can't see that the blades are moving at the centre if you look straight at it, but just remove your eyes a little and in that moment when you take your eyes away, look, you can see it, they are moving, aren't they? Nought point five is the distance ratio from the zero centre to the point where you can see the movement."

Seiho's explanation scorned to fill in any gaps and Kaji could not quite make out what it had to do with the question, but the speed and skill with which he had grasped the example of the fan blades before him and almost hurled his response out, that was an adroitness, a sleight of hand perhaps, to which Kaji possessed no answer.

"Do you make all your discoveries in that way?"

"Well now, look. I was walking along the street and I stumbled on a stone and fell over. A tram was passing at the time and I saw sparks fly off its undercarriage. After that, when I got home, I thought I'd switch on the radio, so I turned the knob but it just went phut and nothing came on. I joined up the sparks and the radio going phut and going dead and started thinking about the two things. That's my light ray."

This was the same extraordinary thought process. Yet Kaji's first response was only to want him to keep quiet. If he talked any more in that way he'd really be in danger. Young people had no awareness of where danger began. Seiho, without Kaji realizing it, had already gone beyond that danger point, and it was questionable whether there was really any point in warning him, since it was already perhaps too late.

"Falling put the whole process in motion. If you hadn't fallen, nothing would have happened."

Here, indeed, everything had come out of nothing, thought Kaji, and with that thought he felt a pity for Seiho that was almost unbearable.

From that day onward Seiho's light ray began to weigh on Kaji's mind. If all that he said were true, then his life was worth nothing, a candle set in the wind. Everything about Seiho's existence was perilous, and safety for him could only mean the least dangerous place and nothing more positive than that. Everywhere the weapons of the mob, envy and slander, and what they would give rise to one could never know. Supposing the war were to end in defeat, he would undoubtedly be shot straightaway. Suppose, on the other hand, it ended in victory. Once he had fulfilled his purpose, would so dangerous a person he allowed to remain alive? No, it would be too risky. How could he be protected, then? Short of assuming that all human beings were men of goodwill, there was no method one could think of. Darkness in everything, a dark sky, but one recalled that intense smile of his and it was a light flashed on, a piercing and all-embracing brightness. There was not one single point of darkness, one trace of sadness, in his whole countenance. He was full of a nobility that something unknown and unseen preserved in him.

One day Seiho and Takada came again together to Kaji's house. This time he was wearing the white uniform, complete with bayonet, of a naval sublieutenant and looked slightly older than he had before, but even so the insignia on his shoulder hardly seemed to belong to him.

"I imagine you've been in any number of risky situations in your life, and I've no doubt you can remember things now which make you go cold just to think of. I wonder what it is that pulls us through. Just the strength of life within us, perhaps, or just fate?"

Kaji's question came out of the confused reflections of the previous days.

"Yes, I've had a number of those. There was one on the very first day I was taken to the Naval Research Centre."

Seiho gave a brief account of what had happened. As soon as he got to the centre he was to go up in a new prototype fighter plane to test its reactions in sudden dive. On arrival he was seized with acute stomach cramp and had to beg to be let off for that one day. The military cannot alter their schedule for the sake of one man so the test flight went on with just Seiho left out. Seiho watched the performance, and as the plane entered into its practice bombing dive, it suddenly disintegrated in the air before his eyes and plunged into the sea. There were no survivors.

Then another story. On the flight to Rabaul he had just leaned his body round from the pilot's seat to reach for a sandwich someone was offering him, when the cabin was struck by enemy bullets. Because he was leaning in that way they missed him, but the person sitting behind was struck in the chest and died immediately.

Then a third story of similar coincidence. This interested Kaji the most of the three since it seemed peculiarly Seiho-like. It was when he was still a boy at primary school and he was on his way to school with his mother. The road was deep in snow, and a bird suddenly flew down and began to hop and flutter all around him. The bird attracted him since he was still only a boy. He tried to catch it with both arms outstretched, but it always just evaded his grasp, yet kept on fluttering quite close.

"You know, I kept thinking, now I've got it, now I've got it, nearly got it in my hands, but hippety-hop it would go, cleverly just out of reach all the time. That made us pretty late for school, and we got there just in time to see an avalanche smash down on the roof, already heavy with snow, and flatten it. All the children inside the school died. If I'd been a bit earlier I'd've been one of them."

When Seiho talked about this later to his mother, she said there had been no bird or anything like a bird. Kaji decided that even if this last story was a pack of lies, it was still remarkably well told, indeed a minor masterpiece.

"There's a poem by Dogen about seeing a bird in flight and being like a bird. Your story is rather like Dogen in that respect, isn't it?"

Kaji felt relieved by being able to joke like that. The westering sun as it began to enter the room shone on the one bamboo blind hanging under the eave.

"Since I came to your house last time, I haven't been able to sleep. I keep seeing that blind."

He went on looking outside.

"I'd forgotten how many slats it had, and no matter how hard I tried, I couldn't remember. It was driving me crazy until finally I did. And I was right. It's twenty-two."

Seiho smiled happily.

"I couldn't put up with things like that bothering me," Kaji said.

He decided that Seiho had reached a point where he himself could no longer grasp what was truly troubling his mind.

Kaji went on: "There are cases of people working out mathematical problems in dreams, aren't there? There's the example of the mathematician Kronecker, who came up with some theorem in a dream, the Youth Logic of something or other. . . ."

"That happens to me all the time. For example, I got up this morning and looked at my desk and saw that someone had been making some pretty complex calculations on it, so I asked my landlady who'd been writing at my desk last night and she said, 'Why, wasn't it you working away all last night?' I hadn't known a thing about it myself."

"People must treat you as if you were some kind of lunatic."

"Well, that is rather how they seem to think."

Seiho looked up and flashed out his smile.

Since today was Seiho's day off, the three of them began writing poems. Seiho turned his face toward that part of the room which had caught the green colour of the leaves, and wrote:

> A bird pursuing
> Its own shadow. The slope
> Of the mountain.

He wrote it quickly, a geometrical poem with no seasonal reference. He explained that it was something he had observed on the slope of Hayama mountain when the birds arrived there in April. Takada, his sharp eyes glittering, was careful to hold himself modestly back since on this day he wished to set his pupil forward, and the sensitivity toward others created by scores of attendances at haiku meetings was very apparent in what he wrote:

> Being served with tea
> Three times. Is it the scent
> Of the chrysanthemum?

In that poem one could feel the true refinement of one delighting in the old way of treating a guest and also restraining that delight since the guest is himself. Kaji was pleased at how good an afternoon it had become. His wife appeared and apologized because they had run out of food that day, and then offered little balls of rice with cucumber inside them. Seiho began talking to her in dialect, apparently telling her not to trouble herself about something like that. Kaji took a sheet of coloured paper:

The thick local
Accent of home: how rare and good!
Cucumber rolls.

Slightly less than a fortnight later Takada came alone to Kaji's house, looking very crestfallen about something. The military police had come to his house yesterday and told him that Seiho was indeed a lunatic; they advised him not to believe any of the rumours he had been spreading about, and then they went away.

"Since they are going round all the places where Seiho had been saying the same thing, I thought I'd better come and let you know."

Kaji felt he had been struck in the face, and both remained silent. Then was everything that Seiho had said all lies? Or was it?... He began to think that perhaps the military police had been obliged to say that he was mad as a stratagem by which to protect him.

"Don't you think we'd better treat him like a madman as well? It would be for his sake in the long run."

"I suppose you're right." Takada spoke without enthusiasm or interest, in a broken and hoarse voice.

"Let's do that. That'll be best."

Takada looked as if he were trying to apologize for having introduced Seiho to him, and he didn't at first come up into the house. And Kaji found that he was becoming uncertain within himself as his own mood of depression deepened.

"But the fact is, he does look crazy. All right, perhaps he really is, but if he didn't look mad the outlook would be really bad for him. If we were in the same position wouldn't we look crazy as well? Wouldn't you?"

"I suppose so. Still all of it, the whole lot, I'm beginning to think it's all just the dreams that anybody in science has."

Takada was clearly determined not to let himself be cheered up, and the day passed in heavy silences.

After Takada had gone home, Kaji realized that the principal reason he had come to believe in things in which there was no good reason to believe was the faith he had in Takada's judgement. And yet Kaji, Takada, the military police, all three represented only three different standpoints, three different ways of looking at Seiho, three different zero placements.

The whole of it was an emptiness, nothing really there at all. Thinking thus, a weariness overtook him as all the empty strain of the last, and as it had now come to seem, meaningless month dissolved away, and he looked up at the sky.

Regret, a movement of release, of almost comfort, then a sense of darkness slipping and falling. From tomorrow the sequence of days with nothing to believe in would begin again. And yet in these moments why does a man raise his eyes all at once to the sky? It was a reflex, something one just naturally did. Raising one's eyes to the sky. The round swell of the sky that had nothing to say.

The second day after Takada's visit a letter came from Seiho, to the effect that he had recently received an Imperial summons and had in fact just now returned from his audience at the palace. "I was in tears so I was unable to say anything, but the president of the university kindly replied on my behalf. I should like to come and tell you about it in the near future, if I may." That was all he wrote. He had hoped to forget all about Seiho for the time being, and now he felt all the annoyance of being obliged to take a step back into the past. He looked for some time at the hastily scribbled writing. The next day Seiho came.

"So you went to the palace?"

"Yes. And I didn't say anything. The words just wouldn't come out. Once His Imperial Majesty came over to where I was and then went back to the throne, and all I could do was count his footsteps: eleven of them, five metres. Then the screens were let down and he questioned me from the other side of them."

The same beautiful smile as ever flashed over his face. Every time Kaji saw that innocent smile he forgot about all the other things. Beyond what Seiho did and aimed at, beyond the question of his being a lunatic or a fraud, there was this smile, and for Kaji the conversation between them proceeded simply as something by which one awaited that, waiting for the next one to deepen around his mouth. That alone was all he wanted to see.

"How did the Emperor address you?"

"As 'the sublieutenant.' That's what he called me at first, and every time after that he addressed me in the same way. Everything went to my head. I thought I was going to go mad or something. I've been feeling a bit strange ever since."

Seiho screwed up his eyes and began scratching his head as if astounded by his own inability to say anything.

"Well, it was a very great honour for you. Don't let it go to your head or it really might make you mad."

When Kaji said that, he could not be certain if he himself were treating Seiho as a maniac or not. Whatever you think is the truth is true. And if you think the same thing is a falsehood, then it will be so. What should be mistrusted became a thing not to be mistrusted, became something restricted to this time and this place. Right there in the middle of the question, that middle that the laws of logic excluded, lay fixed one intuitive truth, and now it was offering Kaji one superb example of the truth of itself. It urged this truth upon Kaji; it said: "How about this? How about it? Why don't you answer?" And Kaji would not answer, despite all this.

"I believe what I see. I see the smile. I believe that." But that was no way of replying to things. It was an evasion, a technique of turning the problem and rolling it away from himself.

"What I wanted to ask you was whether you would be prepared to have dinner with me. I mean this evening. We could go together, if that's all right. I've got a car waiting for us at Shibuya station."

"Are there still places left where one can eat out?"

"The Naval Officers' Club."

"Of course, you're in the navy, aren't you," and he smiled at Seiho, who he saw was not wearing his student's uniform but the wing-collared outfit of a naval officer.

"Yes. I've got on a first lieutenant's uniform today, although the truth is I'm a lieutenant commander, only I look so young I thought I'd better lower my rank a bit."

Seiho was still only a boy so there was nothing unnatural in the pride he took in the number of stars on his shoulder. But if this boy was the only person who could save the country now—and heaven knows if anything could get the country out of the military situation it was in now it would have to be something like his new weapon, since there was no other conceivable way. And yet a boy like Seiho—and numerous doubts started to rise up within him again, but of course he had not actually seen anything of his experiments so he was in no position to judge. And what method would he have of investigating them, anyway? The idea was absurd, a mere dream on his part. And then a thought struck him that was much nearer home. Suppose Seiho's going in and out of the Officers' Club was only a dream as well, a personal fantasy of *his* own?

"You know, you're a very mysterious person. The very first time you came here I thought your footsteps sounded different from those of a normal visitor." Kaji murmured the remark almost to himself.

"Ah, that was because I was counting the number of paces from the station to your door. Six hundred and fifty-two," Seiho promptly replied.

Of course that explained the precision of his footsteps. The puzzle was easily solved. Similarly, when Seiho had first come to his house, although all Kaji knew of his home was that it was in A prefecture, he had said to him: "I have this feeling that your home must be very close to that of Hirata Atsutane."*

Seiho had replied to that with the same prompt precision as on this occasion: "One hundred metres."

*A distinguished scholar in the Motoori Norinaga tradition who had a deep influence on the intellectual world immediately prior to the Meiji Restoration. An Akita man like Seiho. There is a chapter on him in Donald Keene's *The Japanese Discovery of Europe*.

He again recalled what Seiho told him about his first experiences in the navy, when, the day after his stomach cramp, he had been occupied with the test performance of the new fighter. The testing could be carried out only while the machine was in steep dive, and he had been obliged to do it four times. On each occasion a fault appeared in the wing, and each time Seiho had merely said: "Don't worry. That can easily be put right." His head was overflowing with numbers, yet he could not stop the flood of mathematical data that kept inundating him. No wonder his mind should start to lose control of itself. There is the paradox that whatever is precise must go off balance, that what is correct in something eventually leads to derangement. Kaji accepted and understood that. Whatever was of undoubted beauty in the modern world was included in that paradox.

"Have you been to the officers' Club today? Didn't the M.P.s follow you?"

"No. I've just got back from the testing ground in Chichijima. I came straight here."

It sounded like Chishima (the Kurile Islands) in Seiho's pronunciation. When Kaji asked him what he had been doing up there and how on earth he had managed to get all the way back, he repeated the name slowly and correctly.

"Just finished an experiment and came straight over. It went off all right. The first things to die are cats. Just give them a little brush with the ray and they roll over and die straightaway. Dogs go next. Monkeys take a bit of time, I can't quite work out why. I rather want to try it on a human being, but that's a bit off, as they say."

He gave a low laugh and began scratching his sunburnt head. What sounded like the careless remarks of a madman were, if you worked them out, the letting slip of secrets about this dreadful ray.

"I've become very interested in the hearts of animals. I'm thinking there must be an awful lot of different varieties of hearts, and there might be a lot to be said for investigating all of them. It could be entertaining."

Seiho's new weapon, assuming it existed, seemed to be making progress. Yet Kaji, despite the fact that he was now as close to Seiho as this, did not have it in him to ask him outright about the weapon and whether it was a fact or not. The whole business had lead to so much trouble that, in reaction to that, Kaji was now unable to feel it as something that had anything to do with himself. And the feeling that Seiho really was mad remained with him; yet despite that, one still accepted him, permitted it in him.

"How long does it take from Chichijima?"

"Two hours. The electric power's very weak out there and one can't get on with the experiments as one would like. Still, it's effective up to ten thousand feet, which is not bad. At first I thought it wouldn't work under water, but sea water's salt and we in fact discovered that it actually works better there than in the air."

"What, ten thousand feet! That's a pretty long way. And it works all right? You can bring an aeroplane down with it?"

"It already has. We signalled to the pilot and after he baled out we set the ray on the empty plane. It went all right I can tell you. I spent last night drinking whisky with the pilot, just the two of us. We made quite a night of it."

How totally different was Seiho's cheerful face, how detached from the melancholy faces of the crowds in the streets.

"We tried it out on a submarine, but we made a slipup and hit the tail section, so although it was supposed to float to the surface, in fact it never will. Lousy thing to happen. Still, it can't be helped. It's all for the old country. One has to learn to live with things like that."

Seiho's face clouded over, but the clouds immediately passed away.

"A Japanese submarine!" Kaji exclaimed.

"Yes. I felt really rotten about it when the thing happened. I thought I'd just about had enough of damn experiments. That really sickens me, that sort of thing."

For the first time these weird experiments began extraordinarily to take on the unintelligible aspect of reality. But could it possibly all be real, all this stuff he rattled on about?

"But if this thing gets into the hands of the wrong persons, my God," Kaji murmured.

"That's just it. The problems of supervision are enormous."

"It would mean the destruction of the human race."

"Just fill up six boatloads of these things and we could take London. Take it right under their noses. A landing in America would be possible by the end of the month."

This must be more than a mere joke. Just what of all this was substantial and what was not was still in question, but Seiho's talk proceeded so serenely, so easily, so regularly filling up all the empty spaces. Kaji no longer understood if he was surprised by all this or not. And yet why did he start thinking about the weapon falling into the wrong hands? Finally it was not just a question of winning or losing a war. Certainly he had no doubts about his own love for his country. The idea of wanting defeat was unthinkable. He wanted victory, and yet when the country had been winning he always had doubts about whether they could go on winning in that way. Now at this stage, with defeat always staring one in the face, the clamour of such anxieties was unappearable. War made no distinction between good and bad, and it became simply that the destruction of one's country was something one could not endure. And now this new weapon of Seiho's appeared and one's heart leaped just on hearing about it. So why should one think about it as something falling into the wrong hands? Why should one even think of that, and why should a cold clutch of unrest seize the heart? Which of the two truths that now existed in his mind was the real truth for him? Kaji looked directly into himself. It was the old problem with all its torments, that one of the truths had to exclude the other, that there was no middle truth that could exist between them, and it welled up within him and pierced through to his heart. Up to yesterday Seiho's secret weapon had been no more than his fantasy, and all that had concerned him was solely Seiho's life. But now it seemed that it might be in the process of becoming real, so Seiho could fend for himself, since it was now he, Kaji, and his own existence that were at issue, Kaji himself who had got the scent of the devil in his nostrils. The devil—yes, he existed all right, he existed.

"That weapon of yours: if it doesn't get into the right hands, this country will be finished. If evil men get hold of it, then on that day we are defeated."

He said that for no reason and stood up.

Surely God also is.

The truth of that statement seemed also unanswerably so.

Seiho and Kaji went out. On the platform at Shibuya station the light of the sun was just going, and crowds of people swarmed off or swarmed on the trains. One of the crowd was not attempting to do either, and Kaji noticed him, a tall, pale young man wearing the peaked cap of the Imperial University. He just stood gazing into space with a wonderfully pure and bright expression in his eyes that seemed to have passed beyond melancholy. He glanced at Seiho, and immediately the beautiful, withdrawn expression was gone out of his eyes and he just went on looking at the outside world, unmoving.

"You see that student over there?" Seiho said to Kaji.

"Yes."

"He's one of my colleagues at the centre. The navy pulled him in as well."

The two of them began moving toward him through the crowd. He had the insignia of the navy and of the science department on his collar.

"Ah. Wait. Don't say anything. I think he's being evasive. He's got something against me."

Seiho passed behind the youth, who remained looking in the opposite direction from them.

"Everyone's against me, everyone. They've all got it in for me. Nobody even tries to understand me."

Seiho spoke like that, but the rhythmic sound of his tread only grew more energetic. Walking along beside him and matching his stride with his, Kaji found his own movements growing more and more rhythmical. He realized that what was disordered, out of step, and thus broke that rhythm, was something not only in the Japanese masses but also at the very heart of the most important research unit in the country.

The car that Seiho said would be waiting for them was

nowhere to be seen outside the station. They decided to take the tram to Roppongi, but Seiho told Kaji the number of the car, saying that if he ever saw it anywhere he should just stop it and take a free ride. On the tram he told Kaji how much the problem of how to address his service inferiors, who were yet men in their thirties, bothered him.

"The person I most respect at the moment is a man of thirty-five by the name of Izu. He's only a low-grade mechanic, but what I most hate is having to tell him off, and on the side I've explained to him about it and that I don't like just calling him 'Izu,' but if I didn't the others would simply stop taking any notice of me. I hope he can accept that as a sort of temporary arrangement for the sake of the old country. He's a marvellous man, has wonderful character. When I first went there I never thought I'd ever be able to pluck up enough courage to call him just 'Izu.' "

How was it possible to think of Seiho as insane. Here he was, a doctor of philosophy at the age of twenty-one, a lieutenant commander in rank, someone entitled to call scores of inferiors exactly what he pleased. If one were looking for a youth whose actions were worthy of the highest honours the country could bestow, where could you find a more perfect example than in Seiho? However, if you thought about his future, you realized that he would go no higher than he was now. He could only descend. It was his fate, an unlucky one. The feeling of intense pity for this youth with the perfect and pure smile overtook him again.

They got off at Roppongi and walked along Mamiana Street with its rows of chestnut trees. In the dusk there were few people about. A squad of about ten soldiers pulling a cart loaded with very heavy-looking iron objects was coming up the incline toward them. When the corporal in charge noticed Seiho's epaulets, he called his men to attention. The hand that returned the salute of the motionless men was also absolutely firm, totally fitted to the man who gave it. Kaji felt he was seeing him for the first time as a true military man.

"There's not much of the student left in you, is there?" Kaji complimented him.

"I prefer the army to the navy. The navy's terribly slack

about distinctions of rank, not like the army, which has real, correct discipline. The army's just sent in a request for my transfer to them, but the navy won't have it."

The Naval Officers' Club came in sight. It was the first time Kaji had ever been there. At this period of the war one almost never saw smoke coming out of a chimney, but the one tall chimney here was belching out clouds of it. Seiho placed his sword on the counter of the cloak room and Kaji noticed that it had the chrysanthemum crest on its hilt.

"It's a sword bestowed by the Emperor. It's not mine: I borrowed somebody's. I'll be getting my own soon, of course." Seiho spoke like a child.

He led Kaji into a room marked For Senior Officers Only. Among the deep, black lustre of the polished leather armchairs and sofas, Seiho in his lieutenant's uniform looked not simply young but, with his childish grin of a young boy, actually out of place. He was clearly doing his utmost to give Kaji a pleasant night out. While they were eating, Kaji noticed that all the other officers without exception ate with serious, dejected expressions on their faces, and only Seiho grinned in his inimitable and lively way, pouring beer into Kaji's glass with expansive gestures. After the meat course had been served, Kaji said: "Is it all right for us to be sitting here? After all, you've only got lieutenant stars on."

"Everybody knows about me here."

Seiho answered with perfect composure. Another officer came and sat at Kaji's side. After nodding to Seiho he went on with his meal in complete silence, in an atmosphere of gloom that seemed to be particularly prevalent that night. There were rumours circulating that the navy had been totally defeated on every front. Reports were spreading that the battle of Layte had ended in an overwhelming defeat and that the mainstay of the fleet, the battleship *Yamato*, had been sunk.

After finishing the rare Western meal, which even included bread, Kaji and Seiho went down onto the grass in the quadrangle and then across to the lawn in front of a large shrine. The small shrine gates around it were decorated with paper prayer offerings. From the centre of the lawn the Officers' Club looked the complete seven-storey hotel. In the night sky that stretched out before them, only the Russian Embassy competed with it in height. Behind a cluster of small shrines was a long, rambling building with some kind of special annex, where a few lights were still burning. Seiho pointed to that room at the rear of the building which could be seen through the branches of the box trees.

"That's the Mess Hall for Junior Officers. There seems to be some sort of conference going on there."

In the whole expanse of the building just those windows still shone brightly. The white uniforms of the officers flowed into the room among the fresh white tablecloths. Kaji noticed how the breasts of the defeated officers caught the light and had the living whiteness of breaking ripples as they seated themselves, and he thought of Seiho, who lay sprawled out on the lawn by his side with his body twisted looking toward the lighted windows, and of how when the whole great edifice fell, only this pillar, this one and not those others in that room, would be reliable and hold. He looked about him. It was a peaceful evening full of that nameless fear, full of a madness beyond the individual's grasp, that had now entered into the everyday ordinariness of mealtimes.

Kaji said, "Everybody here wants to be allowed into that room, I suppose, but there's no joy under those lights. I was looking at the Soviet Embassy just now and thinking. . . ."

"What I really want to do is write stories, novels. I once submitted a story to the university newspaper. It was an attack on the Theory of Relativity. I called it 'The Umbrella Maker's Daughter.' "

Seiho had suddenly turned toward Kaji, leaned his head back on his hands, and made that remark, the last link in what fantastic chain of ideas one could not say. Kaji could only mutter something in response. What on earth had made him say that?

"It was more than a story, the length of a novel in fact. My math teachers were very taken with it. What I'd really like to do is write mathematics in the form of fiction. I read your novel *Travel Sadness* four times. I was very interested by the sections in it about mathematics."

It was a time when one could not bear to be still, and yet

there he was, this pillar that was to sustain the great edifice, and he spoke about novels, lying there at the bottom of the darkness between the busy coming and going of the officers, and the Russian Embassy. Surely this was the new age that had already arrived, the unintelligible, inexplicable future.

Kaji tried to change the subject.

"If we could get off the subject of my novels for a moment—about your light ray? What colour is it?"

"You can't in fact see my light ray during the daytime, but at night it's like any other light, bluish and clear at the edges and yellow in the centre."

"It's quite possible that the conference going on over there is about your light ray. There doesn't seem anything left other than that."

It had grown quite dark. The two got ready to leave. Seiho received his sword from the cloak room and put it on.

"I expect they'll give me a sword of honour," he said cheerfully as he put on his coat.

They went out and began walking through the pitch dark toward Roppongi. Seiho moved close to Kaji, and lowering his voice, spoke as if making a sudden confession of what up till now he had suppressed.

"We sank four cruisers and four destroyers. I timed it carefully by my watch. It took four minutes. All over just like that."

There was nobody else about. Like a man drawing a dagger in the dark and thrusting it under someone's ribs, Seiho flashed his watch out of his trouser pocket and went through the motions of reading off the time from it.

"Then some sort of announcement will be made soon."

"No, it won't. The enemy would get wind of it."

"But even so. . . ."

No more was said and they went on walking. The coldness in the firm stone walls could be felt; it passed through the air into them. They were going up a gentle slope in Mamiana Street, the only sound being the echoes of their own footsteps. All that had been disturbing Kaji for some days had reached a peak. It was now no good his trying to get rid of what Seiho said as merely a pack of lies, since it would make him feel his own uselessness too deeply. That he should be trying to sustain this illusion that had already been roughly torn away from him, that he should now incline himself so forcefully toward it, had one cause and one cause only. He was being drawn along in that direction by nothing except Seiho's smile. That was what he found so bitter to acknowledge in himself, and what made him wish to have the power to dismiss Seiho just like that as a lunatic. He was normally a calm and unimpressionable person, but now he felt a strange fluttering of fear and unease within him, and as he walked he wished to draw closer to the trees of the avenue and to their silence.

After a while Seiho again drew close to Kaji, and said: "Sir. There's just this one thing that keeps troubling me."

"What's that?"

"I've never once felt afraid of death, and I don't know why, but since a few days ago I've suddenly become frightened. I don't want to die."

Kaji was aware that Seiho was starting to return to his right mind.

"I don't know why it is, but I want to go on living a bit longer. I haven't been able to sleep these past nights for thinking about it."

Something deep within him had started to move; the reverberation of it was in his voice. He's started to get hold of it, thought Kaji, and waited for what Seiho would say next. But the silence began again and for a while they walked on like that.

"I need someone I can trust, someone I can hold on to. I can't help myself anymore. I need someone. And there's nobody."

Like a little boy who has been playing all over the sky, and he stops and looks round and no one is there, and then suddenly he looks down . . . it was that lonely fear soaking through the voice, a fear of loneliness about to burst into tears.

"Yes, well. . . ."

Kaji had nothing to reply and he was upset by that, but all he did was go on walking, observing the thickness of the bark of the wayside trees. He wanted to get as soon as possible to the crossroads ahead where he could see street lights.

They reached just that point where they had met the squad of soldiers pulling the load of iron, and recalling the cheerful Seiho of the daytime, Kaji at last replied.

"You see, that's the point from which human life starts, from that. It's starting for you now. It's not something to worry about, feeling like that."

"Do you really think so?"

"You've reached a point beyond which no one can go. You've reached zero. You've seen it. Look, this road is called Mamiana Street and that's because only badgers used to live here, but then one day human beings started to live here and got used to it right away. Human life is like that. In our lives we have to pass lots of places along a long road. Moving along the road, passing those places, is what we can't avoid. People are always shouting, banging on their drum, 'It's starting, it's all starting, the show's beginning!' Well, that's just the way they move along the road, that's how they do it. And I suppose it's the same thing with death."

"I suppose you're right."

Seiho seemed to have stopped weeping, and Kaji started to notice the regular sound of his footsteps again. The lights of the tram stop at Roppongi appeared before them, with two or three other people standing there. Soon after they arrived, the tram came travelling up the rise toward them.

An autumn breeze blew. September was near at hand. Takada came to visit him, saying there was a party tomorrow to celebrate the acceptance of Seiho's thesis and that Seiho particularly wanted Kaji to attend. The party was being held at Yokosuka and he apologized for the distance, but as Seiho particularly wanted him to attend, they would make the occasion into a haiku meeting. Since this was a celebration he decided he had better go, so on the next day he waited for Takada to come for him.

"What sort of people will be there?" he asked Takada on the train to Yokosuka. Takada replied that the meeting was being held in a house up in the hills, the home of a mechanic employed in aircraft production.

"He's a rather special sort of mechanic, talented fellow,

very good at haiku. I know him well through that, and he's the sort of person you can get on with easily."

"But if the M.P.s turn up, what then?"

"Well, I suppose they. . . . But after all, this is a haiku meeting. It'll be all right."

During the journey neither of them touched upon whether Seiho was a lunatic or not. Indeed, Takada, who had said to Kaji's face that he did judge him to be mad, was now actually taking him all this way to a naval port to attend a celebratory party on the lunatic's behalf.

The mechanic's house was some distance from the station. The steep ascent from which one saw the sea was of high, twisting stone steps, and it took Kaji's breath away. The bank by the side of the road was covered with flowering arrowroot: water drained down over the bank. From the bottom of the valley filled with the descending sun, the voices of autumn cicada came clearly up to them.

They reached the top of the ascent and entered the door of a house surrounded, almost buried, by bitter orange trees loaded with green fruit. This was the mechanic's house and the meeting had already begun. Seiho was seated in the place of honour in front of the tokonoma, and above him hung a congratulatory sign and the various poem themes that had been written up. The gathering was of about twenty persons, all silently absorbed in poem making. Kaji and Takada sat at a corner of the veranda and began immediately on the poem subject "arrowroot flower." Kaji leaned against a pillar with his back toward the room and his notebook open on his lap. The bitter oranges that loaded down their pliant branches, various greennesses brushing together, seemed to draw all his weariness out of him. The evening sky still received the reflected brilliance of the sea. The echoing voices of the autumn cicada could still be clearly heard.

"This is my brother. He's come all this way just for the party."

Seiho addressed him quietly from behind. The brother thus introduced made some formal remarks in a north-country accent. Above the head of Seiho's slight-statured brother, Kaji noticed a slender bamboo vase with an arrow-root flower trailing from it. The brother seemed to have no interest in gatherings of this kind, and announcing that he had a train to catch, soon made his farewells and left before anyone else.

> Bitter-orange green and far-
> Blue the hill of parting;
> With arrowroot flowers.

Kaji soon wrote this first poem in his notebook. There seemed still to be the voices of summer cicada. It struck Kaji that if one were to doubt everything, this party for Seiho would have to be an object of doubt as well. Perhaps all Seiho had done was real only as fragments of his own mere fantasy, and was thus all untrue. And yet this small gathering on a hill, of people assembled to celebrate that fiction, that nothing, that zero, was it not now to bloom with all the beauty of a flower? Thinking thus, Kaji had no sense of dissatisfaction, no feeling of emptiness or waste.

> The autumn cicada.
> Seeing in the honoured guest
> The arrowroot flower.

Kaji wrote this second poem on a slip of paper and cast it onto the tray.

The sun fell and the light from the room began to pierce the garden dusk. One of the guests whispered to his neighbour and they both started looking at something on the other side of the hedge. They had heard the footsteps of a military policeman creeping round the outside of the hedge. The host asked Seiho if they should invite the M.P. in.

"No, he must certainly not come in. They'll start making a habit of it."

Seiho was sitting bolt upright in front of the tokonoma, and as he shook his head sternly he had a commanding, military air about him which Kaji had never seen before. He made this firm decision and thus the meeting continued.

Takada brought the session to a close by reading his own poem aloud, the others following suit. Kaji's and Takada's poems received the highest marks and the competition was between them, but finally Takada's went ahead and the meeting ended on that note. Half the guests left the house and descended the hill; the remaining half, being specially close to Seiho, were to stay and take their evening meal there. The footsteps of the M.P. still circled the hedge.

Drink went round and the atmosphere became more relaxed. Seiho brought someone to be introduced to Kaji.

"This is Mr. Izu, whom I'm always telling you about. He's the person I am most indebted to."

Izu was dressed in overalls, spoke little, and looked solid and reliable. Kaji felt like thanking him. Seiho started joking with the girl who was doing the serving, the daughter of a friend, and the exchange was mild enough but the girl was overawed by the twenty-one-year-old doctor, and her face coloured and she became flustered. The host remained apart with his arms folded, peacefully absorbed within himself as if possessing some great virtue there.

The guests from Tokyo kept having their glasses refilled despite the small amount of drink. Takada, his cheeks flushed, lay on his back looking up at the sky. A flying boat with lights on was skimming in low among the hills, its engine roaring.

"Hey, now Seiho's light ray, do you think it could bring that one down?"

Takada, his head still cupped in his hands, glanced in Seiho's direction, and immediately the noisy room became unnervingly quiet. Takada recalled where he was and stood up. He assumed a correct, upright sitting position, his eyes full of self-reproach, but immediately he got the silent room back to life again. Kaji sensed a note of desperation in the very skill of Takada's diplomatic moves at this crisis, but Seiho in his shirtsleeves looked pleased with everything, as if he might even suddenly perform a dance.

That night Kaji, Takada, and Seiho slept in the upstairs room of the mechanic's house. Takada slept to Kaji's left and Seiho to his right. Those two were soon asleep, but hemmed in the middle, Kaji found it hard to fall off and lay a long time with his eyes open. Seiho lay with the top half of his body naked and with no eiderdown over it, since he had folded it into four and embraced it, holding it over his face and head. He looked extraordinarily comic, as if someone had piled four of five cushions on his head. During the night

Kaji occasionally looked at him. The light flesh round his navel swayed up and down with his gentle breathing, and was lit up by the harsh glare of the electric light. With his head covered up like that, the body looked like a headless trunk, from the centre of which the navel whispered to Kaji: "I'm afraid of death now, afraid. I don't know why."

After that Kaji and Seiho never met again. From that autumn the bombing became heavy, and Kaji remained in Tokyo looking up at the sky, but there was never any sign of the light ray. Kaji asked after Seiho on the frequent occasions he met Takada, but Takada had had his house burnt down and replied that he'd lost all interest in Seiho and knew nothing about him. The only news Takada did have was about a month after he'd stopped seeing Seiho, when he received a letter from the mechanic saying that Seiho had been court-martialled on a charge of having worn one more star than he was entitled to, and sent to a military prison. Later he also heard that the mechanic himself had got married during an air raid, and then died of a sudden illness the very next day. The death of the mechanic, who had been working at the same place at Seiho meant that his one source of information was now closed to him. Kaji heard nothing else after that.

The war ended. Kaji assumed that Seiho was certainly dead. How he had died he could not know, but he felt certain that he was no longer in the world.

One day while Kaji and his wife were staying in a mountain village in the north to which they had evacuated, he came across a short news item in the newspaper. It was a report from the Technological Council that claimed that even in Japan during the war, work had been carried out on an attempt to perfect a death ray, and it had been brought to the stage where its range was three thousand feet, and that the young inventor, on hearing the news of the defeat, had gone mad out of sheer frustration and died. Kaji was certain that this must be him.

"Seiho's dead."

Kaji said just that and handed the newspaper to his wife.

Amid the cramped, black type he seemed to see the blue flame of a light ray spurting out its one jet of light, then flickering and dying out. And with the same speed, his emotion, which had seemed as if it were to expand and flower, died down quietly within him. Everything had returned to zero, nothing.

"It must be Seiho. So he died as well in the end. And he told me that not one plane would get through. It must have made his head almost boil over when we lost, mustn't it?"

Kaji also thought back, like his wife, to the time when they first met him, and he decided that Seiho's madness must have begun before then. The things he had said and done, some of them were true and some mere dreams. Then Kaji himself had been partly infected by him and had shown symptoms of the same mania perhaps. He felt like Urashima Taro lifting the lid off the treasure chest and seeing the puff of smoke as everything disappears, and for a while he just looked at the sky. The mechanic was dead, Seiho was dead, and as he looked up at the sky he saw the day at Yokosuka when he had last parted from them. They stayed the night at the mechanic's house, and while descending the hill the next day the four of them watched an aeroplane make practice bombing runs on a submarine at anchor on the surface of the sea. The mechanic had grunted: "No matter how many I make, they all get shot down. Seiho's job is to shoot them down, so he's one up on me all the time."

One pace ahead of the disgruntled mechanic was the still-energetic figure of Seiho in his dark blue jacket descending the road. Kaji recalled his bandy legs and their roll-type gaiters, looking like the foldings of a paper lantern when the winding has come loose. They had looked over the battleship *Mikasa* and parted at the station.

"I don't suppose I'll ever have the pleasure of seeing you again. I hope everything goes well for you."

Seiho spoke with complete firmness in his eyes, then bowed deeply. As Kaji had walked away he seemed to feel something in his back, as though the deep, solitary resignation that was in Seiho was penetrating into him.

On his return to Tokyo from the north, Kaji suddenly became ill. Takada sometimes came to see him during his illness and Kaji would venture to talk about Seiho. For Takada it all had the same uselessness as reckoning the present age of a child who had died some years before, and he would only smile ambiguously.

"However, one has to admit that Seiho had a marvellous smile, if nothing else. I suppose anyone would have been taken in by it, just like us. Just that would have been enough."

Kaji wanted to imply also by those words that the human smile can kill the heart just like any death ray. But it was still mystifying, if one thought of the perfect beauty of that smile with all the early spring that was in it, to think that it reflected a heart that looked up into the sky in the hope only of seeing things fall from it, a heart that had decided on such a fate for itself. It was the hope of a simple and clear judgement, the hope that all of us possessed today. And yet the real world only smiled coldly on this desire, since the real world drifted like the excluded centre of the problem perpetually splitting into two irreconcilables. Kaji remembered Seiho pointing at the revolving blades of an electric fan and smiling cheerfully, remembered it as something that Seiho still went on saying to people: "Look, the moment you take your eyes off the blades, you understand that they are flying round. Look, I've just started to fly myself now. Look."